Science Fiction   JUL 15 1987

Shadows 9   .95

PN 1 (98)

Shadows 9

Shadows 9

Edited by
CHARLES L. GRANT

DOUBLEDAY & COMPANY, INC.
GARDEN CITY, NEW YORK
1986

Introduction copyright © 1986 by Charles L. Grant
"The Jigsaw Girl" copyright © 1986 by Stephen Gallagher
"The Lesson" copyright © 1986 by Christopher Browne
"On the Turn" copyright © 1986 by Leanne Frahm
"Moving Night" copyright © 1986 by Nancy Holder
"Sanctuary" copyright © 1986 by Kim Antieau
"Now You See Me" copyright © 1986 by Sheri Lee Morton
"The Fishing Village of Roebush" copyright © 1986 by Leslie Alan Horvitz
"Icarus" and "The Last Time I Saw Harris" copyright © 1986 by Galad Elflandsson
"Ants" copyright © 1986 by Nina Kiriki Hoffman
"Nor Disregard the Humblest Voice" copyright © 1986 by Ardath Mayhar
"The Skins You Love to Touch" copyright © 1986 by Janet Fox
"Walk Home Alone" copyright © 1986 by Craig Shaw Gardner
"The Father Figure" copyright © 1986 by T. L. Parkinson
"An Ordinary Brick House" copyright © 1986 by Joseph Payne Brennan
"Overnight" copyright © 1986 by Lou Fisher
"Tavesher" copyright © 1986 by Peter Tremayne
"Bloodwolf" copyright © 1986 by Steve Rasnic Tem

Shadows (Garden City, N.Y.)
Shadows.—[1] (1978)- — Garden City, N.Y.: Doubleday,
1978–
v.; 22 cm.—(Doubleday science fiction)
Annual.
Editors: 1978–   C.L. Grant.
ISSN 0884-6987 = Shadows (Garden City, N.Y.)

1. Horror tales, American.   I. Grant, Charles L.   II. Series.
PS648.H6S52   85-643084
813'.0876'08—dc19
AACR 2   MARC-S
Library of Congress   [8510]

ISBN: 0-385-23486-4
Copyright © 1986 by Charles L. Grant
All Rights Reserved
Printed in the United States of America
First Edition

Contents

INTRODUCTION

by Charles L. Grant

Over the past few months, there has been on the part of several reviewers, writers, and critics an attempt to define the boundaries of horror. I say *attempt* because no matter how hard each of them tries, all they seem to do is define their own approach to the genre, to the exclusion or grudging inclusion of everything else. And in the defining, no matter which side(s) they take, each also seems to have forgotten one vital fact—

Horror writing is fiction.

And the only boundaries fiction has are in the mind of the writer.

The best writers, here as anywhere else, work with people first and gimmicks second (if, indeed, gimmicks there are). They take a look at us and tell us what they see; they look at the truths as they believe them to be and tell us what they see; they look at the past, the present, peer into the future, and tell us what they see. All of it, however, in terms of us. People. Not superheroes, not supervillains, not gods or devils. Us. People.

They, the best writers, are seekers. They want to explain—if not to us, then to themselves—why we are the way we are, why we love and hate and destroy and rebuild and do all those things that have characterized human history from the first human being; they want to explain why there are no explanations; they want to explain, in some small or great form, why they feel the need.

This isn't always a conscious act, and indeed, those who are conscious of it don't always succeed because they often end up doing little more than preaching.

But the only boundaries fiction has are in the number of people who live in and out of it.

What frightens you? What frightens your children, your friends, the people you love, the people you hate, and the people to whom you are indifferent? What horrifies you, terrifies you, makes you race for the nearest closet with the strongest lock and the thickest walls? What disgusts you?

The only boundaries horror fiction has is in the writers, the people, and the horrors.

The only boundaries are those described by the shadows that stalk each of our nightmares, each of our waking hours, each of our relationships, each of our lives.

And shadows are never the same from one person to another, one writer to another—each time a light casts a shadow, the shadow is different. Sharp edged, diffused, dark, pale . . . and those who would explain will be explaining for the rest of their lives, with no result save the indisputable fact that there are horrors out there, there are fears, there are terrors, and trying to explain them won't make them go away.

There is no exorcism for a shadow. When the light is switched off, the shadow only becomes a hidden part of the dark.

—Charles L. Grant
Newton, New Jersey
February 1986

Shadows 9

Introduction

One of the most favorite exercises we indulge in is the reconstruction of our past. Sometimes it's done in melancholy, sometimes in anger, sometimes just to see "what if." Sometimes it's fun. And sometimes it's murder.

Stephen Gallagher is the author of Chimera *and* The Follower, *and a number of short stories. He lives in England and, unsurprisingly, knows where there's a haunted pub. He also lives on the edge of the moors, and when he laughs about it, it isn't always with humor.*

THE JIGSAW GIRL

by Stephen Gallagher

It was finding the old jigsaw that did it, one rainy afternoon when Mike and I had sneaked out of the art studio for a long lunch hour and wound up in one of those flea markets, nosing around stalls that were filled with junk. I recognized the picture on the lid right away. I pulled it out, blew the dust off, rattled the wooden pieces inside; a few pennies would probably have bought it, but all I did was replace the box where I'd found it, carefully, as if in deference to its age. Later in the day, when I was sitting at the drawing board trying to work up some enthusiasm for a letterhead design, I found that my mind was drifting back. It was then that I realized that I'd been holding the answer to a puzzle more than two decades old.

I got out of the studio on some excuse and went back, but of course now I was too late. Where the stall had been standing was just an empty trestle table in a low-ceilinged, windowless hall beneath one of the city's newest concrete plazas. The rain was still falling when I reemerged, and everything seemed to be streaked and blurred like paint on glass; I couldn't face the studio again, not today, and so I turned up my coat collar and struck out into the drizzle toward my car. Mike would cover for me, if he had to. I'd covered for him often enough.

Damn it, I was thinking as I drove home, how come things always seemed to slip through my hands so easily? Opportunities could go past me and I wouldn't even recognize them until it was too late . . . and now this, a simple kid's toy, a piece of my past that had been delivered into my hands and then lost again because I'd been too slow to make the connection. I could still see it, that deep box scuffed at the corners and faded along the sides. The kind of jigsaw that you'd buy for a small child—not too many pieces, not too difficult to put together. The picture on the lid showed a gypsy woman beside her caravan; it was night, and she was holding her hands over a fire to warm them. One side of the lid was torn, and the whole box was held together by an elastic band. I'd have guessed that it would be complete —I mean, who'd bother to pass on a jigsaw with pieces missing? I also wondered if it might be the same one, because someone had obviously valued it and protected it for a long time before letting it go. But then, I told myself, they must have sold thousands of them, all identical. This was hardly likely to be hers.

Not the Jigsaw Girl's.

The rain had more or less eased off when I finally left the car out on the drive and let myself into the house. Helen wasn't home yet, and the girls were away on some school trip and wouldn't be back until Friday, which meant that the place felt even emptier than usual. I brewed some tea and took it up into the study and switched on the anglepoise over the drawing board.

I loved my study at home about as much as I loathed the studio where I worked for most of the day. It wasn't because of the conditions or the people I had to be with; it was all down to the product. If you've ever wondered who produces the artwork for the notices you see in post offices and doctors' offices, for the cheapest Christmas cards and calendars, and for the old-fashioned-looking covers on the romantic novels in corner-shop libraries, then you'd find the answer on the drawing boards of McClain and Forward. We were six salaried artists employed on a production-line basis, two time-served sign writers, an office junior, and a dispatch clerk so elderly that we all called him Pharaoh.

I wasn't too worried about having left an empty chair at the studio. Mc-Clain—there wasn't actually anybody called Forward—allowed us the degree of freedom that you'd expect "creative people" to take anyway; as long as we produced to quota, we could tackle the work load however we liked. This was probably good psychology, because in our darkest moments I suspect that each of us would have admitted to losing any claim we had to creativity in a slow degeneration from the day we started taking the salary check. Work produced to order, in a hurry, and consciously pitched at the minimum acceptable standard is not the mark of an artist.

We all had our little escape hatches, of course. Mike was a passable cartoonist in his own time, making occasional magazine sales. Joe Henley did unpaid covers for small-press magazines, while Randolph Atkinson, the "grand old man" of the design staff, was preparing a limited edition of his daughter's poems backed by his own illustrations.

And me? I had *Killer Caine*.

Ever since I'd made up and stapled my own one-off comics as a small boy, I'd wanted to work in the strips. Not just little three-panel stories, but a complete long narrative. *Killer Caine* had been at the back of my mind for some time, but it hadn't really come to anything until Helen and I took a package weekend in Paris; on the Boulevard St. Michel I spent almost an entire afternoon in a bookstore that stocked nothing but large-format, hardcover comic books. I'd known that there was a continental market for such things, but I'd never understood its scale until now; *Asterix* and *Tintin* were only the tip of the iceberg. All the space you could ask for, a long narrative, color . . . I started on *Killer Caine* within three days of getting home.

I tended to put in about ten or fifteen hours a week. I had twenty pages completed, and another thirty or so in rough. I had a ring binder full of notes for the development of the plot line, and sketches for characters that I hadn't even introduced yet. I'd begun it like a sprinter, but now it was beginning to turn into a marathon on me.

Somewhere along the line, I supposed that I was going to have to make a choice. Just like today, I'd sit in my study and imagine what life could be like if I put all my efforts into the project and made it succeed, meanwhile trying not to think about how I'd manage to pay the mortgage and the family bills if it should flop.

With the tea cooling at my elbow and the *Killer Caine* roughs laid out before me, I told myself that a little contemplation would lay me open to new ideas and allowed my mind to drift yet again.

Of course, it drifted back twenty years. It drifted back to that day, and to the Jigsaw Girl.

It was still called a village, but only by the people who had moved into the big houses overlooking the golf course. Perhaps it had been a village once, but a long time had passed since the boundaries had spread and merged with the general suburban sprawl. It was the place where I grew up.

Even an area so small had its own Poverty Row; in this case it was the Prefabs by the canal, an estate of prefabricated concrete bungalows that had been thrown up as a temporary measure after the war and that, like most temporary measures, seemed to be destined to hang around forever. Some had been tended with obsessive pride, but they were the rarities. The general picture was of patched fences, weeds, and old cars on blocks with their brake drums showing. The estate's main street was dead-ended by a set of railings with gaps that led through to the corporation tip; it's tempting to start building this up as a symbol of decay, but that would be to bring grown-up cynicism to bear where it isn't really appropriate.

Because the truth is that the Prefabs and the tip beyond were the liveliest and most interesting places around, at least from the point of view of a ten-year-old. The street was like one large playground where nobody ever came out of the houses to shoo you along, most of the gardens were open to all traffic, and the tip—the tip was paradise, a moonscape mosaic of metal shavings and smashed pottery, of oil drums and planks and, once, a doorless old car with the seats still in. There was a railway siding along one boundary where you could sneak over and play among the standing wagons or even give the brake wheel in the guard's van a quarter-turn to feel it roll, and a polluted stream where tadpoles somehow managed to make it into frogs. What more could a kid ask?

I suppose it was inevitable that a lot of my friends would come from the Prefabs, since most of the children there went to the school at the end of my street. Some I knew well, others only slightly. One of the closer ones was David, a boy who holds a unique place in my memory for being able to get far more glue onto the outside of a model airplane than was ever needed on the inside to hold it together. David and I were working on a comic; if ever I get a biographer and he wants to trace back to the origins of *Killer Caine*, here they are.

Among the others—those I knew only slightly—I'd include the Jigsaw Girl. She was eight or nine years old, one of those really tiny children looking like a perfect miniature of an adult. From the way her straight hair was cut and the way she was dressed, you'd think that she'd been lifted from a Salford backstreet of the 1930s. She was bright, too—brighter than I was, although I didn't recognize this at the time. She always said hello when I went past her garden on the way to David's. I always said a reserved hello back, and hoped that she wouldn't do this sometime when there were people with me. That kind of thing was embarrassing; she was a girl, and she was two years younger than me—a different species, a different generation.

And how did I come to give her that name? It happened on a spring afternoon, in the school holidays.

She called to me as I was passing, and asked me where I was going. She was so small that she could hardly see over her own gate. When I told her, she said why didn't David and I come around and play in her garden?

I was instantly evasive. Some things you learn early. "Well," I said, "we've got things to do."

"You could do them here."

"It's okay. Thanks anyway."

"I've got a swing. My dad put it up for Christmas."

I'd seen her swing. It was strictly scrap value only, rescued and repainted. The seat had been fixed so low for her short legs that it would have been useless for anybody else.

"Perhaps later," I said, thinking that if I made it vague enough, she'd stop pressing and then forget. But she beamed as if I'd just promised her something really worthwhile.

"I'll ask my mam if I can bring my jigsaw out," she said. She pronounced it *jik-saw*.

"Why?" I said.

"It's what I had for Christmas."

It dawned on me then that the jigsaw and the swing had been it, her entire Christmas bonanza. One creaky swing, and one dull old jigsaw! What could her parents have been thinking of? I'd read in old Christmas stories about kids hanging up a stocking and getting perhaps a cheap little flute and an orange, but I didn't really believe that such things went on. The modern requirement was for a pillowcase, at least. My own had been a special Santa bag with a printed picture on the side, and some of the stuff had had to be heaped alongside it when it was full. Oranges were right out; they could be had anytime. And a jigsaw—well, a jigsaw was just about acceptable, right down there with the make-weight presents, but as a main event, it had no chance of pulling a crowd.

All this ran through my mind, but fortunately none of it came out.

She said, "What did you get?"

I thought of that stack of goods, the things that used batteries and the things that didn't, the wooden cowboy town that my father must have been working on since October, the board games and the wind-ups and the edibles.

And I said, "Oh, nothing much. Nothing as good as a swing, anyway."

"And a jigsaw. I'll ask if I can bring it out for when you come."

"Yeah, great."

She leaned over the gate and waved as I walked away. She had to raise herself on tiptoe to do it. "See you," she called, and I waved back and then walked on more quickly, hoping that nobody had been watching.

I honestly didn't know what to make of her. She chatted like an adult to an adult. She'd told me of her hopes of growing up and becoming a nurse, of marrying somebody who'd have a car like her uncle's and living in a cottage a long way from the Prefabs and the canal. It put me on the spot, such treatment. I wasn't sure that I could live up to it.

Anyway, I got to David's place, but David couldn't come out. He was being taken to visit an aunt in half an hour, and he was too clean to be let beyond the front door. So I went through to the tip to see if anyone else was around, and met up with Roy and a couple of his friends from the unknown territory at the far end of Petersburg Road. Roy was the nearest we had to a village idiot, a boy of average intelligence but with a lunatic streak that made him good entertainment, in limited doses. One of his favorite routines was to expose himself to the girls in the school cloakroom; "Just a little look," he'd announce, and then he'd drop his shorts, underpants and all, enjoying the shrieks of surprise and shock. He wore loose elastic suspenders, which meant that he only had to release his grip and the pants would snap back up into place. It was like watching a film being run backward.

"See what we found," Roy said, so I went to look. A lorry had been along sometime that morning and dumped a load of mispressed metal sheets, about a hundredweight of medallion-size discs and the plates from which they'd been stamped. They looked too good not to be of some use, and eventually we discovered it; thrown edge-on, they made tolerably accurate missiles. We set up some paint cans as targets, and the half-hour that I'd intended to spend gradually unraveled itself through the whole afternoon.

Finally Roy and the others set off toward Petersburg Road. I didn't want to stray off my home turf into alien country, so I didn't go with them; I hadn't much liked the look of Roy's friends, anyway. One of them, named Ralph, had a sniffling cold and no handkerchief; Roy had called him Silversleeves, and got away with it. You can get away with a lot when you're as nutty as Roy. I sometimes wonder where they keep him, these days.

I had, of course, completely forgotten about the Jigsaw Girl's invitation. In fact, it had been out of my mind by the time that I'd climbed through the railings and onto the tip.

Memory of it came back to me as I was making my way back up toward the main road and home. The poisoned stream ran around the back of the Prefab estate on its way to an eventual meeting with the canal, and its banks were so overgrown that walking alongside it had something of the flavor of a jungle trek; it was, therefore, a favorite route.

It also went along behind her house, separated from the back garden only by a sparse hedge; there had been a fence, but most of it had rotted away. I felt a sudden guilt as I got close. I know I don't seem to have come through this story with much on my side so far, but that surge of entirely decent guilt was, I believe, my one sincere and saving grace.

Even so, I ducked down and tried to sneak past as quietly as I could. She was still out in the garden, although it was starting to get late. She was kneeling on an old towel, placed so that she could see around the side of the house to the street, waiting for visitors who hadn't come. True to her word, she'd brought out the jigsaw; the open box was at her side, the pieces were spread out on the towel, and she seemed to have them already half-assembled.

Her back was turned and she couldn't see me. I stopped for a minute and watched. I was looking for some signal that everything was fine, that no hurt had been caused, that I had nothing to feel bad about. I didn't get it.

Her head was down, her whole posture one of misery. She picked at the pieces, slotted them into place mechanically. Every now and again, she glanced toward the empty street; she did the same when anyone walked by, but a little more eagerly.

I felt bad, but it was all too late. I felt like I'd dropped a small animal from a cliff, and now I was watching it struggle during its long fall and knowing that however sorry I might be, it was too late to change anything. It was almost dark already.

She sighed, and carried on. She was using the picture on the box lid as a guide. It didn't take her long to finish.

I hung back, wanting her to sweep the pieces back into the box and go inside before I tried to scramble past; she was bound to hear me and look around, otherwise. But instead, she just knelt there and stared at the completed puzzle on the towel before her.

Something seemed to be wrong. She looked from the lid to the puzzle, and then at the lid again; and then back to the puzzle, which she studied hard and for so long that my legs began to knot with cramp.

And then she started to cry.

It wasn't just little-girl crying. It started as slow, deep sobs, and built up from that. She seemed too small to contain so much anguish. For the first time in my life, I saw what real despair was like.

It was almost too powerful for sound. All that came out of her was a thin, keening hiss of air, like a broken whistle. She took her breath in ragged jumps, and hugged her sides as if they hurt. Her back was still toward me.

Finally she got to her feet. She ran through the treasured jigsaw and into the house, slamming the door behind her. There wasn't another sound, and there was no other sign of life.

I was feeling less than noble. But you can't go on like that for long, not at ten years old, and so it began to turn to anger. Anger at the Jigsaw Girl, for making unreasonable demands on me. Anger at David, for not being there. Anger at everything and everybody but myself.

I had nothing to feel sorry about. It was the jigsaw that had triggered her off, not me. Perhaps a piece was broken, or missing, or perhaps it fit together wrong; from the way she seemed to regard it, something like that might well set her going.

Seconds later, I was through the hedge and crouching over the towel.

She'd scattered the pieces, but there weren't more than thirty of them, and they were big ones. I scarcely had to look at the picture on the box as I put it back together. I glanced up at the house once, but nobody was watching. The jigsaw was easy.

And it was a different picture from the one on the box lid.

If I hadn't known better, I would have sworn that it changed as the last piece was fitted into place; but it was late, and the light wasn't good, and I hadn't been paying that much attention.

Instead of the gypsy woman, it showed an ordinary-looking house. A family of four stood before it, also ordinary. A man, spreading a little, losing his hair; the woman beside him looking a touch worn out with the upkeep of it all. Two children, both girls, about my own age. It was about the most unremarkable picture I'd ever seen.

I swept all the pieces together and shoveled them into the box before I left by the way that I'd come. It was utterly weird, I thought to myself as I hurried along in the twilight, knowing that I was going to be late home and in trouble. I hadn't seen anything in the picture to get upset about, nothing at all, and I couldn't see any reason for her tears.

But then, she was so much brighter than I was.

I phoned Mike at the studio the next morning, saying that I was going to be a little late getting in, and asked him to make excuses for me if it turned out to be necessary. He was very cool about it, but I couldn't blame him for that.

It took me about an hour to get across to the other side of town. Although I didn't live so far away now, I hadn't been back in years; no reason to.

An hour's drive, and it wasn't worth getting out of the car at the end of it.

The Prefabs were gone, cleared long ago. Only the name of the street was the same. The houses on the site weren't even new; they'd taken on that greyed-down look of established brickwork, as much at home as poppies on a grave. Down at the far end, where the railings had been, stood a high concrete wall. I could just make out the sounds of a hidden six lanes of motorway over on the far side. There was no tip, no railway, no single feature that I might have recognized.

What had I expected to find, anyway? An eight-year-old girl, still waiting in her garden for an apology from someone who'd missed his chance to value her in the way she'd deserved? It just doesn't happen, not outside "The Twilight Zone." Everyone else had grown up and moved on, just as I had; it was only in my memory that they were fixed in time, as ageless as old photographs.

I restarted the engine, and set off to look for a working phone.

The people at the Town Hall transferred me across three departments before I got to speak to somebody who could answer my one, simple question; when they'd cleared the Prefabs and sold off the land, where did the people go? But of course, there wasn't a simple answer; they hadn't all been herded onto trucks to be taken away to the same place, some makeshift resettlement camp for the refugees from the great urban renewal program of the sixties. They'd mostly dispersed, some to other towns, others not so far. If there was somebody specific that I was trying to trace, perhaps . . . but I didn't have a name. All I had was the Jigsaw Girl, and the memory of that afternoon, and a too-late understanding of what it had all meant.

Half of the morning was gone. I was on a no-hope mission with no real purpose in my mind. It was time to get back.

Let it go, I told myself as I joined a network of fast roads that hadn't even existed when I was a child. You'll get nowhere, anyway. Go back to your safe job and your secure home, and your ambitions for *Killer Caine.*

Even then, there was something in me that wanted to head down any sliproad leading to groups of featureless tower blocks, to dull concrete shopping precincts, to rambling, graffiti-sprayed estates of modern maisonettes; I couldn't shake the feeling that if I stood at the post offices or hung around outside the chain stores, then I'd see her there. She'd be one of those not-so-young mothers, worn out and flat-footed before her time, pushing a trolley or waiting in line. They wouldn't talk of evening classes, or of child minders, or of resuming a career when the children were old enough. The future had been wide open but her part in it had been fixed, there and then . . . much, I suppose, as my own had been.

So, what did I think I could do about it now?

Nothing, I suppose, but give in. And let it go.

I had my jacket off even before I came through the door; within moments I was at my board and looking as if I'd been there for the whole morning.

Mike raised his eyebrows and glanced around furtively, but that was all. I could see that there wasn't any trouble.

"Thanks for the cover," I said in a low voice.

"No cover needed," Mike said, leaning back and stretching. For a moment he looked as if he was in real pain, but then I remembered he was probably on his nineteenth dewy-eyed puppy. "McClain hasn't been in yet. Had to run one of his kids to the hospital."

"Anything serious?"

"Not according to Pharaoh, but you know what Mrs. Mac's like. One of them gets a stomachache, and she wants an X-ray."

Situation normal, then. I took the first commission from my overloaded In tray, and gave the client's instructions a quick read-through.

It was straightforward enough, but then they're hardly ever anything else. Cover for an insurance folder, line and tone. Perhaps an hour, certainly no more than two. I picked a pencil out of my jam jar and started roughing in.

I drew an ordinary-looking house. A family of four standing before it, also ordinary. The father spreading a little, losing his hair; the woman beside him looking not *too* worn out with the upkeep of it all. Two children; usually you make them one of each, but I made them both girls.

When one o'clock came around, I was inking and Mike was on his feet. "Coming out to wander?" he said, but I shook my head.

"I'm way behind," I said. "I'd better work through."

He stopped beside me for a moment and looked at what I was doing.

"I'd have said Helen's hair was darker," he suggested.

It was two years before I found it again.

This wasn't because I didn't look, but because when I went along to the next market there was a different stall holder on that spot, selling sets of movie lobby cards out of cardboard boxes. I asked around, but nobody could help. And that was how it was pretty well everywhere that I tried.

I'd given it a name in my mind by now, that of the Fortune Teller. It had shown me an image of my future in the garden that afternoon, an image that I'd failed to recognize simply because it had been so ordinary, with none of the dreams of a child visible anywhere in it. I knew with equal certainty that it had done the same for the Jigsaw Girl and that she, unlike me, had known what she'd been seeing; and while her dreams had been far more modest than mine, the Fortune Teller had dashed them even harder.

Helen and the children became used to me disappearing off into the back streets of any new town that we visited, looking for charity shops or rummage sales or anywhere that the Fortune Teller might present herself to me again.

The *Killer Caine* samples that I'd sent out had raised some interest, with the result that the project was making bigger and bigger demands on my professional life, and I knew that the time of choosing couldn't be put off for much longer. All that I wanted was to know how it would go . . . to see where I was heading so that I could have the confidence to move toward it.

We were in Brighton for a few days leading up to the Easter weekend. Helen had set up a base camp of towels and picnic stuff on the pebbly beach at the west pier, and I'd done my usual fade-out for half an hour or so as the girls paddled around barefoot in the cold April surf. What I found, some way in from the seashore, was a dusty-fronted junk shop in the shadow of the railway line; the place was so dismal that it didn't even look open, but I could see that there was somebody inside reading a newspaper in a back room. The entire shop, once I was inside, stank of mildew and neglect, but I was drawn by the promise of the cast-off goods that looked as if they'd been stacked against the walls for so long that they were probably holding the roof up.

I asked if they had any jigsaws, and was shown a water-stained tea chest that was three-quarters full of them.

The Fortune Teller came to light less than a minute later.

At first, I could hardly believe it. The same torn lid, the same picture. The same elastic band, holding it all together. The box seemed to move in my hands, to pulse with hidden energy, but the pulse was only my own. I got a strange sense that for all the time that I'd been looking for the jigsaw, it had also been looking for me; and here we were at last, reunited, like two lovers on a station platform amid the turmoil of war. Paying over the few pennies that it cost to buy seemed like an absurd come-down.

I almost ran back to the hotel with it.

The maid service hadn't yet reached our room when I got there, so I hung out the Do Not Disturb sign and then moved the furniture around to make space for the pieces on the floor. It was a good carpet; better, I noted as I opened the box and spilled out the puzzle, than the stuff we had at home.

It was easy enough to put together, almost as if my fingers remembered exactly what I'd done all those years before. I went by the shapes, not by the picture; the man in the shop had even said something about the contents not matching the lid, and as I worked, I wondered if he'd given the puzzle a try on some long wet afternoon when there were no customers and nothing better for him to do. If he had, what had he seen? Nothing he'd understood, obviously.

The last piece was in place, and I stood up to get a better look.

And realized, then, exactly what it was the shopkeeper had been telling me.

I didn't know whether to laugh, or to strike myself on the forehead, or what to do. In the end I sat weakly in the chair and covered my eyes and started to giggle. What he must have been saying, only I'd been in too much of a hurry to listen, was that the box and the pieces came from two different puzzles; because the completed picture bore no relation to anything that I could recognize, from the box lid, from my own life, or anywhere. I snorted and laughed until my sides hurt, thinking what an utter idiot I'd been.

An oracle, indeed. I shook my head, and used one of those shoe-polishing cloths to wipe my eyes. Well, at least I'd managed one thing—I'd released myself from what I supposed had been a two-year obsession. I felt curiously light and cleaned out as a I swept the pieces and the box up into the waste bin for the maid service to take away. Then I removed the sign from the door handle before heading for the lift down to the lobby.

What might have seemed like magic reflected back from the vision of a ten-year-old had become rather less so to adult eyes. I'd been looking here at a printed picture on an old puzzle, nothing more; and any temptation to believe that it might be any kind of a window into the future had been removed by the simple fact that I wasn't in it.

It had been three women in a church, that was all, probably one of those gloomy old Victorian paintings since the women were all dressed in black. They were all veiled, and all three sat apart as if they weren't speaking. The rest of the pews, all the way to the back of the church, were empty. There was probably some story implicit in the scene, as was common with this kind of picture, and it was probably something morbid and depressing, which was the kind of thing that the Victorians seemed to like.

But as I said, I didn't even appear.

The elevator reached the lobby, and I stepped out.

I allowed myself one more rueful smile at my own folly, and then I cleared the whole thing out of my mind as I headed back toward the beach.

Fortune Teller. I mean, come *on* . . . *!*

Introduction

There used to be ads in the backs of comic books and magazines that promised you, if only you would send in the coupon, that you could amaze and entertain your friends playing the piano/guitar/whatever at parties after only ten simple lessons. They never explained what those lessons were.

Christopher Browne seldom writes prose fiction, but those who look forward daily and on Sundays to the adventures, as it were, of Hagar the Terrible, know who he is. They'll also wonder, after reading this story, if they really know him at all.

THE LESSON

by Christopher Browne

When I was ten years old, I lived near the Third Avenue el on the Lower East Side in Brooklyn. The summer of my tenth birthday the smell of fish rising from the melting ice on Fulton Street mixed with the unfamiliar smell of asphalt and oil. The cobblestones were being covered over. The cars were coming. A large paper carp, red and white, twisted in the wind as it hung from the fire escape across the alley. My friend Billy Moran had a string that ran from my window to his. We had a little matchbox that had a second string attached to it, and with this simple gizmo we could pass messages back and forth, even sometimes late at night when we were supposed to be asleep. We could even send new tin soldiers back and forth this way. It was lots of fun. He was my only friend.

Many sounds came up from the street. Horses, the ice man, the fruit seller, the policeman's whistle. One morning at breakfast my mother's head snapped back. She twisted it from side to side like a bird.

"What is that? Heywood, what's that sound?"

My father didn't appear from behind his *Journal-American.*

"Hmm?"

"That noise, that strange music. Is that a piano?"

Of course it was a piano. In no time, Mom had gotten the word. A piano teacher, a famous Viennese piano teacher, had moved into the brownstone on the corner of Sullivan Street.

"What does Viennese mean?" my father wanted to know.

"German, stupid!"

"A Kraut. That's just swell."

"Well, I don't care if he is German, I want Chubs"—my parents called me Chubs; I had been slightly overweight as a child—"to have the benefit of a musical education."

Even years after adolescence hit me like a sticky freight train, and my excessive adipose ran off my body in rivulets, the moniker Chubs stuck with me. I will have to remember this when I go see them at the home next week.

Have you ever been hauled up three flights of stairs, yanked like a mule and pulled by an ugly tie you didn't want to wear in the first place? Thus began my first piano lesson with Professor Werner Van Doreen Sternn. My mother, leading and pulling, her high heels clattering loudly on the hard wood stairs; me, screaming and clutching at banisters, letting my body go limp and praying loudly; and my father bringing up the rear with the *Daily Mirror* rolled up into a tight cylinder and tucked under his arm.

In a few brutal minutes, we were waiting in the large waiting room that led by a pair of large glass french doors into the professor's music room. We stood quietly and properly, like a tired little trio posing for a photo cameo. No note of music came from behind those doors. Only a few muffled sounds: a piano bench being moved, some papers spilling on the floor, an old man swearing in German. Finally he appeared in the doorway. The doors swung open like the gates of a musical hell.

Everything inside the room was old. I don't mean that there wasn't a freshness to it. I mean old. Aged. Barely clinging to existence. The wood of all the furniture was dark and of a type I'd never seen before. The seats on all the chairs were velvet; they must have been bright as the sun at one time, but now they were colorless; smoke and threadbare, they had the same look as the white-headed eagle of a man who stood on his toes and clicked his heels when we met. The chairs and the man both looked like all the good had run out of them.

"You are uncommonly intelligent people to have the wisdom to bring your child to me for his musical education. I am the finest piano teacher in Vienna, and now, as you see, America, and so perhaps, who can say? Maybe the world.

"It is incredibly important to begin a child's piano lessons as soon as possible. Mozart, I'm sure you know, composed his first composition when he was only a child of four. Some say three! Musicologists differ on this point, but it is a very small point and it was a very long time ago." He talked like a trip-hammer. I looked up at my father on my right. No help was coming from him; he was almost asleep on his feet. My head swung around to my mother on my left. Uh-oh; she was like a chicken hypnotized by a snake. She clung to his every word.

"Now, I have my own method, it's a revolutionary new concept, the Werner Van Doreen Sternn Method, named after me, Professor Werner Van Doreen Sternn, its creator. I have had such incredible, unbelievable results with this method that in an effort to keep my method a secret, I must ask the parents not to be present during the lessons. But you need not show any concern; the child will be fine. You will come back in an hour and you will see, he will already be beginning to make music on the piano. Of course it takes many, many lessons, and ruthless practice, sacrifice, dedication, until he becomes, say, Chopin, Mussorgsky, eh? But you'll see. My method is so brilliant, I'll let you know a secret: this very day, my prize student, from Vienna? He is only eighteen, but I have taught him by my method since he was six. He is coming here, to Brooklyn, New York, all the way from Vienna. Today! Here! Just to continue his training with me. Amazing, is it not? Yes, it is."

My parents looked duly impressed, and that seemed to please the hyperactive old buzzard. But he quickly ushered them out the door and pushed me toward the piano. The piano was the only thing in the room that was bigger, older, and scarier than the professor.

"All right, my boy. Don't be afraid. Always, the first lesson the boy is afraid. What do you think, I'm going to eat you?"

That seemed to break the tension a little, so I smiled. But when I did, his yellow grin vanished.

"Do you think something's funny? You're here to work, to study and learn! So!" He took a piece of sheet music, yellowed and taped with cellophane, and stuck it on the music stand.

"This is a short Ravel piece. This is 'Dark Forest March.' You have heard of it?"

I didn't know what to say. He looked angry.

"Why are you looking at me? Do I have music notes on my face? Don't look at me, look at page." He grabbed my chin roughly and twisted my head hard. It made my neck hurt, and a chill ran up my spine. Now at last it occurred to me. I was in some kind of real danger here.

"Have you ever read music before? Eh? Well, this doesn't matter. With my method, I have you reading in no time, all right? Now, watch the notes where I show you." He picked up a foot-long black pointer. It was a little thicker than a school pencil at the base and it tapered away to nothing at the tip. He led that sharp tip along the first row of notes, first tapping out each note and chord and calling it by name,

"A minor, C, C minor, B, B, B diminished, A . . ."

And then he'd run the wand over the line of notes again, this time in a sweeping, wavelike motion, humming the music rapidly, much too fast to remember.

"Okay, now. I want you to watch what I do; concentrate! And remember. Understand? Watch what I do, concentrate and remember. Remember." I nodded my head.

He cracked his knuckles in a strange way; inward, as if making a snowball, not outward like my Aunt Baru always did. Then he closed his ancient eyes, shook out his fingers as if drying them in the wind, and slowly let the fingertips float down, float down, like leaves, onto the ivories.

Bang. Bang. Bang. The hands came alive, two rocks turning into two tumbling, bone-white wildcats. They moved faster and faster, becoming a blur . . . they moved so quickly they seemed to slow and start moving backward, like the spokes on the wheels of a fire wagon . . . the music that came out of them was fast, complicated music, space chatter from some superintelligent race from a million miles beyond my understanding. But it was also awesomely beautiful. And just as suddenly as it had started, it stopped.

The professor turned to me again, his eyes snapped open.

"Okay. Now, you. Do as I do."

I didn't understand. He stared at me coldly, then grabbed both my hands in his and slammed them down on the keys.

"Come on, come on, you come here to learn, begin to learn. Play what I just play for you. You play the same now for me."

Was he joking?

"Play!" he screamed. The veins in his nose stood out and the whites of his eyes turned pink. Well, what the hell did I know? Maybe playing the piano wasn't that tough after all. I squinted at the sheet music. I concentrated. I tried to remember what he had done. I let my fingers drift down to the keys like he had done. I began to play.

Bang, bang, bang. Garbage came out of the piano. Pure, unintelligible junk. It was a nightmare. My hands burst into two red roses of pain. He was beating my knuckles with the black wand. I yanked them back.

"Oh, you don't like that, do you, baby? The little man doesn't like pain? Listen to me, you stupid child! Every great musician has to suffer for the music, all right? Now maybe you will do what I tell you when I say watch, concentrate and remember. These are the golden keys to the Professor Werner Van Doreen Sternn special method. Okay? Now, watch."

Again he closed his eyes. I looked down at my hands. Red lines ran across their width, from left to right. His hands fluttered down onto the keys again.

They jumped up and down the keys at super speed, but the ten bony fingers never faltered. The exact same beautiful music poured forth, the room filled with golden mystery, and then all too soon, the silence returned. His head touretted toward me and his eyes stared into mine. His eyes were like the barrels of a sawed-off shotgun muzzle.

"Now, again, you try. And this time, please! *Concentrate!*"

Maybe he was right. I looked at the sheet music for Ravel's "Dark Forest March." I concentrated. What was the secret? It was right there in front of me, but what was it? I closed my eyes as he had done and put my fingers on the keys. I played my heart out, fast, just as he had done. The first two notes were perfect, I swear. The rest was monkey gibberish. I might just as well have been playing with two hammers. Smack, smack! Again he smashed my hands with the birch whip. I yelped and tried to pull away. He grabbed me by the collar and continued to strike me severely. Tears welled in my eyes.

"You're going to make me very cross with you if you insist on being so difficult! Now, I am willing to give you another chance. You don't want your parents to be disappointed in you, do you?"

"No, professor, but . . ."

"But what?"

"There are so many notes . . . it's difficult for me to . . . to . . ."

He saw me rubbing my hands together.

"Stop babying those! All right, if the piece is too hard, I suppose it's too hard. You Americans are soft and stupid, that much is becoming very clear to me. I'll tell you"—he randomly snatched another sheet of music off the piano and slapped it over the first one in the music stand—"I would never have this problem with one of my old students in Vienna. What a refreshment it will be for me when my prize student, Hans Delmar Vorst, arrives here in town. Now there is a student—dedication, concentration . . ."

But the old man's words were falling on deaf ears. I was consumed by the piece he had set before me: "The William Tell Overture." The Ravel piece looked simple by comparison. The page was covered with thousands of tiny black notes, ants with fat black heads and tiny, hairlike bodies. They seemed to be frozen in battle, as if they had all been fighting and then died all at the same instant, still locked together. A word formed in my mind, something I had heard in school. *Gettysburg.* I shook my head. In fact, I started to shake all over.

Bang ditty-bang, ditty bang-bang-bang! He started to play again, and again, more beautiful than before. This time he played the entire first page. My horror grew with each additional second. It occurred to me that he wanted me to play this insane piece, and not just a few notes, but an entire page of music.

He finished and turned to me, and in the same moment smoothly picked the switch up off the piano. He held the switch directly over the keyboard this time. His lips tightened over his yellow teeth and a pendulum of spit appeared on his chin. It shook as he spoke, but did not fall off.

"Play."

I tucked my swollen hands under my thighs.

"Insolent child! Never disobey your professor! Play!"

"No!" I screamed and slid off the bench. I ran around the room, screeching. I kicked over chairs with velvet bottoms, I threw yellow handfuls of sheet music in his face. He chased me around the room three times; when I slowed to try the french doors, he caught me and pulled me to the floor. He kneeled over me, whipping me savagely with the switch. I screamed for a long time. Then I heard noises even louder than my screams coming from the waiting room. Then my parents burst in. I ran to them.

"What the hell do you think you're going?" my father bellowed. It was the first time I can remember him standing up for me. "Are you insane?"

My mother chimed in. "You have no right to do this to our child! What the hell has been going on here?"

"That is none of your business, frau. It is my own method, a secret method of my own perfecting which I have had grand and glorious success with in Europe. And as to my rights, I have *every* right; *art* gives me the right!"

Now everybody in the room was screaming at everybody else in the room. I was weeping, my father was calling the old man everything but a white man, my mother was swearing oaths and promising both legal action and the wrath of almighty God, and the old professor was smacking himself on the head, ranting on.

"How could I be so *stupid* as to think that I could find appreciation for my method in this stupid country! Only in Vienna did I ever find even a few who had the patience, the stamina to withstand the demands that art makes on us! Only there, amid the clacking tongues did I find a *few*— "

Two men appeared in the doorway from the hall. They were two large Irishmen, and they were sweating. As they mopped their brows, one of them interrupted the old man.

"Pardon me. Pardon me, I hate to bust up a good healthy scrap like this, but are either of you men Professor Van Doreen Sternn?"

"Yes, yes, that is me."

"We're the men from the Kelly company. You asked us to meet a train at Grand Central today?"

The old man's face lit up. He was awash with excitement, and he began tittering like a child.

"Oh, yes, yes, yes, come in, come in!"

He threw the french doors wide open now, all the way open, and locked them in position. Momentarily he seemed to forget we were even in the room with him. Then, noticing us with disdain, he dismissed us like so many servants, with a wave of his bony hand.

"Now, get out, you stupid little people. It was a mistake to think I could ever teach your undeveloped minds anything. Out! Out! My prize student is arriving, and he's very sensitive. I don't want him disturbed by you stupid pigs! Out, pigs, out!"

As we retreated, I licked my battered hands and my parents each rested a hand on my shoulders. The two big Irishmen wrestled a large, squat crate into the room on a dolly. We had to step to one side as they squeezed it through the french doors. VIENNA and NEW YORK were stenciled on the sides, and many oak tags were affixed to its broad pine slats with thin wire. Several times something large and violent bucked and squealed inside the crate.

"Careful," the larger Irishman cautioned the smaller. "Where the hell do you want this thing?"

"Just there by the piano," the professor snapped.

They slammed it down on its side and pushed it up against the piano. The box smelled like the monkey house at the zoo. The creature inside sounded like a demon out of hell. The slats were spaced a few inches apart here and there, but the room was very dark and we couldn't get a good look. Two long hairy arms, filthy, came out of the crate on the piano's side. They seemed to be reaching up toward the ceiling. The hands, wrists, and arms were covered with years of scars, old and recent ones, as well as running sores and deep unhealed cuts. The fingernails had all grown to points and turned back into the fingertips. A horrible, inhuman howl issued forth from the crate. The professor tapped the box with the switch.

"Enough of that, now," he cautioned.

The strange clawlike hands turned in upon themselves, and with that strange, snowball-making motion, the thing cracked its knuckles. Then the two hands slowly fluttered down to the keyboard, as gentle as two leaves. And then, after a pause, they began to play the most beautiful music I have ever heard in my life.

Introduction

How do you explain your lover's interest to your friends—the interest you pretend to like yourself because you don't want to endanger the relationship? Do you do it tolerantly, with feigned enthusiasm, or with humor? Or do you tell the truth?

Leanne Frahm continues to be one of the most popular Australian writers whose work appears in this country. She doesn't write as much as we'd like her to, and a new story is always more than welcome.

ON THE TURN

by Leanne Frahm

The wind met them head-on with an almost overpowering gust as they tramped their way through the last of the scrub and topped the final dune. It was deceptive. In the hollows, there had been no hint of the blast moaning overhead, no hint of a breeze on the highway, or when the car had turned at right angles onto the dusty pocked road that led to the beach. They had traveled between fields of sugar cane, three-quarters grown, that scarcely moved, between great loops of electricity lines on which anxious-looking nankeen kestrels and querulous butcher birds alternated, studying the fields below them intently for signs of tiny prey movements.

Saph had liked the trip. She knew birds pretty well, most of them, and had enjoyed the sudden intimate glimpses of small feral lives as they went, the noise of the car disturbing the quiet. Once, as they had rounded a bend, a small goanna had reared up with a look of astonished terror and had run waddling into the ditch, legs pumping comically at right angles to its body, almost tripping itself. Saph had laughed; Reg had grinned at her pleasure.

Then they were past the cane fields, into flat greyish country, sparsely treed, where gaunt cattle were browsing on tufts of brittle grass. "Look at them," Saph had said mournfully. Reg had glanced at the herd, his hands still firm and assured on the wheel. "They're drought cattle," he had said. "Brought in to the coast for agistment. They'll fatten up soon—soon enough to be nice and plump for the abattoirs." Saph had been silent; she enjoyed steak.

The cattle place had given way to muddy lagoons, sprouting water weeds and reeds, where a few black ducks were paddling industriously and white egrets were poised as if caught and preserved in amber. The road had become worse, and Reg had steered the car carefully between the ruts and hummocks until they could go no further, and had come to a halt in a little cleared patch where the solid ground became soft and sandy.

"Here we are," Reg had said.

They had alighted from the car, and Reg had apportioned the gear between them, carefully retaining his precious rods. It had been still in the clearing, but Saph had heard the muffled roar of waves. The beach wouldn't be far. They had walked along a faint trail that four-wheel drives had made, flattening the dry grass, letting the sand plump up and spill over it. Then they had climbed over the dunes.

And met the wind. It was blowing straight in from the sea with an implacable, unvarying determination. Reg looked dissatisfied. "No good casting into that lot," he said. "It'll blow the sinker right back in your face." He eyed the direction, and looked up and down the beach on which they stood. It stretched from a remote rocky point on their left to a place not far away to their right, where mangrove thickets abruptly blocked its golden infinity.

"We can try the creek," he decided. Saph nodded; it was Reg's decision to make. He was the fisherman.

It was a pleasant walk, despite the gale lashing sideways at them, forcing Saph to stagger from time to time. The night tide had been high, and had left the sand compacted and firm to walk on. She found a huge whelk in their path, the slug coursing aimlessly across the drying sand, dragging its conical shell behind it. It could be drying up, she thought. She picked it up and it slowly withdrew into its shell, snapping its door shut, dangling strands of sand-encrusted mucus.

"Where are you going?" said Reg, loudly, because the wind was howling so.

"I'm throwing it back in the water. It's lost, and the tide's going out."

Reg snorted. "It'll last to the next one, won't it?"

Saph continued to the water's edge anyway. Reg didn't know, not for sure. Better to be sure.

They reached a point where the beach rounded into a point, and mangroves grew as suddenly and as high as a wall in front of them. A narrow meandering creek issued from them, its banks sand for a little way inland, then transforming by degrees into the gelatinous mud of the mangrove swamp. "Down there a little," Reg said, pointing to a spot where the sand and mud formed an uneasy alliance that made it possible to walk comfortably. "We'll wait for the water to go down a little, and cross the creek to those mudflats over there." He waved to what was still a sheet of water on the other side of the creek's mouth, where the mangroves faced the sea. "There'll be lots of lobbies there. We'll pump for them, come back here, and wait for the turn of the tide."

"Can't we fish now?" said Saph. "You've got some bait . . ."

"Lobbies are better, fresh ones. And it's no good trying to fish on the falling tide. Fish just won't bite then. It's a waste of time."

Saph wondered if waiting for an incoming tide wasn't a waste of time when there was all that water there, but she said nothing. Reg knew about fish; she didn't.

Reg placed their gear on his chosen spot, flopped down beside it, and pulled a paperback out of the rucksack. Saph stood watching the water in the creek. He glanced up at her. "You might as well relax. It'll be at least another half-hour before we can cross. And another two hours before the turn."

"Then why are we here now?" said Saph.

"Because I thought we could fish the surf for whiting. We can't. This is the alternative." He went back to his book.

Saph shrugged and wandered back along the beach, examining stray shells and driftwood, kicking at clumps of drying seaweed. She liked the beach; always had. It was a place somehow linked with childhood fun and parental indulgence. Of course, those beaches had always been crowded, peopled beaches, like the ones in children's story books, with deck chairs and buckets and spades and other kids wailing with sand in their eyes. And sunburn cream. She glanced at her pale freckled forearm, where the sunburn cream glistened colorlessly.

This beach was different, though. Nothing moved, except the sea and a sea gull far out and hovering above the rough waves. The wind was lifting fine sand and driving it into the dunes, making it look filmy and out of focus. It felt desolate, almost eerie under a bright sun that shouldn't have allowed eeriness. You probably have to get used to this sort of beach, Saph thought.

They waded through water up to Saph's thighs in crossing the creek. Saph was amazed at how shallow it was. "And it still has further to go out?" she said.

Reg nodded. "Two o'clock it turns."

"It must get awfully low," she said.

In affirmation, little sandbars and pieces of driftwood were already emerging at the edge of the creek, sending the current into new directions and complex eddies. She stopped to look at a tiny crab busily investigating a rotting tree trunk embedded in the sand, saw Reg almost across, and scampered through the water to catch up, wetting her jeans to the waist. The wind made it cold, but already the sun was heating the damp material. She could feel it hot on her rump.

Reg had walked a little way onto the mudflat as she came up to him, sinking a few inches with each step. He was examining the ground intently. She could see that it was covered with tiny holes. "These are lobby beds," he said to her. "They burrow into the mud and sand and live in the holes." Saph nodded, although she didn't even know what a lobby looked like yet. But the size of the holes indicated that they weren't very large and were therefore unintimidating.

Reg positioned the lobby pump in the middle of a particularly dense group of holes. He plunged the tube into the mud at an angle with a liquid squelch, at the same time drawing up on the plunger. He pulled the pump from the mud, pressed down on the plunger, and with a gurgle, a cylinder of mud and sand squirted out at their feet. Saph stared at it. Little forms were squirming frantically in the middle of it.

"Quick!" yelled Reg. "Grab them!"

"What?" said Saph.

"Those! They're lobbies. Put them in the basket."

Saph held out the small wicker basket Reg had given her to carry. "This?" she said.

Reg grabbed it from her and bent toward the lobbies, already almost invisible as they wormed their way back into the mud. He managed to pick up a couple, threw one back—"Too small"—and put the solitary catch in the basket.

"Now," he said, straightening, "I'm sorry, I didn't explain it properly. When I pump, you have to be ready to catch them before they dig in again. That's"—he pointed to the lobby in the basket—"what you have to pick up."

Saph examined the lobby curiously as it scuttled up and down in the confines of its cage. It was less than an inch long, pale orange, and looked just like a miniature prawn, except that it was armed with a pink-white claw that was nearly as long as its body. "Does it bite?" she asked doubtfully.

"They'll nip if you're not careful," Reg said. "Now, be ready."

"All right," said Saph.

After half an hour the basket was half full. Reg seemed pleased that the beds had proved so lobby-abundant. Saph looked into the basket, glad that Reg was pleased, despite the many lobbies she'd missed, but the sight of the packed mass of little creatures heaving while the uppermost ones scurried back and forth over the bodies of the bottom layers unsettled her.

"How do you kill them?" she asked.

"*Kill* them?" Reg echoed. "You don't *kill* them. You use them for live bait."

"What—alive?" said Saph.

"Now you know why I didn't want to bring you fishing," said Reg, the exasperation that she'd known lurked beneath his calm bursting forth. "You're too soft," he added roughly, as if to emphasize that softness by contrast.

"I wanted to share it with you," Saph said, tears trembling her voice. "Marriages are for sharing, aren't they?"

His annoyance gentled, and he smiled at her. "Most things, but you weren't meant for some things, Saph."

She smiled tremulously back at him. "Now, how are you going to kill them?"

Reg snorted and turned away, picking up the gear. Saph was left with the basket of writhing lobbies. She knew he wasn't going to kill them, even for her. She tried to imagine what it felt like, to have a huge hook sliced into your chest, feeling it worm its way down into your entrails—

"Do they die right away?" she called above the wind.

"No!" A gust of wind trailed the word away from her, toward the land.

—your legs and arms twitching in a mock paralysis of screeching pain . . . But the thought was too uncomfortable, so she busied herself with hurrying after Reg, feeling the wind burning the other side of her face now, as they strode back toward the creek.

"What time did you say?" Saph asked, as much to make conversation as to know. Reg didn't look up from his paperback. "Two o'clock," he said. She threw another shell into the creek water. It was less windy here; a rise in the sandy point as it turned into the creek kept the wind mostly above them as they sat at the water's edge—or what had been the water's edge. Still, the wind howled into the massed growth of mangroves opposite their position, tossing the leaves on their stunted branches, whipping the creek waters into waves that marched inland, making it look like the tide was indeed coming in.

"It's quarter past," she said.

Reg closed his book on a finger. "They take that time at the Harbor. We're quite a bit south of that, and the coast curves inland, so the tide's probably going to turn a bit later here." It was nice of him, Saph thought, to explain things so considerately to her. She threw another shell at the water.

"Don't do that," Reg said automatically. "You'll frighten the fish."

"What fish?" she said.

"The fish are there, all right, but they won't bite until the tide turns."

"Oh."

She looked closely at the surface of the water. Yes, the waves gave the impression that the water was racing in, but when you looked through the water, you could see dead leaves and sticks whirling along in the current, toward the sea. And bubbles, as if the fish below were breathing gently, gathering strength for the turn and the feeding frenzy . . . And she'd placed a sea-bleached shell upright in the sand where the waves washed the bank, and now the water was several inches beyond it, still receding.

She got up, brushed the sand from her bottom, and walked to where the lobby basket sat. Reg had scooped a hole in the wet sand, and it had half-filled from seepage. He'd placed the basket in it, in the shade of the creel. "To keep them alive till we need them," he'd explained, and Saph wondered if his smile hadn't been just the littlest bit cruel as he'd looked at her, and then had dismissed the idea as unwholesome and false.

The lobbies were still milling around, although more lethargically. Some didn't seem to be moving at all, were floating limply in the water that now enveloped them within the wickerwork. Saph thought they looked forlorn, but resigned, as if they'd been brought up to expect little from their muddy lives, and this little seemed to be just about right. She sighed, and looked at the creek.

More sandbars had risen, and only one narrow channel still flowed seaward with any confidence. Some water was trapped in little pools, and it flowed nowhere; only the wind ruffled it into waves that looked as if they meant to march somewhere.

Saph said loudly, "I'm starting to fish now. I'm sick of waiting." Reg jerked his head up; he'd pulled a dead tree trunk, scoured white by many weary miles of ocean travel and deposited high on the beach by some king tide, down to a spot closer to the creek, and had been leaning back against it, reading.

"What's the time?" he said, and answered himself by glancing at his watch. "Ten past three . . . Is that water still going out?"

Saph looked at a brown fragment of leaf drifting past with a hesitant swirl. "Yes."

Reg looked surprised and stood up. "Should be turning by now, surely." He stooped to pull another book from the rucksack. Saph recognized it—his Tidal Diary 1985. "Maybe I got the date wrong," he said, flicking through the pages. "No—no, that's right." He pushed the book back in between the first aid kit, the torch, the spare lines, and stood staring at the creek, hands on hips, frowning.

"Well, I'm going to fish anyway," Saph repeated.

"Okay," said Reg absently. Then, "Do you want me to bait your hook?"

"No, I'll use the dead squid." It came out more forcefully than she'd meant, but that was because she had to shout against the wind. Reg shrugged, and with a final puzzled glance at the creek, went back to his reading.

Fishing was fun, she decided. It was fun to get squid juice all over her fingers, fumbling to push the flesh? skin? muscle? of the piece of squid onto the hook, and to wipe it carelessly, stinking of salt-ocean, off on her jeans. It was exhilarating to feel the line zing out as she cast, right into the middle of the channel, and pleasant to sit quietly holding the rod with her fingers over the line as Reg had taught her, to feel when the fish bit. She felt at peace with all the silence around her, with the sluggishly ebbing water, even with the wind moaning and whipping the mangroves opposite.

Overhead two brahminy kites were sailing, pausing head-on into the wind sometimes—how could they not be blown away, she wondered, when they hovered so motionlessly—mewling with a sound like a new baby that came strangely from those relentless tearing beaks. The gull had been joined by some others, and they spent most of their time strutting up and down on the beach behind her with a curious mixture of aloofness and supplication now that they saw she was fishing, and that there might therefore be scraps of bait . . . Smart birds, she thought with a grin. A couple of terns—two different species, she could tell, but which, she couldn't identify—glided out over the rumpled sand that marked the mouth of the creek, disdaining the pouty beggarship of the gulls. She watched them soar against the hot blue sky.

From where she sat, the sandbars exposed by the falling tide seemed to stretch to the horizon. Only a fuzzy white and grey-green line beyond the yellow of the sand proved that there was still an ocean out there. She wondered about the tides. The moon pulled the high tide after it, she knew, and left the low tide eternally hurrying behind it, round and round, up and down. She tried to picture it, but instead of a globe she could only see a teacup slopping brown liquid from side to side until it slurped over the rim and ran down the side, leaving a muddy brown stain on the white china surface . . .

The line tugged under her fingers. She jerked her hands up, more from fright than experience. The water was so shallow that the sinker exploded into the air on her jerk and sailed toward the beach, drawing a silver-flashing shape with it. She turned the reel inexpertly, crying out to Reg. "A fish! Look! I've caught a fish!"

He dropped his book and came over to her, seizing the line and pulling the dangling tackle and its burden toward him. He laughed. "It's a bit small," he said.

"What is it?" she asked.

"A little perch." He grabbed it with his thumb and finger around the body, well back from the gasping gills. "Careful, it's got nice little spikes there." He took the hook in the fingers of his other hand. "You've hooked it nicely," he said. Saph felt the glow of his compliment fade as she stared at the mouth of the little fish. It was gaping, and she could see that the hook had pierced the flesh on the inside, behind the jaw and the tiny teeth, and had come out on the other side, through the pulsating white skin above its throat. She thought of a hook jabbed through *her* jaw, coming out in *her* throat, and almost gagged with the imagined pain.

"It's far too little," Reg was saying. He deftly twisted the hook, withdrawing it from the mouth of the flapping fish, and tossed it back into the water. It disappeared with a silver flicker. "Want more bait?" he said, then looked up at her.

"Saph," he said, almost angrily, she could sense.

"I'm sorry," she said.

"You wanted to fish," he said, turning the statement into an accusation.

"I didn't think—I didn't realize . . ." It was impossible to tell him how that pain felt. Fish didn't feel, he would say. Not like us, he'd point out. She turned away from him.

"Well, then," he said, with a forced jollity. "I almost dozed off then."

He looked at his watch. "Ten to four . . ." Saph barely heard his mutter in the wind. He glanced at her quickly, then walked to the edge of the trickle of water that ran from the creek, still on the ebb. Saph had not seen him look like this before; Reg never looked bewildered.

"What's wrong?" she asked.

He was frowning again, a hard set to his face. "The tide should have turned well and truly by now," he said. "There's something wrong somewhere. Either the diary or . . ." He couldn't seem to think what else could be wrong. "Well, we've been here so long that even if the time was wrong, it must turn any minute."

"Yes," said Saph. "There's hardly any water left to come out."

He grinned at her. "That's one way of putting it. We'll give it a bit longer."

Saph was suddenly tired of the fishing trip. The afternoon sun was slanting across the mangroves now, more golden than the white hotness of noon, but out over the sea and sandbars the wind seemed to have sucked the color from the sunlight, making it grey and oppressive. The last of the afternoon's comfort was lowering with the sun, and Saph wanted to follow that sun home. Besides, she knew she wouldn't be fishing again, ever.

"It's getting late," she said. "Can't we go home now? Even when the tide comes in, it'll take a long time to start filling up the creek and we'd be here for ages . . ."

"I came here to fish," Reg said. His face was stony; sometimes he could be very obstinate. Saph recognized that this was a sometimes, and sat down at the creek, putting the rod behind her where she couldn't see the hook.

The mud skippers were out in force. They could skip practically right across the creek now. All the bed was exposed except for a thread of water, oily-looking and black in the heavy shadows of the mangroves. The tiny mottled fish hopped around, leaping into puddles and awkwardly out again, having a great old time, Saph thought, with so much air available to them. They'd get sick of it, though; they'd need the water to come in and dampen everything down again.

She looked at the shell she had erected so hopefully as a marker for the tide. It was a long way behind her now; she'd followed the water right down, heedless of the spreading muddy stain on the seat of her jeans, so she could watch the skippers and the tiny black crabs with the huge threatening claws they waved in a sort of crustacean semaphore, whether signaling "Attack" or "Truce" or "Hi beautiful" she didn't know. The wicker basket of lobbies was beside her. Its original Reg-made pool had dried up, and loose sand had begun to blow over it. As she'd moved forward, she'd made new puddles for it at each stop, pushing the sand and mud to one side and putting the basket into the water that gathered. It was little use, though. Most of them looked dead—motionless, at least. Still . . .

She glanced back at Reg. He was not reading now. He was sitting on the log, staring at the dark strip of moving water that was the creek, concentrating on it as if to turn the current by force of will. He looked angry—no, more than angry, but she had to try.

"Can we go home now?"

"Not yet," he said.

She turned back to the water. The setting sun threw a final effulgence that glimmered briefly on the stream, turning it momentarily from black to blood-red. She shivered. The wind seemed even stronger.

The wind-grey had seeped across the unending sandbars, across the beach, and reached them in the creek. There was little light, only a suffocating dimness that strained the eyes more than blackness. The mud skippers and crabs had retired to their mud homes, seeking moisture deep within the ooze. Saph had watched the last of them pop into their burrows with a final flick of tail or wave of claw. The birds had long since gone, crooning and calling, to faraway nests. Saph looked at the creek. There was no thread of water now, only unconnected pools, small isolated lakes left in the depressions in the sand whose surfaces shuddered in the wind.

"It's stopped," she called loudly without turning her head. There was no reply from Reg. She stood up and faced him. "It's stopped," she repeated.

He was a pale shape against the paler sand, leaning against the driftwood and staring into the mangroves across the creek bed, his arms crossed over his chest.

"I'll wait," he said.

Saph bent down to the basket, opened the lid, and upended it in one of the shallow pools. One or two lobbies stirred; the rest lay like a child's sand castle, a cake of dead bait, gradually dissolving into the water.

She left the basket where it lay, on the mud, and walked back to where Reg sat. She felt sorry for him, but she said firmly, "I'm going now. I know an end when I see it."

"I'll *wait!*" yelled Reg, making her jump.

She turned away and began walking back along the beach toward the car, with more difficulty now that the sand was dry. The wind buffeted her, blowing faster now that it was coming over smooth sandbars instead of rough water.

She noticed in the gloom another large whelk at her feet, began to pick it up, then realized that there was no water handy to put it into. "You should have kept up," she said out loud. It made her chest hurt to think of the millions of little things, like the mud skippers and the crabs, who hadn't kept up, who were unaware of the end that Reg stubbornly didn't believe in yet.

She looked back toward the invisible creek. "It's not coming back," she called, but the wind picked up her words and sprayed them uselessly across the night, and she continued to trudge along the long empty beach.

Introduction

The most comforting thing about a home is the fact that you know it, all its nooks and crannies and secrets and surprises. The most discomforting thing about a home is that you don't know nearly as much as you think you do.

Nancy Holder lives in San Diego and, after publishing several novels, is making her way into the short fiction market. She has a gorgeous smile that is also one of the most feral you'll ever see.

MOVING NIGHT

by Nancy Holder

It moved.

Petey lay in his bed, shaking with terror, his eight-year-old eyes bulging so widely they ached. His head throbbed; his grubby fists clenched tight to keep him from screaming, as the moonlight gleamed on the chair that rattled near the closet door.

It had moved, oh, no, oh *no*, it had moved, and no one would ever believe him. All those nights his mom and dad would come in and talk to him in syrupy voices, and tell him, *Why, Petey, nothing moved. Only live things can move. And your stuffed rabbit isn't alive, and that pile of laundry isn't alive, and Mr. Robot isn't alive, and . . .*

And they never believed him. *They never did!*

But the chair had moved. He had seen it. When he'd pretended to look away, then looked quickly back, he knew the chair had inched closer to the bed. He knew it was coming to get him, to eat him all up and spit out his bones, to fling him to the monsters and the bogeymen and witches with rotten teeth and no eyes who lived in the closet . . .

. . . who stuck their heads out at midnight and laughed at him when his mom and dad were asleep; and waited until the last minute for the sleepy *pad pad pad* of slippers, the creak of the bedroom door . . .

Petey? Are you having another nightmare, dear? Don't give yourself one of those headaches!

There, it moved again! Petey wanted to scream but his throat was so dry he couldn't make a sound, not even a hoarse gasp. It moved, he swore it, please, please, someone, it *moved!*

He whimpered like a wounded kitten. Only live things could move. Only things that were alive.

Why didn't they ever believe him? When he whooped with white-hot fever over the dwarf in the toy chest, they just laughed. When he pleaded with them to listen *listen!* about the skeleton in the mattress, they said he had an active imagination. They only believed about the headaches. Headaches were real.

Maybe he needs glasses. Maybe he's allergic to pollen.

Maybe, maybe . . .

It moved again!

Petey bolted upright and pressed his back against the headboard. His head was splitting. They had believed him about *that,* but they had never done anything! They had never helped him! They had never taken away the pain!

"Stop!" Petey begged. "Stop!"

His head always hurt, like a little gremlin lived inside, sticking pins in his brain. And they talked about taking him to the doctor, and talked about taking him for tests, and talked and talked . . .

"Stop!"

. . . but they didn't care about him. They didn't love him, because his mom had had a boyfriend while his dad was on his battleship; and when he came back, she was going to have a baby. Him. Petey . . .

It was still moving!

. . . and he heard them late at night, fighting. His dad (not his read dad, his real dad was a bogeyman) would shout, "Ya shoulda gotten an abortion, Barb! Ya shoulda gotten rid of him!"

And his mother would cry and say, "I know, Jack, I know. I'm sorry."

Then last Sunday, after the kitten, his dad (the fake one) had shouted, "He's a monster! He's not human! We should send him away!" And his mother, sobbing, had replied, "Yes, Jack. I know. We will."

It moved. Tears streamed down Petey's face.

But only things that were alive could move. And the chair was not alive. And neither was the thing sitting in it.

"I didn't mean to hurt the cat," he whispered. "Or the dog, or Mrs. Garcia's niece . . ." He crammed his fists in his mouth; no one knew about *that.*

It moved again. Much closer.

"I didn't mean to," he cried wildly. "Grown-ups are supposed to help little kids! And nobody . . ."

He thought of Mrs. Martin, the school nurse. She had *tried* to help him. When his head hurt really badly, she would let him lie down on a canvas cot in her office while she knitted. She had a big bag full of yarn and light green needles that flashed between her fingers. She wouldn't call home unless he asked her to. She would let him lie there, not moving, and every once in a while she would smile at him and say, "Feeling better?"

Sometimes he would say no just so he could stay with her. She was older than his mother but she was pretty anyway, and she always smelled like roses. She sang to him sometimes while she knitted, in-and-out, in-and-out

Bye, baby bunting, Daddy's gone a-hunting

like he was just a baby, and she told him he could grow up to be whatever he wanted.

He should be locked up! Did you see what he did to that cat? My God, Barb, he's not normal!

I know, Jack, I know.

Whatever he wanted, even President of the United States. And once he laughed and said, "Not me, Mrs. Martin!" But she shrugged and asked, "Why not? You're a bright boy with your future ahead of you."

Who was that guy you cheated on me with? Who the hell was he?

The headaches! The headaches!

At Halloween she lent him a doctor's bag and a stethoscope and told him maybe he could go to medical school and become a doctor.

"You're a good boy, Petey," she would say. "A fine young man."

He tried to tell her about the skeleton and the dwarf and the witches—oh, the witches, with their laughing, waiting for the *pad, pad, pad* of the slippers before they disappeared! But she didn't believe him either, and that *hurt* him, worse than the headaches. Mrs. Martin cared about him. He knew that. But she didn't believe him, and the pain never got better, never did.

And then she stopped working at the school and he was all alone again.

"Nobody helped me!" Petey screamed as loud as he could. "You should've helped me!"

"I'll help you now," slurred the thing in the chair.

It used to be his mother, but now she was all bloody from where he had stabbed her *wasn't my fault, wasn't, was not!* and the rest of her was white. Her lips were blue and her eyes were full of blood and flies were buzzing in her hair.

She hadn't moved for four days.

"It's not my fault!" he shrieked, scrabbling against the headboard. Maybe if he made a run for the door, he could escape. But she was moving, even though she was just a dead thing, not a live thing, and only live things moved.

Except his pretend dad, who *was* still alive—Petey could hear him moaning in the hallway—had not moved since Tuesday.

Anything he wanted to be . . . a fine young man.

"I'm coming for you, Petey," his mother whispered through broken teeth. He had punched her when she screamed "Monster! Monster!" until she stopped. "I'm going to give you to the skeleton in the mattress and the dwarf in the toy chest. I'm going to fling you to the eyeless witches in the closet."

President of the United States.

"Not me, Mrs. Martin!"

"Why not?"

He heard a mad, gleeful gibbering underneath the bed.

"No!" He buried his face in his hands and sobbed. "Oh, please, no! I'm sorry! Please, someone!"

The gibbering faded. The room was still.

Maybe it was just another headache. A bad dream. There was nothing . . .

Bye, baby bunting

When he raised his head, his mother, all oozy and gory, smelling terribly, was standing beside the bed. She smiled a toothless, gummy smile. "No more headaches."

And the chair skittered up next to her just as the closet door opened.

Anything he wanted . . .

And then *everything* moved.

Introduction

Explaining a mistake we all make at one time or another requires few words because we all make it. Explaining a mistake we all make that we refuse to admit to requires fiction, because sometimes the horror of what we've done is much too personal, and much too universal.

Kim Antieau's fictional voice is unqiue, which is as it should be, and one wonders if all that Oregon rain has anything to do with the difference between her cheery telephone conversations and what she puts down on paper.

SANCTUARY

by Kim Antieau

I went back to the house yesterday. At first it seemed too different. The long twisting drive was almost overgrown. The lawn was covered with weeds; Kiri's flowers had all since died. Then I looked up at the pine trees swaying in the wind and heard the gentle noise of the sea air winding through them. My chest tightened and the memories came rushing back. I wondered, as I have wondered nearly every hour of my life for five years, how I could have done what I did to Kiri.

In the summer before my last year of college, I came to the tiny coastal town of Canyons to work in my uncle's store. I accepted his offer of work because I wanted to experience smalltown life. I had spent most of my life in cities and, as a future psychologist, I thought I should learn to deal with all kinds of people. And I needed a job.

My uncle's store served as a food, drug, and feed outlet for the town. Everyone knew my uncle Bob and within the week everyone knew me. First suspicions appeared to be instantly allayed when people were told: "This is Bob's nephew Jason." For the first week it seemed my entire name was "Bobsnephewjason."

Since I served as delivery person as well as stocker and cashier, I was able to see most of the town and some portions of the beach within the first week. I began to learn what home belonged to which people. Most of the houses were single-story frames, bent and crooked, as if shaped by the constant sea wind.

There was one house, however, that stood out among the others. I spotted it on a delivery run one afternoon. I stopped the car and looked up the drive. The house was built on a hill overlooking the beach and town. Tall evergreens shielded the wooden and stone two-story building from the winds. To one side of it was an enclosed greenhouse, and when I squinted, I could just make out a figure inside, bending over. Someone honked behind me, and I started up the car and left. Later I asked my uncle about it.

"That's the Marlin home. Kiri Marlin lives there."

"All by herself?"

"Yep," he answered, heaving a box of juice off the shelf and onto the dolly. I grabbed another and stacked it on top.

"Have I ever seen her in here?"

"No," he answered. "She doesn't leave her house."

"What?" I had visions of discovering a truly remarkable psychological case. I could study her, do a paper about her. I would become famous before graduating.

"I'd like to meet her," I said. "Does she see people?"

My uncle stopped bending and looked over at me. "Of course she sees people. I deliver her groceries once a week. She's just a lady who doesn't leave her house. Her parents were sort of eccentric, too."

"Actually, it isn't eccentricity. It's a condition called agoraphobia. It literally means an abnormal fear of open places. I didn't know it could run in families."

"She's not afraid of open places, Jason. She just doesn't leave her house. She used to, but she hasn't since her parents died."

"Why? How did they die?"

"They just died."

"Could I deliver the groceries next time she calls?" I asked.

He reluctantly agreed. "I'm only allowing this because you are a relative, not really an outsider. I'm trusting you not to bug her. We all like Kiri. She's part of this town and we don't want anything to happen to her."

"I'm not going to hurt her," I said. "I'm nice to old ladies."

Bob smiled. "Quit talking and get to work."

Two days later, Kiri Marlin called in her order. I helped get the requested items together and then I anxiously drove to her house. When I got out of the car, I noticed there wasn't any wind. I could hear it in the pine trees, a gentle whooshing sound I liked to listen to on nights just before a storm, but I could not feel it like I could in town—a damp wind that never seemed to stop. It was peaceful here, as if I had stepped into some kind of haven. I listened for a moment before reaching into the car for the groceries.

I rang the doorbell and a voice called for me to come in. I was mildly surprised that the door was not locked. I opened it and went inside. I expected cobwebs, darkness, perhaps a stale wedding cake or an old woman in a dingy wedding gown. Instead I was greeted by two cats, sunlight, bleached oak floors, vivid green ferns, and various hanging plants. The air was cool and fresh, as if a breeze were running through the house.

And then Kiri walked into the room, a totally different apparition from the one I had expected. She removed gardening gloves and held out her hand. I was struck dumb, but I managed to shake her hand.

"You must be Jason," she said, tucking the gloves into her jean pockets. "I'm Kiri Marlin." She smiled, and I guessed her age at around thirty. Light brown hair was pulled away from her face by two combs. Her pretty cheeks were flushed, as if she had been outside running.

She laughed. "Close your mouth, Jason. Emily Dickinson I'm not. Come on into the kitchen," she said, taking one of the bags from me.

I blushed and followed her into a large airy kitchen, where windows and plants outnumbered appliances and cupboards. One of her cats, a Siamese, leapt onto the counter and sniffed at the packages as I set them down.

"Are you enjoying your visit?" she asked as she began putting away the groceries.

"It's very different from where I come from," I answered.

"That doesn't answer my question," she said, "though I suppose it does in a way."

"Oh, I like it here, really, especially the ocean and the beaches."

"I like the ocean, too. Sunsets from here are spectacular," she said.

"You can see it from here?"

"Sure, I have quite a view," she said. "Come on, I'll show you."

She took me out of the kitchen and up a short flight of stairs into the living room. All of the west wall was made of glass. We were above the trees and had a panoramic view of the ocean. Today the water was dark green, flecked with white. A flock of birds flew over one of the shore rocks.

"It's nice, isn't it?" she said, smiling.

I nodded and turned from the window. I suddenly felt guilty for my earlier desire to examine her like some kind of specimen.

"Do you like games?" I asked, noticing several boxes on her bookshelves: a backgammon game, a go set, Scrabble.

"Yes, I guess I do."

"I've always wanted to learn go. Could you teach me?"

She turned and looked into my eyes for several seconds, as if she were trying to look deeper, to see into my soul.

"Sure, I'll teach you," she said. "You bring the pizza and be here at eight."

Kiri was a good and gentle teacher, but when I did something totally wrong, she reprimanded me, telling me I had not been listening. After nearly an hour in her company, I forgot she had this little quirk: she did not leave her house. We played and ate in the living room so we could watch the sun go down. As the evening passed, she asked me about school and my life, and I told her. She teased me when I told stories about parties I had attended in college.

"I don't want to hear about that," she said. "I want to know what you've learned. Not just at school, but in your lifetime."

"I'm not sure what I've learned," I said, "except how little I truly know." I was surprised at the things I could tell her—feelings and ideas I wasn't even aware of until I said them aloud to her.

The cats each chose a lap and curled up to sleep.

"I've had Harlow, the Siamese, since my mother died," she said. She leaned against the couch and stroked the cat.

"When was that?" I asked.

"About eight years ago," she answered. "She's getting to be an old cat. I got Tori three years ago."

"How did your mother die?" I asked.

"Just like most people die," she answered. "She stopped living."

I remembered that my uncle hadn't told me how her parents had died and I wondered what the big mystery was. I didn't pursue it, however, and the conversation moved away from her mother. We discussed books we had each read. I will remember that first evening always. Sometimes, now, I wish I could forget, or at least distort it so I don't remember how beautiful it was. That night, as always with Kiri, I was relaxed. There was no flirtation, no awkwardness between us. I just truly enjoyed the company of another person. The house creaked, the pines moved with the wind, and Kiri and I talked into the night.

Finally, when night was edging toward morning, I told Kiri I should leave. We cleaned the living room and then she walked me to the door. I hesitated, not wanting to go.

"May I come again?" I asked.

She looked into my eyes.

"You must know one thing, Jason," she said. "I do not leave this house. You must promise not to try to change that."

"I promise," I said, without thinking. She smiled. I would have promised anything that night just so I could see her again.

For the next week, I went over to Kiri's every night. Sometimes there were other people there, friends of hers. Some of them were people I had met in town or had seen roaming the beaches. They were nice, but I resented their presence. I wanted Kiri all to myself. She seemed to enjoy our time alone, too, showing me how she managed without leaving the house.

She was obviously proud of her greenhouse. It was filled with flowers and vegetables. I had never seen flowers so colorful or vegetables so lush, yet she used no fertilizers or other chemicals.

"Just my hands," she said.

I was not much of a gardener, but since Kiri enjoyed spending time in the greenhouse, I asked her to teach me how to be useful.

"I think teaching you to be useful would be a full-time job," she said, grinning.

I grabbed her. "I'll get you for that," I said. "I'll yell at your plants and give them neuroses."

She laughed, and I realized she was in my arms. My stomach seemed to twist inside itself. It still does when I think of that moment. I had never felt anything so wonderful—until I leaned over and kissed her. She put her arms around me, and we embraced.

She whispered my name and kissed me again.

"We're all dirty from the garden," she said. "I think we need a shower." She took my hand and we went upstairs.

I had never fallen so quickly and so much in love. We never ran out of things to say, yet often we just lay quietly in each other's arms, listening to the wind through the pines. One evening, we fell asleep on the couch together. I awakened to darkness; Kiri was gone. When my eyes adjusted to the dark, I could see Kiri by the window. I went and stood behind her. The moon was out, shining down on the beach and ocean. Two people walked along the tide mark. I put my arms around Kiri's waist.

"Do you wish you were down there?" I whispered.

"Good God, no," she answered, stiffening in my arms. "If all around you were flames and you were in the only safe spot, would you want to go into the flames?"

"Is that what it's like for you?" I asked. "Is it that frightening?"

"It is not so much frightening as . . . ." She turned to me, searching for the right words. "As certain. I will die if I leave this house."

"But you will die inside this house someday, too," I said. "Think of all the things we could do together, places we could see before we die."

She covered my mouth with her hand. "Ssssh. You promised. You must accept me the way I am."

"Won't you even consider going for help?"

"Help? I don't need help, Jason." She pulled away from me.

I took her hand. "Can't you see it's not normal to be locked up in this house?"

She laughed, making it an almost unnatural sound. "Of course it's not normal. But it isn't just my psyche that's in danger, Jason. It's all of me." She sighed. "I've been out, and I'm nothing out there—insubstantial. Here, I'm something. I have control. Some people never find their niche in the world; I have. My parents tried to live outside this house. They failed. This is our spot. This is where I belong. I've accepted that. There is comfort in knowing where you belong, Jason."

"Kiri, I can help you if you let me," I said, as I took her face in my hands. "There is nothing outside this house that can't hurt you inside this house, too."

She stared at me, an unwavering look that made me think she was looking clear to my core. I dropped my hands.

"You can't understand," she said, "but you must accept that this is my place on earth. End of discussion."

The conversation ended, but I continued to think about it. I needed to finish college. I couldn't do that in Canyons, but I didn't want to leave Kiri. I had always imagined myself traveling one day. I couldn't do that with Kiri, and I didn't want to go without her. I was so blind; if only I had realized how many places we saw together in her own home.

I was determined to cure her. I went to the library and found out what I could about agoraphobia. There wasn't much. They described physical reactions: perspiration, accelerated heartbeat, severe anxiety attacks. Therapists suggested gradually curing patients by taking them on small excursions outside the home.

One night I began looking through my uncle's library, hoping to find something to help me.

"Whatcha looking for, son?" Uncle Bob asked as he stood in the doorway.

"Psychology books."

He laughed. "Nothing but Zane Grey and Janet Dailey in this house," he said.

I smiled. I had never known anyone as well read as my uncle. The house was packed with books. Bob came into the room and sat down.

"Let it be, Jason. What does it matter?"

"I want to do things with her," I said. "It hurts me to see her holed up in that house all the time."

"Why? Is she unhappy?"

"She says she isn't. But how could she be happy? It must feel like a prison."

"Or a sanctuary," he said. He leaned back in his chair. "She knows what's best for her, Jason. Her folks have been in this town, in that house, for generations. Made their fortune in the stock market, I believe. Before they died, Kiri's parents were important people in town." He squinted. "You know, I can hardly remember them anymore. It hasn't been that long since they died."

"How did they die?"

"Mr. Marlin was in a car accident," he said. "There were rumors he died before the car actually crashed into the ocean. There wasn't much left of him when they pulled the car out. It was the first time in decades he'd left the house. No one knew why he left. Some said Kiri's mother talked him into it." He shrugged. "Maybe it was a nice day and he wanted to go for a ride. Soon after his death, Kiri's mother walked into the ocean and drowned."

"So you think Kiri's fear comes from what happened to her parents when they left the house?"

"You aren't listening," he said. "Maybe she's got reasons to fear."

I shook my head. "There must be a way to help her, to free her from this fear. There must be."

Bob stood and stretched. "She doesn't have a problem with it, Jason. You do." He started to say something else, but instead, he left the room. I sat on the floor, wondering what to do next.

For weeks I worried about the end of the summer and the rest of our lives. Then suddenly I had the answer and I was elated—and afraid. Kiri never suspected what I was going to do—at least I thought so at the time. I chose a day that was particularly cool and breezy. The air moved nicely through the house, filling it with the smells of the outdoors. Clouds covered the sun, taking the summer brightness away. Kiri and I worked in the greenhouse. I helped her take flowers and put them in the wheelbarrow. Later I was going to plant them outside, around the living room windows.

"I get enough sunlight from the windows, but sometimes I think my flowers need to be outside," she said. Harlow bounded into the room like a kitten and jumped onto my shoulders. Tori pawed at my leg and meowed.

"They're hussies, aren't they?"

"Just like you," I said. I reached over and kissed her nose.

"How did you get off work today?" she asked.

"I asked for it off."

"That was clever," she said, laughing. Then she scowled when I tugged too hard on a root and it broke. "Patience, Jas. In any case, I'm glad you're here. I love these kinds of days." She whirled around. "I can't believe how happy I am!"

I caught her in mid-turn. The cat jumped away from me. "Happy! Well, I've got something that will make you even happier. Close your eyes."

"What?" She closed her eyes. "A surprise?"

"Yes." I tied a kerchief around her eyes and across her ears. Then I twirled her around a few times. I led her around the house, going up and down stairs, trying to disorient her. We both laughed. My heart began pounding too hard. I broke out in a sweat. I hoped I was doing the right thing, but I was afraid she would be angry with me. I stopped her for a moment and kissed her. She lifted her head up, blind, and grinned.

"I love you very much," I told her, suddenly frightened of what I was doing.

"I love you, too," she said. "Now take me to my surprise."

I twirled her one more time, led her in and out of two more rooms, and then I took her through the open front door. I talked and laughed so she wouldn't notice the change. I had even put some old boards on the sidewalk, hoping they would feel like her living room floor. I stopped her just out of the shadow of the house, about ten steps from the door.

"Jason, where am I? Can I see now?"

I slowly untied the kerchief. "See, you're safe," I said.

I will never forget the look on her face as she turned to me. It still troubles me at night: I open my eyes from a nightmare and I will see her face, inches from my own. Her eyes were opened wide in terror—and disappointment. I had betrayed her.

"You promised," she whispered.

Suddenly, it seemed that the sky was black. Or was it? I couldn't breathe or move. Perspiration rolled down my back. I became overwhelmed with anxiety. I was dizzy. I covered my eyes, trying to still the twirling world. What was happening to me? I reached for Kiri, but my arms flayed air.

Seconds later, I opened my eyes. The dizziness subsided. I looked around. It was a gorgeous summer day. The cats stood in the doorway watching me. A breeze moved through the pine trees.

And Kiri was gone.

I ran toward the house, calling her name. Inside, I wandered about almost blindly, bumping into doors and walls: I knew when I found her she would not ever want to see me again.

But I didn't find her. She wasn't in the house. I looked around the yard, too, but there was nothing.

And then I went to the greenhouse and found something near the windows. I'm not certain what—it looked as if some living thing had suddenly become unglued and melted into the ground, leaving behind its shadow like a kind of marker. I closed my eyes and quickly backed away.

They never found Kiri. For a time I was suspected of murdering her. The more I went over the events in my mind, the more I believed that to be true, but when I confessed, they didn't believe me.

Soon after, Kiri's recently made will was read. She declared that her substantial fortune and the house be left to me if she was not seen in the house for thirty days. When my uncle told me, I cried out, calling for someone to take away the pain. I realized then she had known all along I would not keep my promise.

The house stood empty until my return yesterday. The cats had fled long ago. I stood at the door trembling. I turned the handle. It was unlocked, as it had always been. I wanted to be sick as I opened the door. It all came rushing back, every second of the happiness we had shared in this house. And then I stepped inside. This time I found the cobwebs and darkness I had expected that first day. The house smelled of decay. I breathed the damp air deeply. I had done this. I was the cause. I looked around. The house was empty, as if Kiri had never existed.

I started to back away, to run out of the house, but something made me hesitate. Perhaps I could fix it up, make it alive again. I had traveled for five years, running toward anything that could make the memories go away even for a little while. Now I was weary of it. This was my home, my place in the world. I looked outside once more, and then I closed the door and shut away the light.

Introduction

Adults are supposed to know that things change, and they're supposed to be able to handle those changes in one fashion or another. Children, on the other hand, know that often, handling changes is only another way of running away. They know. They've tried it, and it doesn't work.

Sheri Lee Morton lives, works, and attends school in Tennessee. She tells terrible jokes, and I love them. And for the appearance of this story in Shadows, special thanks to Peggy Nadramia—I owe you one.

NOW YOU SEE ME

by Sheri Lee Morton

For as long as Amy could remember, she had seen ghosts. Not just the ones that looked like sheets with arms, but people in strange clothes with funny faces, and monsters, too. Mostly she saw monsters. Some of them lived in her house—like the ogre who guarded the television set (Amy sometimes thought that her mother had put it there to keep her from watching too much TV), the werewolf in her mother's closet, or the big black thing that lived in hers.

Even though she was used to the monsters, Amy spent most of her time watching them, avoiding dark corners, and not talking very much. Amy was afraid that one day she would forget and say something about the monsters—grown-ups couldn't see them—and then the monsters would get her for talking about them. The time that she had tried to tell her parents about the thing under her bed, she saw the vampire in the den lean forward to hear what she was saying, and Amy knew that if she told, the thing under her bed would reach up and drag her down with it when she went to sleep that night or, worse, that the vampire itself would swoop down and drink all her blood. After that she wouldn't tell anybody, because the vampires were everywhere that grown-ups were. The doctor had one in his office that leered at her when she walked past the door, her teacher had one that stood in the back of the coat room, and even the dentist had one that grinned at her in the waiting room.

Upstairs in her sunny room, she was safe. There weren't any dark corners for monsters to hide, and there were lots of fairies that danced outside her window in the afternoon. She was lying on her stomach, daydreaming about killing the vampires like in the movie on TV the other night, when her

mother yelled from the kitchen. Reluctantly she leapt off the bed and went
down the hall. Skirting the gargoyle in the living room, she ducked and ran
past the vampire and into the clean, shiny kitchen.

She didn't want to go to the eye doctor. "Why do I have to go?" she
whined, scuffing her feet on the blacktop beside the car. "Because I said so."
Amy's mother pushed her toward the open car door. "You don't want to
grow up and be blind, do you?" Amy shook her head. "Then in—let's go."
Amy pouted on the way to the doctor's office. Feeling spiteful, she stuck
her tongue out at the ghosts on the sidewalks they passed. "Nyah, nyah,
nyah, I get to ride in the car and you don't." Squinting her eyes, Amy could
just make out whether the ghosts were men or women. The dark sky darkened a little more and it started to rain, but the ghosts just stayed where they
were, staring into space.
All too soon, they were at the doctor's. Amy saw the vampire when they
went inside, right where she thought it would be. Amy picked a chair facing
it so she could make sure it didn't move. When it was her turn, she got taken
down a dark hallway (why did grown-ups always make everyplace so *dark?*)
and into the examining room, full of giant insects. They were big, green and
silver, and they reminded Amy of the praying mantis she'd found outside last
summer. They smelled like metal.
The nurse made her sit in a chair like the dentist's, turned off the lights,
and asked if she could read the letters on the far wall. Amy didn't see any
letters, just a black slime that crawled, trying to get out of the light, and
almost said so, until she remembered the vampire in the waiting room. She
made up some letters instead. The nurse went away then, and the doctor
came in, a little bald man who smelled like wintergreen. He had one of the
insects hold something so he could look at her eyes, and Amy relaxed a little
bit—the bugs must be tame if he could make them do things like that and
they didn't pinch his head off. The doctor shone a light in her eyes and made
her look through lots of little pieces of glass that made her head hurt and
reminded her of a three-D movie her mother once took her to see. When the
doctor was finished, he scribbled something on a piece of yellow paper and
told her mother to take it next door. The vampire grinned at Amy and shook
its arms as she ran out the door.

Later the next week, Amy went back to pick up her glasses. She hadn't
wanted to go, and she had whined and fretted until her mother threatened to
whip her if she didn't get into the car. When they got to the office, the
vampire grinned at her again like it had known she'd be back. After they

waited for a while, Amy's mother reading a magazine and Amy sulking, they went down the same dark hall to the same bug room. The doctor came in, still smelling like wintergreen and sweat, bringing a pair of little pink glasses. As he settled them on her nose, she squeaked—the whole world suddenly jumped into focus. The big bugs around her were tall metal things. When the nurse turned off the lights, she really could see letters on the wall. Her mother laughed at the expression on her face and said, "And you didn't want glasses, silly."

The hall to the waiting room wasn't nearly as long or dark as before. When she burst into the waiting room, Amy realized that the vampire was just a big wooden thing to hold people's coats. She ran up to it and grabbed. Wood and wool were all she felt.

On the way home, all the ghosts that she had always seen dissolved into street signs, washed-out posters, and telephone poles. Amy began to realize that her parents were right—there weren't any such things as monsters and ghosts. When they got home, she raced in the front door, past the gargoyle that was an overstuffed chair, the vampire coat rack, and the cyclopean TV set, into her father's arms.

"Well, little four-eyes, what're you so excited about?" Amy giggled, and wormed her way out of her father's tickling fingers. "Whatsamatter, cat got your tongue?" Her father laughed.

"She can see," her mom said. "She probably doesn't even recognize you."

Her father laughed again and hugged her. "I've got an idea. Why don't both my pretty ladies go and get fixed up, and we'll go out and celebrate. And Miss Amy here can pick the restaurant. Okay? C'mon, slowpokes! Run, run, run!"

Once she was inside her room, Amy threw open her closet door and ran inside, laughing when she saw that the big black thing in the corner was only her old bean-bag chair. She even left the door open while she dressed, to show it she wasn't scared anymore. She looked in her mirror, and for the first time ever saw nobody but herself. Skipping down the hall, she stuck her tongue out at the old table squatting there.

"Are you ready to go?" her father called from the bathroom. "Well, I'm not yet, so you'll have to wait." Amy and her mother giggled at her father taking more time than they did to get ready. In a few minutes he came rushing out, smelling like toothpaste and aftershave, and the three of them went out to the car.

At the car, Amy's dad patted all his pockets and got a funny expression on his face. "Oh, no," he said. "I left the keys on the hall table. Amy, honey, would you run back inside and get Daddy's keys for him?" Amy nodded, and zipped back up the drive into the house. She looked for them on the hall table, but they weren't there. When she passed back by the living room, she saw them sitting on the arm of her father's chair. She bounced in, leaned over to pick them up, and froze. She saw, for just a moment, something tall and black moving near the corner of her eye. Fear settled in her stomach and made her feel sick. She turned around, and there was only the coat rack. Amy grabbed the keys and turned to run out of the room, but whirled back around when she heard a scrabbling sound behind her, like claws on wood. The overstuffed chair was off the coasters her mother had put underneath it to keep it from scratching the floor. Suddenly Amy knew what was wrong. Her parents were wrong. There were ghosts, and there were monsters. They had tried to fix it so she'd be safe from the monsters, but the monsters were still there, only she couldn't see them anymore. She started to back toward the door, keeping her eyes on the furniture that strained to rush forward if she looked away. She went back slowly, step by step. She was in the hallway before she remembered the table behind her. It scuttled down the hall crab-like, its arms open to grab her. Amy didn't get her glasses off in time to see it catch her skirt.

Introduction

If the fiction writers are to be believed, love is equal parts heaven and hell. If life outside fiction is any different, no one has yet discovered it.

Leslie Horvitz, the bestselling co-author of Double-Bind *and other novels, is currently working on a new book, though he won't say if it's about the time he was lost, after dark, in a game park in Kenya.*

THE FISHING VILLAGE OF ROEBUSH

by Leslie Alan Horvitz

What brought us to the fishing village of Roebush that summer was something that until now I haven't wished to disclose. Most, if not all, of my friends assumed that I had selected such an isolated spot because I wished to finish the rest of my long-overdue novel without the distractions that are an inevitable part of city life. People were forever pointing out bizarrely designed clapboard houses set somewhere up on what looked to be an inaccessible slope, miles from nowhere, and saying, "Now, wouldn't that be a terrific place to write?" Although I usually refrained from expressing a contrary opinion, the truth was that I liked the city, I liked the distractions, and found that nothing buoyed my spirits so much as a phone call coming in the middle of a sentence I couldn't figure out how on earth I was ever going to complete. But as I kept this need for interruption a secret, it was no surprise that my plan to stay in Roebush for three months was regarded as a judicious decision on my part, particularly by my impatient editor.

But the fact of the matter was that the novel had nothing to do with it. It was because of Marianne that I chose to uproot myself from New York and relocate for the summer. I let her do the choosing; she liked the idea of fishing villages and she wanted one where she could be virtually assured that no tourists, no outsiders at all save ourselves, were likely to be found.

In Marianne's view, the further she got from her friends, from people who might be friends of friends, the better off she'd be. A good deal of the time she barely abided my companionship, which was not to say that she didn't love me. There was enough evidence for that, God knows. It was just to say that she frequently became disappointed in me because I failed to live up to her expectations. But then, of course, no one could do that.

She was a splendid girl, thirty years of age, vital, warm, with skin that easily turned copper in summer and a fall of golden brown hair. She had lovely breasts and legs that in a slit skirt could cause a delicious pain to rise into my chest. I don't say that she was pretty, though she could often be beautiful. It depended on any number of factors: the angle of the light, the way she'd decided to arrange her hair; the particular mood that held her in throe. Sometimes, however, the beauty would drain away from her and what was left was not ugly but more of a blankness, a frightening emptiness.

And yes, Marianne came from a troubled background. Family discord. Divorces. A remote father. A callous, materialistic mother. A history of un-happy love affairs. Afflicted with grief and terrible longing, she lived life as if it came down to one question. Like the Sphinx that greeted Oedipus on his way into Thebes, that question was perpetually poised on her lips. The ques-tion was this: What are you going to do to save my life? And damned be the man who didn't know the answer.

I used to believe that she was just too high-strung, that she went in for nervous breakdowns the way others went in for collecting stamps or finishing furniture; it was how she staved off boredom and at the same time made sure she did not go ignored.

Anyway, when I first fell in with her, she showed no outward signs of any mental unbalance. She freely talked about her episodes, as she liked to call them, laughing about them, too, which was her way, I suppose, of exorcising demons: turn them into anecdotal recollections to entertain a new beau.

There were days—or nights, I should say—when the darkness intruded. There were fearful things about her that I really didn't wish to know about.

Only when the nights of panic and weeping and desperation began to outnumber the calm and pleasurable nights did I start to think that maybe I'd gotten it turned around in my mind: far from being a healthy woman subject to occasional mood swings, she might be a genuine manic-depressive able to lead a normal life only for short periods of time.

I don't think that Marianne knew what to make of her condition, either. Intelligent and sufficiently self-aware to realize she needed help, she sought out a number of psychiatrists over the years, ranging from orthodox Freud-ians to Sullivanians and therapists of uncertain stripe who ascribed her illness, whatever it was, to repressed lesbian tendencies or an unresolved longing to sleep with her father. None of them seemed to have done her much good.

I didn't know whether I should cut my losses and leave her or else stay and cope. To do the latter I might be risking my sanity, something friends of mine were quick to point out. But then they were not in love with her. Why I was in love with her was beyond me; women far more attractive, with their heads screwed on straight, failed to interest me at all.

It was at my suggestion that we decided to leave New York at the end of June, although, as I said, it was Marianne who chose the spot. At one point she told me that she selected Roebush simply because she'd once come across it in an atlas and liked the name. Another time she said it was a friend who'd told her about it and recommended that she should stay there. Her story would change depending on when I happened to raise the subject.

What I envisioned when I thought of a fishing village was almost nothing like what Roebush turned out to be. There was something about the place that made it seem as if winter were its only proper season. The houses were bent, almost deformed in some way; they were mostly composed of gray clapboard, in need of paint just as their roofs were in need of shingles. The most prominent structure in the village was the church. It also seemed to be the one in the best shape. On closer inspection, however, it proved to be abandoned, its windows broken, its twin front doors left ajar; a smell of something stale seeped out from it.

By far the most charming part of the village was its piers. Here there were several boats moored, high masted, most of them constructed of wood. In the lapping water close to shore, they bobbed up and down, their hulls groaning. Sea gulls wheeled overhead, dive-bombing for food. Fishermen, some of them looking very nearly as weathered as the houses they lived in, could be seen repairing their nets and applying fresh paint to the decks.

As Roebush was hardly a site likely to be visited by vacationing tourists, there was no hotel or even modest lodging house available. Neither would we have been interested in one if there had been. An agent in New York had managed to locate a house for us he said would be perfect (although he was only taking his Canadian counterpart's word for it). He assured us it'd be close enough to the sea to provide a "picture postcard view."

In spite of our apprehensions, we were not disappointed. The house, one of a row of half a dozen all modeled alike, was of more recent vintage than those in the center of the village. It was two stories tall, with a roof that still preserved all its shingles. The rooms were small, even cramped, but for the two of us they were quite adequate.

I selected a small room upstairs for my office. With its antique rolltop desk, filled with secret drawers, and a small library set into the walls, it was perfect. The only danger was that I might become too distracted by the view, which could, in fact, have adorned a postcard: there was nothing to be seen but the bay until the horizon, where a haze had settled like smoke.

Marianne declined to go exploring with me, saying that she preferred to unpack. But most of the unpacking was done. It was a pretext. I had a feeling that she wanted to see Roebush on her own, stake out its territory for herself, discovering in the process her private dominions. It was possible, had she her way, that she might have chosen to come to this place on her own, but she was broke and I was the one who was paying. Besides, it wasn't as if she didn't love me; it was just that she didn't know quite what to do with this love, and very possibly resented the hold I had over her.

At times it wasn't so much of a hold as all that.

The light in the sky was changing when I walked out. There was nothing to be seen of the westering sun; weather was moving in, blanketing much of the sky. The haze hanging over the horizon seemed to have grown thicker. The effect was not unlike that of a premature dusk. A smell of impending rain was in the air.

It hardly took any time at all to carry out my exploration. There simply wasn't very much to see. What I'd glimpsed from the car was just about all there was of the village. No more than a hundred or so people could be living here, I reckoned. Probably the population had shrunk as the economy declined. Aside from a corner pharmacy, a grocery shop, and a gas station, there seemed to be no active business going on. Of inactive businesses there were at least four: all boarded up, their signs fading into illegibility.

Making my way down to the docks, I was surprised to see how few people were about in the streets. Those who were gave me questioning looks and tentative smiles; there was no doubting that I was a stranger, and as such, an object of some curiosity. Not as much as Marianne would prove to be, though.

The fishermen were gone by the time I reached the docks, their boats left untended and unguarded. When I glanced back, beyond the ribbon of pebbly beach, behind the seawall, I saw that lights were coming on in the village. Not yet five o'clock and it appeared as if everyone had retired for the night. I began to think that perhaps Roebush might be *too* restful.

Not for Marianne. She couldn't sleep that night. She never slept nights in New York; I don't see why I believed it would make any difference on the Canadian coast. The fresh sea air wasn't sufficient to cure her of her insomnia.

But I was dead tired and not at all disposed to being woken up in what must have been the middle of the night, if the darkness of the sky was any indication.

"What is it?" I grumbled.

"Listen," she said, her eyes glimmering, her hands gripping mine. "Listen, can't you hear them?"

At first I couldn't hear anything but the tide coming in. Then, faintly, I detected voices.

Marianne rushed to the window and peered out in the direction of the bay. "Come look."

I did as she asked, but it was difficult to make out what had so compelled her attention. Then I saw what it was.

Where the haze had been throughout the afternoon and evening there now emerged an island. At least it looked like an island, perhaps half a mile in length; close to the northern end of it, there could be seen a hill shaped like a woman's breast.

There were no more voices to be heard. The night resumed its customary silence.

"I checked the map," she said, her eyes on the island, not on me, "but it's not on it."

"Too small, maybe," I suggested. Or could it have sprung up because of some plate activity beneath the ocean that had taken place since the map was printed? Such things were possible, after all.

I rested my hand on her back. "Are you coming to bed?"

"In a little while. Right now I think I'll go back to my reading downstairs."

In the morning the island had sunk back into the obscurity of the low-lying haze. But this was something that, while mildly curious, seemed of little importance when weighed against the fact that Marianne had failed to come to bed. If she'd slept at all, it was downstairs, sitting in the antique rocking chair near the fireplace we'd been warned not to use unless we wanted to burn the house down.

Whatever the case, she appeared rested. The smell of pancakes and brewing coffee reached me as I came down the stairs, and while I watched, unnoticed, she moved about the kitchen, humming to herself, apparently quite in love with the new summer morning.

But no sooner had she put breakfast in front of me than she announced that she wasn't hungry and, rather than watch me eat, had decided on going for a walk. I posed no objection, but it was all I could do not to stop her. One of the principal reasons I'd come to this obscure coastal village was so that the two of us could spend time together without suffering the intrusion of friends and acquaintances. I'd assumed that we'd discover Roebush and its environs together. Now I was beginning to wonder.

It wasn't until evening that she returned, and then she wasn't alone.

"This is Stephen," she said, introducing me to the burly, ruddy-faced man who stood beside her, at least a head taller. Deep brown eyes and an apologetic smile disclosed themselves from beneath his mop of dirty blond hair.

I took his extended hand. He smelled of fish and saltwater.

"I met Stephen down at the docks." He was, of course, a fisherman. "My friend Jack's a writer—a novelist."

I didn't appreciate the ambiguity of that word *friend*, the open-endedness of it. No telling what she'd told Stephen about our relationship.

"Never met a writer before," said Stephen. Or something like that. He mumbled.

"They're a lot like the rest of us," Marianne said with a laugh, in a very good mood, I could see, "except that when they stare out into space you give them the benefit of the doubt and figure they're being inspired and not just daydreaming."

Stephen did something like laugh; it was a kind of strangled chuckle.

At first I guessed his age to be in his late twenties, but when he sat down directly under the kitchen light, he looked older, maybe forty or so. His skin was very tan and mottled with white patches that might have been pre-cancerous. All those years at sea, under the sun, I thought, wondering what he would write if he had a gift for setting words down on paper.

"Are you liking it here?" he asked.

He had a certain accent that was peculiar to residents of this part of Canada, thick, vaguely reminiscent of Scottish; words seemed to have to plow through syrup before they emerged.

"It's very pretty, very peaceful."

Marianne frowned. "You'd think a writer would be more original than that," she said.

"Yes, it is pretty," Stephen agreed, ignoring her. He took a tentative sip of the ale Marianne had poured out for him, as if still uncertain how much to take advantage of the hospitality we—or I should say she—were providing him. "But there are other benefits to living here. We don't pay any taxes."

"No taxes? I didn't think such places existed in the world. Like the Garden of Eden, the stuff from which dreams are made."

"We're poor," Stephen said, "but not poor like other folks. At least we can keep all of what we make."

"And why's that?"

Marianne was looking from one of us to the other the way she would if she were following the flight of a Ping-Pong ball through the air.

"Oh, we worked out a special arrangement with the government in Ottawa a long time ago. In return for our services."

"Fishing, you mean?"

Stephen took his time answering. "Well, yes, fishing." Then he paused before adding, "And other things."

My impression was that it was more complicated than that, but Marianne seemed to accept what he said at face value.

"If your book turns out to be a bestseller and you've got so much money you don't know what to do with it, maybe you should settle here permanently. That way you won't have to give it all to the IRS."

"I don't know whether people who aren't born here don't have to pay."

Stephen was taking Marianne far more seriously than I was.

"We'll worry about that when I'm on the bestseller list. As it is, I'm not even halfway through my book."

"People like you amaze me," Stephen said, draining his beer in one great draft and simultaneously getting up from the table.

I wasn't sure whether he meant this as a compliment.

"I've got to get home for dinner. Thank you for the beer."

Marianne saw him to the door. It always came as a surprise to me how someone who said she didn't like meeting new people managed to make so many friends. Well, part of the reason was that she was female, and good-looking. But I think also that people discerned in her a promise of excitement. Excitement of a kind they'd never experienced before.

"Isn't he lovely?" Marianne asked me once he'd left.

"He seems nice enough."

"He says tomorrow he'll take me out on a fishing trip with him. Him and his father and his uncle."

Obviously I was not invited. "And what hour of the morning do you have to get up?"

Get up? More likely than not she'd be still awake.

"Oh, it's not until nighttime, around eleven. That is when the fishing is best, Stephen says."

While I knew little about fishing, it was still difficult for me to believe that setting out into the Atlantic in the middle of the night was any guarantee of success. And if I deplored the idea of Marianne accompanying Stephen on his boat while it was daylight, I was even more disheartened to learn that it would happen long after the sun had gone down.

"Don't worry, I'll be all right. Nothing's going to happen," she said, seeing how disturbed I was.

What I didn't know was whether she believed it was her safety that concerned me or her fidelity.

As if she was doing me a favor, and perhaps at that she was, she stayed home all the next day, carrying on a desultory conversation with me when she wasn't trying to read one of the many books we'd brought with us.

I remember how anxious I became around ten, how there arose in me a familiar dread that I now knew how to translate into words: When she leaves here tonight, I will never see her again.

This dread, this fear, whatever name you could give it, seized me every time she suffered from one of her dark moods. Then there was no telling what would happen to her, where she would go.

Eleven o'clock. Nothing. Marianne, legs snuggled under her, kept reading, pretending to be oblivious of the hour. Eleven-ten, eleven-fifteen. Perhaps Stephen had forgotten about her or else had promised the outing as a lark, having no intention of actually delivering.

Then I became conscious of a knocking, very faint, not on our door, but somewhere in the distance. The knocking grew louder. I looked across the room at Marianne, but she showed no sign that she heard anything.

All at once, with a furious tattoo, someone was rapping on our door. The sound of it caused me nearly to leap out of my chair. Marianne reacted with calm. "Well, I guess it's time for me to go."

She got on her Windbreaker, grabbed her bag, whose contents she gave a last-minute inspection, kissed me, then opened the door.

I could still hear the knocking; others were being summoned from their homes all up and down the beachfront. But when I looked out I couldn't see who was responsible for it, whether there were three or four people entrusted with alerting their fellow fishermen or only one man selected because he went about his business with great speed.

A number of voices could be made out on both sides of me, building in volume but never gaining in coherence, as the fishermen, one by one, emerged from their houses, carrying their gear over their shoulders.

I didn't like it. Even the sight of so many of the townspeople collecting for this nocturnal event did nothing to relieve my anxiety. Finally I couldn't stand it anymore and left the house, joining the others in their procession to the docks. I don't know whether I hoped to stop Marianne or assure myself that she would not be going off with Stephen alone, that that story she told me about his family accompanying them was true.

I was so preoccupied with pursuing her that it wasn't until I was nearly to the docks that I glanced toward the horizon and saw, just as I had the previous night, the island, silhouetted against the starlit sky. Was it a function of the atmospheric conditions or the action of the tides that dispelled the haze at night, only to restore it at dawn? It was beyond me to say.

I managed to catch a glimpse of her before Stephen's boat could get too far out into the bay. She was leaning over the gunwales, staring blankly toward the island; at no point did she ever direct her gaze at me, and that, I suppose, was just as well.

Standing next to her was a thin, gray-bearded man wearing a visored cap who, for some reason, I presumed must be Stephen's uncle. A man closer in resemblance to Stephen was in the process of hoisting the sail—an optimistic gesture on his part, for there was no wind to speak of—while Stephen himself was at the wheel, maneuvering the craft away from its berth.

Half a dozen boats, a small armada, were also setting sail, their way ahead illuminated by small lights installed on their prows and burning feebly into the gloom.

I watched until they could hardly be seen, vanishing at a point on the horizon where sky, sea, and distant island seemed to turn into a smudge of charcoal.

I could not shake my feeling of unease, but somehow I still succeeded in getting to sleep, thinking that the wait would be more bearable if it were done unconsciously.

But I kept waking, listening for the turn of the key in the door.

At one point or another during the small hours of the morning, though, my vigilance must have slipped, for I opened my eyes to see her standing over me. She looked more radiant than I'd seen her in some time, her cheeks flushed from the chill and salty air, her hair wet and matted from the spray. "Oh, it was marvelous, Jack, next time you'll have to come along!"

I asked if the catch was as large as Stephen had predicted it would be.

Shrugging, she said that it looked big enough for her. When I inquired as to what kind of fish were to be gotten from these local waters, she said she had no idea, that she was never much good at distinguishing one fish from another.

In spite of her invitation to have me come along on subsequent expeditions, I wasn't surprised when she failed to raise the subject again. Her excuses varied when I brought it up. Sometimes it was along the lines of: "Oh, I know how you like to sleep during those hours, you're not a night person like I am." Sometimes it was: "Stephen's . . . well, he's uncomfortable around you, he says you're too smart for him, he doesn't understand the words you use."

That I could not for the life of me recall any words so sophisticated or polysyllabic I might have spoken to him was beside the point. The fact was that Marianne didn't want me to come along.

"I know what you're thinking," she said to me one morning after she'd spent the night on his boat. "You're thinking that I'm having an affair with him. Don't deny it."

"Did I say anything?"

"You don't have to. I can tell. After all this time, I can tell. The truth is, though, I'm not. I like Stephen, he's a good friend, he doesn't take life so seriously as you do. But we have nothing in common." Then she decided that this wasn't quite the case. "Well, we do have one thing in common."

"And what's that?"

"The hours we like to keep."

Actually I did not believe that the two were having an affair. What I believed was that they were hovering on the brink of it, waiting—not until one or the other took decisive action, but waiting rather until they were both so caught up in the passion of the moment that neither would have to take responsibility for what happened.

The summer, I understood almost from the start, was ruined. Yet I also knew that had we remained in New York, the same result would have been obtained. The same would have held true had we gone to Paris or Hong Kong or the Maldive Islands. Whatever fate operated here, in Roebush, operated the whole world over.

Yet I did nothing. It might have been hope keeping me where I was, hope that she would eventually tire of Stephen and that, somehow, her disillusionment with him might succeed in reigniting her passion for me.

Or maybe it was love that prevented me from going anywhere. Love or its counterfeit: obsession.

Obsession. I trained myself to become as insomniac as she was, shunning sleep in the belief that I would discover for myself what advantage she gained from staying awake for all those many gray hours.

I dropped all pretense of being open-minded and generous and pleaded with her to stay home. From time to time my appeals worked and she would relent and not acknowledge the eleven o'clock rap on our door. Often, when she gave in like this, she acted sullen and reproached me with her glances if not always with her words; she reminded me of a little girl forbidden by her father to attend a party on such occasions. But then there were those rare nights when she would embrace me and, kissing me lovingly, declare that she was grateful that I'd persuaded her, that really she didn't care for Stephen so much and that the novelty of going fishing every night was beginning to pall.

In the days when I first was drawn to Marianne, such a declaration, so fervently delivered, would have delighted me. I would think the episode ended, my forgiveness would follow, and we could get on with our lives. But by the time we'd gotten to Roebush I realized that however sincere she might be at the moment, this was no guarantee that her word could be counted on come the following day.

And, indeed, the next night, her resolution to stay put abandoned, she would act as if nothing had happened. Reminded of what she'd said about Stephen, she'd exhibit not a trace of embarrassment. "Oh, but he can still be fun to be with. I'll ask him over tomorrow night for dinner. Then you and he can talk. You'll see he's not so bad."

I almost looked forward to this dinner, if only for the sake of divining (if I could) what Marianne saw in him. But the dinner never came off.

I succeeded well in inducing a state of near-constant insomnia in myself; even when I did go to sleep I didn't remain asleep for long. I started a practice of taking long walks along the seawall before dawn.

One morning, well after six, I observed a haze descending over the island; at first it resembled a thin mist, but as it rolled in from the Atlantic, it grew thicker, darker, more inexorable. There was no way of knowing for certain, but I had the feeling that if I came to the seawall every morning precisely at 6:25, I would witness the same phenomenon. It was eerie. I now knew enough to be afraid.

About halfway back to the house I glanced up to see, far in the distance, the boats returning. One by one, infinitely small black specks on the horizon, they were emerging from out of the haze. I counted nine in all, average for these nightly trips.

Although I'd had occasion to see the boats when they lifted anchor, I'd never seen them on their return. It struck me that all nine craft were riding high in the water—much higher than when I'd watched them put out into the bay. All I could recall seeing on board were the necessary accoutrements of a fishing expedition: rods, tackles, nets, buckets full of bait, and the kerosene stoves used by the fishermen to warm themselves against the seaborne chill.

Once I'd casually asked Marianne what the boats were carrying in their hold, thinking that maybe there was some kind of construction going on on the island and that the boats were pressed into service transporting equipment and building material. But Marianne said that she never saw anything of the sort—"Nothing's down there but a lot of bilge water," was what she said.

Why, then, I wanted to know, were all the boats so low in the water when they left port?

To my question she answered by saying, "Frankly, I never noticed."

Knowing her as I did, it was entirely possible that she hadn't.

When I got back to the house I saw that I had two visitors. In another town, certainly in New York City, I would have assumed that they were casing the place, the way they were nosing about. But Roebush was an improbable site for a burglary; neither did it seem likely that these two gentlemen, both better dressed than the majority of villagers, would be committing such a crime in broad daylight.

Seeing me approach, the two turned. "Know the people who live here?" the taller one asked. Barrel-chested and bloated around the edges, he gave the impression of an ex-alcoholic not long separated from the bottle. His companion, with cropped hair and a small frame, was in the process of cleaning his glasses with a slightly soiled handkerchief.

"Who are you?" I decided to answer their question with one of my own. I sensed, though, that they were people who tolerated nothing but direct answers.

Two wallets opened in the palms of their hands. Police. The one I judged to be an ex-alcoholic hailed from the provincial capital, the other from New York's sixth precinct. In the few seconds I had to see their badges I caught only the names Ian (the Canadian) and Albright (the New Yorker).

Identifying myself, however redundantly, for I'm sure that they'd already guessed, I asked what business they had with me.

"Not with you, sir, with your wife," Ian said.

"Your girlfriend," corrected Albright.

We went inside. Without invitation, the two occupied the worn couch in the darkened living room.

Said Ian, directing his gaze up the stairs, "Is she asleep?"

"No, she's out."

The looks I elicited were, not unexpectedly, full of skepticism. What, in a village that went to bed by nine, would Marianne be doing out at quarter past six in the morning? I'm sure they thought I was lying.

"The reason we'd like to talk to her," began Albright in a voice so soft as to be almost inaudible, "is that she is wanted for questioning in connection with the killing of Max Percy." He raised his eyes toward me. "Do you know Max Percy?"

If I'd said no, he'd continue to think I was lying. But the fact was that I did. I knew him through Marianne; from what she'd told me they were just good friends, traveling together on the New York social circuit, he even more than she addicted to the fast track. I had never cared for him; Max was too jaded, long gone to seed, masquerading as a bohemian artist (in his case, a free-lance journalist) when everyone knew that bohemians, like dinosaurs, were long extinct.

I said yes.

"You were aware that he was murdered."

Yes, I said again. Three bullets pumped into him with his own gun, the coup de grace a knife driven home under the breastbone straight into his heart.

"Marianne was with him the night of his death," Ian said, evidently reluctant to be left out of this conversation.

"That doesn't mean anything."

"Did you know that she was . . . uh, romantically involved with Percy?" Albright said, enunciating each word carefully. He seemed delighted to have the opportunity to spring this information on me.

It took me a while to answer. "No, I did not."

"Apparently Percy grew . . . uh, disenchanted with Marianne."

"They had a fight—a bitter, knockdown fight—the night of Percy's death," Ian said.

"We have a witness—actually, several witnesses—who saw the fight. It happened right outside a New York nightspot called Area." Albright was waiting for me to react, but I could not, being too stunned to utter a word. "One witness reported seeing her flash a knife he later identified as the murder weapon."

I doubted that an identification like that could stand up in court, but it was not the legal technicalities that interested me at the moment.

"We would like to have a little chat with her," Ian said, echoing his counterpart's earlier declaration.

I decided to lie. I told the detectives that she had gone to Halifax and wouldn't return until the following day. The two seemed to accept what I said with only mild skepticism. They asked to have a look around, a request to which I posed no objection.

When they had satisfied themselves that she wasn't at home they departed, saying that they'd be back the following morning. I wouldn't have been surprised if, on their return, they carried a warrant for her arrest.

Now I didn't know what to think. I wanted to believe her innocent, and yet there was no doubt in my mind that there was considerable reason to believe her guilty. Would the New York City Police Department shell out the money to dispatch one of their officers to this remote village if there wasn't?

My first impulse was to demand an explanation from her. But then I decided to wait; I needed to think. I was torn between saying nothing and allowing the detectives to come for her the next day, and arranging for our escape from Roebush. What astonished me, what even disappointed me in a way, was that I was still in love with her. Or perhaps more in love with her than I'd been before Ian and Albright showed up on my doorstep. Was it possible, I wondered, that I found the idea of her being a murderess titillating, a libidinous fantasy come true?

But as it turned out, whether I decided to say anything or not about the detectives' visit mattered not at all. That morning she did not come back.

I walked down to the docks. Stephen's boat was there, tied up where it always was, but I found no one to tell me what had happened to Marianne.

But I had a good idea as to where she'd gone. I knew where Stephen lived and it was to his house that I went, resolute, determined on a confrontation —until the very moment that I found myself standing in front of his house.

There I lost my courage. A sense of futility overwhelmed me. Against Stephen I was no match. And should I be foolish enough to challenge him, my lunacy was not so profound that I'd expect Marianne to applaud and come running home to me.

Three hours later she was back. Unapologetic. She offered no explanation, no excuses. I was grateful. She respected my intelligence at least enough not to bother trying to deceive me. Neither did she betray any sign of awkwardness. Upon walking into the house, she took one look at me, nodded, asked how I was, and went upstairs without waiting for an answer.

I followed her after a few minutes. She'd thrown herself on the bed and was either asleep or pretending to be. I whispered her name, but elicited no response.

When, toward evening, she awakened, I saw that her hours asleep had done something to her. Rage now contorted her features, made her ugly—or as ugly as it was possible for someone as desirable as her to get.

But she did her best to be polite, to get along with me.

About Stephen all she would say is, "He's a shit." It came spontaneously, without any prompting from me.

These words, so heatedly delivered, buoyed me, causing my spirits to soar. A temporary aberration, a flash of hope, nothing more. But at that moment I believed that everything could be back to the way it was when we were first in love. We would escape Roebush, slip out now, before morning, when the detectives would return. I looked at her, saying nothing. I thought, this is not a murderess, she is innocent, the detectives or their witnesses made some dreadful mistake.

But then, a few minutes later, her mood darkened. She became restless. Impossible for her to sit still. For an hour, perhaps a bit longer than an hour, she tried to make conversation with me. Empty words. She repeated stories she'd told me many times before, like a litany whose very familiarity gives solace. But I could see that it wasn't working—nothing was—and I knew then that I would lose her again.

All at once she sprang up from the chair less than a minute after she'd sat down in it. She rushed past me. The bathroom door slammed shut.

When she emerged twenty minutes later she'd managed to compose herself. But now there was a terrible coldness in her eyes, a fixed look that scared me. In her manner there was desperation; I could tell that she barely had it under control.

It was quarter to eleven when she said, "I think I'm going out for a while."

To try to stop her was out of the question. What surprised me, though, was that she was leaving before the knock came on the door alerting the fishermen to their mission.

Had she been like this the night Max Percy was killed? I couldn't be sure. But it was possible; surely it was possible.

She didn't notice that I was not far behind her, keeping her always in view. I wasn't hoping to get her back now; my only concern was preventing her from doing harm to herself—or to someone else.

Inevitably she found her way to the docks. She clambered over the side of Stephen's boat and went below. There she remained. Even when the fishermen began gathering, she did not appear.

Seeing Stephen, I called out to him.

He gave a twisted, unhappy smile. "Hello, mate, what are you doing here?" he asked.

"Marianne's on board. She's in a dangerous mood. I'd watch out for her if I were you."

I had little doubt that he was expecting accusatory words and outraged demands from me, not words of warning.

A look of bewilderment was replaced in a flash with one of solicitude. "Don't you worry, mate, I can handle it."

Saying that, he climbed on board. His father and uncle, I saw, were coming up from behind, about a dozen or so yards in back.

I returned my gaze to the boat. No sooner had Stephen put his feet down on deck than Marianne reappeared.

"Marianne, what—?" Stephen said, but got no further.

The spear gun held in her arms discharged. It was crazy that I hadn't noticed it; the light wasn't so poor as all that.

Stephen groaned and clutched his stomach. The spear wobbled in his belly. Lurching forward, he grabbed hold of something. I couldn't quite make it out. Then, seeing what it was, I called to Marianne.

But I don't think she heard me. She wasn't moving; that was the oddest thing. She seemed to want to happen what was going to happen. With great difficulty, and in obvious agony, Stephen advanced forward, swinging the iron hook in his hand just once, landing it with great deftness. Marianne staggered forward, the tip of the hook poking out from under her breasts.

She let out a terrible scream and pitched forward a moment after Stephen himself had fallen. Neither of them moved after that.

I was in the middle of packing up my belongings when I heard a knocking on the door. It was midday, not an hour at which I customarily anticipated a visitor.

The lean, bearded man I'd always thought of as Stephen's uncle was standing in the doorway. He announced himself as Stephen's father.

I should have known. Very few of my assumptions had proved themselves correct since coming to Roebush.

There was in his face a melancholy that can come about only from living too long and too bitterly. He said, "I would like you to fish with us tonight."

Such an invitation should have come sooner, I thought, and then maybe all this wouldn't have happened. (But it would have; my trust in fate—though it was a bad, miserable fate—had not been shaken.)

I declined, saying that I was getting ready to leave, that what with the packing and the final arrangements to be made regarding the shipment of Marianne's body, I was hardly prepared to go fishing.

"You always wanted to know what we did. Tonight you can find out. It is something you will not regret."

Again I said I wouldn't go. It was only five days since Marianne's death. I didn't want to see anyone now.

"Tonight, at the usual time, you will hear the knocking," Stephen's father said. And with that he left, an aged man carefully studying the pavement in front of him before he risked taking a step forward.

When the knock came, I was ready. Nothing good will come from this, I thought, but I must go, I must find out what she saw on all those many summer nights she and Stephen went fishing together.

We were about halfway out into the bay before Stephen's father spoke. His brother was at the helm; except for greeting me when I'd come on board, he hadn't spoken a word.

"You must have noticed how heavy our boat is. How heavy all our boats are," was how he began.

My curiosity had diminished a great deal since first coming to Roebush; I no longer cared, but out of politeness' sake I did what I could to express an interest.

"When we reach the island, you will find that the boat grows much lighter."

Directing my eyes toward the island, I was struck by how ill defined it was. There was about it something amorphous and crude, like a lump of clay abandoned by a distracted little boy before he could mold it into shape. That we were so much closer to it than I'd ever been seemed to matter not at all. The view from shore hadn't been much different.

"What *are* you carrying?" I demanded.

Stephen's father raised his weary eyes up at me and said simply, "The dead."

"The dead?"

"Their spirits, their souls, whatever you choose to call them. My son's and Marianne's among them. You can feel her presence, can't you?"

My first reaction was to laugh, my second to say that he was mad.

But he stood there, Stephen's father, like a rejected saint, the conviction in his eyes that he was right, that I would feel her close to me. Maybe it was only the power of suggestion, but after a few minutes had passed, I did begin to feel her presence, like the breath of a whisperer close to one's ear.

I might have been taken in. The whole thing might have been a game, a joke; I cannot say that it was otherwise. What I can say is that upon reaching shallower waters close to the island, gray in the predawn light, our boat all at once rose up from bow to stern. And, though it might have been an illusion born of some ungoldly magic, I felt at the same time the lightness, the freedom, that come from having a tremendous burden lifted from one's heart.

"Turn about!" Stephen's father called.

But his words were not needed; already his brother was in the process of doing so.

"They're both there now? On the island?"

All I could see in front of me was a dense forest, full of alder and pine, but otherwise I could detect no particularly distinguishing geographical feature.

"Yes, they're there. And there they shall remain," Stephen's father said.

"You do this night after night? You don't catch fish?"

"Night after night, yes, that is what we are obliged to do. That is why we pay no taxes. It is a job no one else wants."

"What about all the others in Roebush?"

"From generation to generation," he answered, "it is a legacy that is passed on. It is not for us to question it."

I do not know, nor could I get out of either Stephen's father or his uncle, what the truth was, whether those souls who were taken to the island were stranded there forever, condemned, like Stephen, like Marianne, for their crimes and stupidities, or whether, at some time in the far-off future, their exile there came to an end and they were released.

There was no communicating any of this to the detectives Ian and Albright. In any case, they were so upset that their quarry had escaped them by means of a premature and unnatural death that they had no patience to draw out their stay in Roebush. The investigation into the double killing was for local authorities; their concern was only with dead, moldering Max Percy. And while they made no secret of their loathing for me—for hadn't I deceived them by lying about when Marianne would return?—there was evidently nothing to be gained by charging me as some kind of accessory.

A day after the murders the detectives were gone, back to New York and Halifax. But I stayed. I had it in mind to leave, but I couldn't bring myself to. What it was, I wanted to be close to her. She was there, on that island, I was sure. I felt her. I felt her at night when the island reemerged from the mist. I thought that there were times, when the wind would rise from off the bay and sound a certain way, that I could hear her voice intoning my name.

One day I could stand it no longer. I rented a boat, a poor excuse for a motor launch, and made my way into the mist. It was amazing how in the middle of day, with the sun bearing down, turning the water gold with September light, the mist could be so pervasive, whorls of it blotting out sight of land in any direction.

I found the island, or else the island found me. There's no sense saying that I was not afraid. I was terrified. I thought that perhaps the dead had the ability to make me one of them. But no. Nothing like that happened.

The island was thick with growth, weedy trees and unruly vegetation, rock formations and pebbly sand, a primal geography out of which it was impossible to imagine beauty ever springing. There was a weird, faintly sweet smell in the air, not unpleasant, but irritating nonetheless because I found it so difficult to identify.

Strangely, or perhaps inevitably, the island in reality offered far less than I had imagined sitting in my house across the bay. The spirits of the dead, if in fact (and I could never be wholly certain) they existed here, were quiescent during the day. Certainly they didn't make themselves known to me. The scraggly trees, their branches virtually denuded, seemed to be as dead as anything ever got here.

But even so I was spooked. I was nervous and so busy trying to restrain my heart from detonating that after half an hour of desultory exploration I got myself off the island.

But not before doing one thing.

Oh, I know, it sounds like something a kid would do. But I couldn't help myself. It seemed appropriate at the moment.

What I did was this: with a penknife I carved into the trunk of one of these scraggly, malformed trees the following:

MARIANNE LOVES JACK

MARIANNE LOVES MAX

MARIANNE LOVES STEPHEN

MARIANNE LOVES ?

I don't know whether I really thought I might receive an answer. I don't know what I thought, frankly. It was just something I did.

I waited another week and a half before I summoned the courage to return to the island. Again I went during the day, afraid, I suppose, of meeting up with the fishing boats at night.

The tree where I'd carved my multiple choice question—for that, no doubt, was what it was—was not far from the beach, maybe a hundred yards away.

Probably, I thought, I'll find it exactly as I left it, the same four propositions etched into the thin gray bark.

But I did not. What I found was that a large swath of bark had fallen away, either that or been stripped off, so that of my words all that remained was this:

MARIANNE LOVES

Introduction

*Many of us can recall some time in our lives when we were struck with love/
passion/lust for a total stranger. This memory is usually romanticized to kill
the now faded pain of loss or what might have been. But not always. Those
clichéd ships that pass in the night have a bad habit, on occasion, of colliding.*

*Galad Elflandsson, after a long hiatus, has returned to writing with a ven-
geance. And whether he writes dark fantasy or hard-boiled detective novels or
light fantasy, there's no mistaking his particular touch.*

ICARUS

by Galad Elflandsson

1.

Donald Franklin's first impression of sunny Florida was the heat. He stepped
out of the terminal at Miami International Airport and it enveloped him like
a long-fingered velvet glove. The air was actually thick, heavy with moisture,
redolent with the scent of cypress, and he found it difficult to believe that a
few hours ago he had boarded an Air Canada flight in Ottawa, where the
temperature had plummeted to ten degrees below zero Fahrenheit and upward of a foot of snow covered the ground.

He stood on the sidewalk just outside the plate-glass doors of the terminal,
suitcase in hand, and was overwhelmed, staring blankly at the swarms of
brightly clad people who swept around him like a tide. His blue eyes
widened, drinking in the strangeness of it, his brown hair already growing
dark with perspiration and beginning to cling to his face and the collar of his
shirt.

Heat. Immeasurable warmth. Sun-tan oil worn like perfume. And high
overhead, the vast furnace eye of the sun, glaring down out of a cloudless
crystal sky, shimmering, dripping with heat. He laughed softly to himself,
ignoring the stares of those who heard his laughter, a pale giant in denim
trousers and a chambray shirt, his boots still stained with road salt and the
memory of cold winter weather fast fading from his consciousness.

"Hey Canuck! You gonna stand there all day . . . or are you lookin' for
someone t'take you somewhere?"

He roused himself from the dreamlike wonder of it all and looked down at a stocky black-haired man in a ridiculous floral-patterned shirt, who looked up at him through dark eyes full with amused bonhomie.

"John Savard," he said, introducing himself and extending a welcoming hand. "First time in Florida, eh?"

Donald grinned ruefully and set his suitcase down on the sidewalk. "Donald Franklin," he replied in turn, taking Savard's hand. "Is it that obvious?" he asked, pulling a blue kerchief from his back pocket and mopping his face.

Savard shook his head, still smiling from ear to ear. "I just know a countryman when I see 'im," he explained. "I'm still a Canadian at heart, but they got the goods on sunshine in this part of the world, so I go outta my way t'help people like you get comfortable in a 'urry. Where you from?"

"Ottawa," Donald said softly, and his eyes wandered past the older man's shoulder as a young woman in blue satin shorts and a white halter top sauntered past them. "Jesus . . . would you look at the legs on her . . ."

Savard laughed. "That's right, they start on the ground and go all the way up and make a perfect ass of themselves," he said roguishly. "You better slow down there, Mr. Donald Franklin. I always thought summers in Montreal were something else, but when it comes to half-naked women, this place makes it look like one big nunnery.

"You're gonna see hundreds like that one, Donald, and they'll drive you crazy if you don't watch out."

"I guess so," Donald replied. "I've been so busy tryin' t'get through my finals at university that I've forgotten what they look like. This trip's a graduation present to myself, before I start with Bell Northern Research in February."

Savard whistled appreciatively. "I bet they're gonna pay *you* pretty good," he said. "T'ree weeks in Florida?"

Donald nodded. "Got myself a reservation at a place in Hollywood, on Arizona Street . . . ?"

"Me and the wife got a condo in Hallandale, just sout' of Hollywood," Savard said knowingly. "D'you have a ride up there?"

"I was going to take a cab—"

"Forget that," Savard said vehemently. "If you don't mind waiting while I fill my car, I'll take you up and give you the tour."

"Are you sure—?"

"*Sacrament!*" the Montrealer swore in French. "Would I offer if I wasn't? And you try t'pay me I'll bust you in your *Anglais* nose . . .

"You see that white Chevy Impala across the way there? Here's the keys. You put your suitcase in the trunk and I'll be back in a few minutes."

Donald watched him disappear into the crowd, heard his voice raised like a street vendor hawking his wares, advertising transportation anywhere in the Dade-Broward county area. Shaking his head, he crossed the pavement, dodging a half-dozen cabs that came whipping out of the lineup in front of the terminal. Ten minutes later, Savard reappeared with two couples in tow, stowed their luggage in the bottomless trunk of the Impala, and effected their escape from the madhouse of incoming and outgoing traffic surrounding the airport. As they roared into the long, arcing curve of the Palmetto Expressway where it turned east toward North Miami and Miami Beach, Donald found himself wedged between Savard and a cigar-smoking jeweler from New York City who felt compelled to bellow into the backseat conversation of his wife and their companions.

"This isn't a real cab, is it?" he observed quietly.

"That's for sure," grinned Savard, pausing for a moment from a blistering tirade of Quebecois obscenity he was directing at the slow-moving Cadillac in front of them.

"Then what you're doing is illegal," said Donald.

"Only if they catch me," replied Savard. "And then I pay the fine and go back to the airport." He lowered his voice conspiratorially and said, "These Yanks are fucking crazy with their free enterprise bullshit. Everybody does it. I'm gettin' twenty dollars a pair t'take these Yankee dogs out t'the Beach: the cabs'd take thirty easy. So I'm happy and they're happy."

"But are the cab companies happy?" Donald asked doubtfully.

Savard snorted derisively. "You know 'ow many people get off the planes at that airport each day?"

"Not a clue," Donald admitted.

"Well I don't have no clue either," said the French-Canadian, "but I'm damn sure there ain't enough cabs in this town t'take care of half 'o them, so nobody's gonna cry over the ten or twelve couples I take each day."

Donald looked incredulously at Savard.

"Ten or twelve couples—each day—at twenty apiece?"

"Sure beats workin', eh?" said Savard with a grin. "Like I said t'you, these Yanks are crazy."

Donald spent the rest of the afternoon beside the French-Canadian. They made two more runs out to the airport before Savard decided to call it a day and head for home, but by the time they pulled up in front of the motel where Donald had made his reservation, he had a pretty fair idea of the layout of the vast sprawl that comprised metropolitan Miami and its environs.

"Listen," he protested, hauling his suitcase from the trunk, "I really think I ought t'give you something for all this, John."

Savard nailed him with an outraged stare. "What did I say t'you there at the airport?" he demanded with feigned anger. "I'm not takin' a cent from you, and y'know why? Because you reminded me of my oldest son the first time he came down t'visit us. You had the same dumb look on your face."

He dove back into the car and came out with a scrap of paper and a pencil in hand, scrawled something on the paper, and handed it to Franklin.

"There's my name, address, and telephone number, eh?" he said pointedly. "I know you're gonna spend all your time tryin' t'crawl into every bikini on the beach. But if you get tired of listenin' to people talkin' funny and want t'feel a little bit like home, you just give me a call and I'll have the wife fix us a real French-Canadian supper."

Donald looked at Savard with a deep sense of gratitude welling up inside him.

"I'll do that, John," he said, and meant it. "And thanks an awful lot for everything. I don't—well—I don't feel quite as lost as I did a couple of hours ago."

"That's what I'm 'ere for, Donald," Savard said with a smile. "You phone me, okay, and don't drink any of that piss-water they call beer down here. Most places got Molson's."

Savard climbed back into his Impala and drove off, waving one hand out the window. Donald watched until he was out of sight, then turned to face the coral-pink stucco facade of the Tradewinds Motel, falling back into the peculiar sense of unreality that had claimed him at the airport.

He stood in the shade of a huge palm tree, heard the Atlantic Ocean washing up onto the beach less than a block away, tasted the salty tang in the air, watched dozens of sun-browned men, women, and children strolling the narrow streets. Shaking himself loose from the sweat-soaked stickiness of his shirt, he started across the outer court of the motel.

"Welcome t'sunny Florida, Donny boy," he murmured aloud. "Welcome to Anita Bryant country and America's great Southeast."

He showered and shaved, squashed three palmetto bugs that could just as easily have been prehistoric-size cockroaches, and stood on the balcony of his motel room as the sun set somewhere behind him.

From the balcony he could look out over the rooftops to the ocean, where the waning sun slanted rays of light over its unceasing movement, turning the infinite ebb and flow of its tides into a glittering red-gold carpet. He had never seen the ocean before, and now, within its reach for the first time, it mesmerized him, reinforced the surreal quality of his presence. He felt himself to be a catch-phrase stanger in a strange land, and this feeling brought with it a tenuous fear that was, at the same time, mildly intoxicating, like an adolescent's first encounter with a rare and heady liquor, or the body of his first love.

When the sun was gone from the sky, and the crowns of the palm trees, the roof tiles, and the ocean itself all had become nothing more than deeper shadows against the backdrop of the tropical night, still Donald stood on his balcony and listened, letting the night wind caress his face, his bare chest and legs—he already had grasped and embraced the instinctive ethos among southern peoples to shed most of their outer clothing—feeling the tensions of the last few months wash away in the chorale whisper of wind and sea. At length, his hands came away from the wrought-iron railing and he turned, stripping off his shorts, to seek the slightly damp cocoon of his bed, thoroughly enervated, but at peace with himself and the world.

2.

In the morning, when the sun roused him from sleep like a clarion call to arms, streaming through his windows as it burst upward from the sea, he lay back in his bed and felt suddenly an overpowering loneliness, an urge to run back to the things and places and people familiar to him. He nerved himself to ignore it, flung it from him defiantly by unpacking his suitcase—a ritual display of intent—and faced it again as a scrap of paper fluttered from the pocket of the shirt he had worn the previous day, the scrap of paper bearing John Savard's name, address, and telephone number.

"Don't be an ass," he told himself, staring down at the scrap where it lay on the dresser top. "You're a big boy now, Donald Robert Franklin, and the man's not going to be pleased if you make him play nursemaid."

He climbed into his shorts again, slung a leather pouch about his hips that contained his wallet and supply of traveler's checks, pulled on a T-shirt and a pair of running shoes, and hit the streets.

Hollywood was a rabbit warren of almost-quaint little lanes and alleyways that wandered off in search of other lanes and alleyways to meet with; at eight-thirty in the morning, only the diehard sun worshippers were out, and those who had to work for a living. Donald walked aimlessly, vaguely aware of his stomach crying out for breakfast, but content to let the cries become a gnawing necessity before giving in to them.

He came at last to the boardwalk—on the edge of the bleached-white sand that flowed outward for a hundred feet to be swallowed by the ocean—and stood trembling against the bare wooden railing there as he stared at the morning-splendored monster before him, felt the sting of salt spray on his face and the last vestiges of night-cool being seared away by the immense ball of golden light rising ever higher on the horizon.

He marshaled his courage, knelt to undo the laces of his running shoes, and slung them over his shoulder as he stepped down onto the sand, gingerly slogged his way closer and closer to the water's edge. The handful of people already on the beach took no notice of him, being too busy with laying out blankets and towels, peeling away clothing . . . and Donald was alone, caught in a wide swath of sunlight that drew him onward, to where the sand became dark and slick with its saturation of seawater and the tiny wavelets came racing forward to greet him, foaming around his ankles with a crisp coldness that made him gasp with awe and wonder.

He became timeless in that moment, might have stood at land's end forever, snared in something that, to his bewildered senses, approached a state of near-religious exaltation. His heart began to pound in his chest, his lungs clamored for dizzying drafts of the ambrosial air/light that enveloped him. His eyes closed in deference to the scorching heat of the sun and it was an hour before he moved again, before the delicious intensity of the experience threatened to drown him.

Donald slumped over the counter of the small diner that looked out over the boardwalk and the beach, the scents and sounds of the water's edge replaced by the sizzle of bacon and eggs on the grill and the slow drawling banter of the cook as he harangued a street urchin pressed into temporary service hauling sacks of potatoes in through a side door.

"Gonna be one helluva blazer t'day," the cook observed as he put Donald's breakfast down on the counter. "S'posed t'hit the mid-nineties by noon."

Donald nodded abstractedly, sipping his coffee as he took in the man's heavily muscled arms, almost black with tan, that rippled from a grease-stained white sweat shirt with the sleeves cut off raggedly at the shoulders.

"Never seen you before," he went on, resting a forearm on the counter. "You sure ain't a native with that skin."

Donald looked up into a friendly, bearded grin and put down his coffee.

"I just got in yesterday," he said faintly, still dizzy from his experience on the beach. "Flew in from Ottawa—Canada."

"That right?" said the cook, looking vastly impressed. "I was in Halifax once. Must be pretty near where you come from."

"Yeah," replied Donald, vaguely annoyed. "Right next door really. About fifteen hundred miles."

The man cocked his head to one side, unsure whether Donald had been serious or simply sarcastic.

"Well . . . there's a lot o' you people down here these days, mostly frogs, but hell! Who cares really? You guys are just like us anyway. And that feller Taylor—the one saved them diplomats in Iran . . ."

His voice trailed off into silence as he realized his customer was not paying him that much attention. Donald was staring out the wide plate-glass window of the diner, his eyes glazed with fascination.

"She's somethin' else, ain't she?" said the cook pridefully, as if the woman standing on the other side of the window was a permanent but mobile fixture of his establishment. "She just showed up a couple o' days ago . . . no idea where she came from—but I sure wouldn't mind findin' out."

He turned back to Donald with a sly wink in progress, but found the counter stool empty and a pair of dollar bills beside the untouched plate of bacon, eggs, and home fries.

Donald became a shadow, a faceless pair of eyes hovering on the perimeters of her existence, as she moved from the boardwalk to the beach and walked miles, up and down the sand, pantherlike, but a panther spun from pure gold.

She might have been stark naked for all that the white knit string bikini shielded her from the avid stares of the men she passed. She seemed to glide effortlessly over the sand, the long muscles in her legs moving sinuously with each step under the flawless gold satin of her skin, rippling the taut rounded flesh of her buttocks. Her back was a shimmering auric perfection that rose from flared hips and supple waist, her arms almost disproportionately slender, ending in long-fingered, delicate hands that touched lightly upon each thigh. And her hair was a tawny-pale mane that fell to her waist when it was not whipped into a coronal of white-gold flame by the wind.

Donald followed her relentlessly through the morning and on into the withering heat of the afternoon, unable to tear his eyes from her, unwilling to do so even for an instant. She was an extension of whatever it was he had experienced earlier, the physical embodiment of a dream he had never dreamed, until that day, and he felt himself drawn to her as he had never been drawn to anything or anyone in all the twenty-one years of his life.

She seemed oblivious to her surroundings, walked past hungry stares by the score without ever a hint or intimation that she was aware of them. Her restless striding up and down the beach, the imperious toss of her head and hair, upward, to catch the full glare of the sun, drove the world to a mindless distraction as the sand became crowded with sunbathers and swimmers. Yet there was always a path where she might walk, and they all might have been phantoms—indeed, they were phantoms when compared to the tangible force of her physicality and perfection—for all the notice she paid them.

Somewhere during the course of the day, Donald peeled the sweat-drenched T-shirt from his back; somewhere during the hours he followed in her wake, deaf and blind to everything/everyone but her. He lost his own sense of being, submerged it in the essence of Her, and ached with longing . . . to touch . . . taste . . . dissolve . . .

"You follow me. You have stared at me. I feel your eyes."

The soft sighing whisper of a voice startled him back into a semblance of awareness. Where he had been, who he had been—of these things he had no knowledge. But now *she* stood over him where he sat on the sand, and her nearness almost made him cry out with—pain?

His eyes grew wide, distended, like gaping mouths, drinking in each detail of her. He saw the tiny veins in her feet where they climbed to her thorough-bred ankles, into the muscles of her calves and the smooth endless miracle of golden-fleshed thighs, the dazzling white triangle of fabric between them. He saw now that her skin was downed with feather-fine wisps of white-gold hair, that it curled through the triangle of cloth over her sex, crept over the swell of her belly and shimmered on her arms. He raised his head further, past the proud vault of her ribs, the rhythmic rise and fall of her breasts . . . and looked into her eyes, that were as golden as the rest of her, liquid pools of molten fire in a face of peerless beauty.

And before this vision, in response to her statement, the soft sighing whisper of her voice, Donald could say only:

"Yes."

3.

"Why have you done these things? I find them—disturbing."

Though he had not truly seen the sinuous movement that brought her to her knees before him, Donald retained a vague memory of it, and found even the memory had left him speechless. He simply stared at her, dazedly, en-thralled by the magic of the wind stirring her hair, the musical, slightly foreign tone of her voice. He knew, with a dire and dreadful certainty, that if he dared gaze again into her eyes he might never speak another word, and with bowed head, he tried to find an answer to her question.

"I—I don't know," he stammered. "I didn't mean—I'm sorry if—"

"Was it because I am beautiful?" she interrupted him, impatiently, and he cringed at the hint of displeasure in her voice, marveled at the ingenuous yet thoroughly self-assured immodesty of her question.

"Yes," he said quickly. "That's the reason I—"

"Then why do you look away from me, now that I am here before you?" she demanded softly, and Donald now caught the faint inflection of her speech, thought to recognize it as French, even as he found a way perhaps to smooth away her displeasure.

"Because you are too beautiful," he said, looking up at her earnestly and realizing his ploy was no more and no less than the absolute truth. "Because I've never seen anyone as beautiful as you are."

And then she smiled at him, and the dazzling splendor of that delighted smile struck him like the blow of a hammer, reeled his senses and would have thrown him off his feet had he not been seated.

"Then I will forgive you, I think," she said warmly, "but you must walk with me—"

"But I've been—"

"Following me all the morning and the afternoon," she said, chiding him. "Now I ask that you walk *with* me, and talk with me. Tell me your name . . ."

Donald came to his feet slowly, and with one fluid motion she stood beside him, watching him intently as he told her his name, and then moving off again, down the beach.

"I am Celeste," she said to him, only that and no more, walking some way in silence before she spoke again.

"I love the sun, Donald," she whispered reverently, and he noticed that she walked to his right, where the rays of the downward-progressing sun might yet fall upon her without hindrance. "It is like life itself to me. When I feel it touching me, filling me with its warmth, then and only then am I truly alive."

"Do you live here, in Florida?" he asked, for no other reason than to hear the sound of her voice in reply.

"No," she said, purring the word. "I am here for only five more days . . . and then I will go home."

He wondered briefly if home might be Montreal or Quebec City—her manner of speaking, the way she used words, suggested it could be so—and found nothing else to say until they had walked for another hour, in silence, and the sun began to sink below the roofs of the town.

"Celeste . . ." he said hesitantly, using her name for the first time. "Will you stay with me? We can go somewhere—have dinner together—go walking again—all night if you like?"

She glanced upward at the sun, frowning as she shook her head, the mane of her hair, and Donald felt a desperate fear crawling in his throat, and infinite relief as her lips moved ever so slightly.

"I want to make love with you," she breathed softly.

And the days went by in this manner: each morning, when Donald would wake from an hour, perhaps two, of exhausted sleep, he would find Celeste on the balcony of his room, naked, her entire body taut with anticipation as she waited for the sun to heave itself up from the sea. And then she would tease him, plead with him if he asked for a few more hours of sleep, to come with her out to the beach, where they would spend another day walking, bathing in the sunlight, soaking in its warmth, before they returned to the motel room at sunset and their dance of love began again.

Donald scarcely noted the passage of time. Days and nights became indistinguishable, interchangeable in the overload of sensory stimulation that poured from the incredible girl named Celeste. He worshipped at the shrine of her body through every waking moment, and dreamed of his worship when he slept. There were times when he thought he would die from wanting her, when his whole body ached to join itself to hers, and their time on the beach became a torture, an intolerably exquisite agony of waiting for the moment when she would turn to him and say, "I want to make love with you," and he prayed it would never end.

Until the morning it did end, and he found himself alone in his room, screaming.

4.

Thereafter his world was a never-ending nightmare of darkness interspersed with fleeting images and sounds—fists pounding on a door, muffled cries of dismay, horns blaring and sirens wailing while faces that belonged to strangers swam in and out of his consciousness. When it was quiet again he tried to sleep, but a vast and all-encompassing pain seemed the throb through every nerve in his body, making it impossible to sleep, impossible to forget. And if the pain became too much to bear, if he began to scream for Celeste to come and make it go away, white-shrouded ghosts came instead, muttering among themselves in white-shrouded ghost voices as they bent over him . . . and then sleep would come, but it was a dream-haunted sleep every bit as ghastly as the long hours of wakefulness.

"Donald, can you 'ear me . . . ?"

"Celese . . . is that you?"

"No, Donald. It's me, John Savard."

"John . . . Savard . . . ?"

"Sure. Don' you remember? I drove you from the airport."

He opened his eyes slowly, found a face different from all the others hovering above him, a face he recognized—framed by jet-black hair, with dark eyes that were wide with horror and disbelief.

"Yes," he said hoarsely, shuddering as the pain returned to his body. "I do remember. John, is Celeste with you?"

He saw Savard shake his head. "Donald, what happened to you? Who is this Celeste?"

"She was standing on the balcony . . . she did that every morning . . . it was dark outside but I could tell by the way she was standing that . . . the sun . . ."

"Tell me what happened, Donald. The police, they found my name and telephone number on your dresser, told me you were 'ere in hospital . . ."

"I hurt so much, John . . . so thirsty . . . she was standing there . . . raised her arms . . . as the sun started to come up . . . over the ocean . . . and . . . when the first ray . . . of light . . . touched her she was so beautiful . . . so bright . . .

"And then she started to go away, John . . . when the sun touched her . . . it started at the tips of her fingers . . . I tried to get up . . . she was melting away . . . bit by bit . . . I saw someone in the mirror . . . with white hair . . . and a face . . . old and horrible . . . and the sun swallowed her, John . . . but the person in the mirror . . .

"That wasn't me, John . . . for Christ's sake . . . John . . . please tell me . . . *Please say that it wasn't me!*"

Introduction

Where are the boundaries when a mind goes wrong? Or where are the bound-aries when you don't know if the mind is gone, or the world is. The easy answer is—there are none; the correct answer is—in the shadows.

Nina Hoffman continues to impress her readers, her work having appeared in Clarion Awards, Tales by Moonlight, *and most major magazines and anthologies. She's currently working on her second novel.*

ANTS

by Nina Kiriki Hoffman

"Always keep your house spotless, Seelie-Marie," her mother had told her, "and you'll never have problems with ants."

Selina stared at the bottle of all-purpose cleaner in her hand, with its bright yellow and green label. Then she looked down at the kitchen linoleum, which bore a pattern of yellow happy faces, and a thin trickle of black ants making mustaches on several, bisecting others. What could the ants possibly find to eat in the kitchen? She always gave the place a thorough wipedown after every meal. If she had found ants in Pony's room, or Harold's, she could have understood. Neither her husband Harold nor her daughter Pony was a subscriber to the theory of spray-n-scrub. She got into their rooms whenever possible with lemon furniture polish, floor wax, and spray cleaner, plus plenty of dust rags, sponges, and mops. But she couldn't catch all the crumbs. It astounded her how fast Harold and Pony could accumulate dirt when neither of them ever left the house.

She knelt and sprayed the line of ants. She took a moment to shudder, then wiped the whole cadre up with her green-and-yellow double-sided sponge. Horrid little creatures. Somewhere in her memory there was an en-counter with ants. It had happened at summer camp, when she was still Seelie-Marie. She woke in a sleeping bag, feeling uncomfortably itchy, only to discover ants the size of peanuts scrambling over her body. Screams. Must have been hers, though she couldn't imagine opening her mouth when there was the chance an ant might crawl into it. The vision of small black seg-mented *things* crawling up and down the bunk-bed ladder beside her head. The long moment of horror before she could bring herself to believe this was happening to her.

And then, the run for it. Skinning out of the sleeping bag where the little invaders lingered, tossing it out the cabin door, dancing frantically to rid herself of them, strangers against her skin, shucking even her nightgown to get away from their touch—she didn't stop to think about how much the stares and jeers of her cabin mates would hurt. That divestiture of her garment had probably been the last spontaneous act of her life. Snatching a towel off the rack, she had run for the showers. She stood a long time under the steaming water before she opened her eyes to search her pale skin for black spots, and it took months before she could convince herself she was clean.

She stared at the yellow side of her sponge, where small black creatures struggled among the pores, inhaling ammonia fumes, dying before her eyes. These ants were much smaller than the summer ants. Grease ants or sugar ants? Somebody had told her there were two kinds. It didn't matter. She held the sponge under a stream of hot water until all the ants were washed down the drain. She would refrigerate *all* the food, and head right down to the market for some ant poison.

It was uphill work making room for the flour in the freezer. She took one look at the canned goods and decided they would have to survive unprotected until she licked the ant problem. Maybe she could soak the labels off them, not leave anything for the ants to desire—but then how would she tell one food from another? She thought about serving Harold beets when he asked for beans. Or giving Pony cream of mushroom soup when she wanted chicken noodle. No, it would never do. They both yelled a lot at her anyway, and that hurt her ears. Quarrels made her very uncomfortable.

She took the car keys off the rainbow key holder by the door, then went to tell Pony and Harold she was leaving.

She stopped in Pony's room first—it was furthest down the hall. Pony looked horrible. No, that couldn't be true. Those blue, bruised circles under her eyes—mouses, the kids on the playground used to call things like that, a particular sort of black eye—the paleness of her skin, the gummy blonde hair —no, one's children never looked horrible. Pony just needed a nice bath.

Selina tried on her most cheerful-charmer smile. "I'm going to the market, sweetie. Anything Momums can get for you? Need anything before I go?"

"Need ta take uh shit," Pony said, only half her mouth working. It had been like that since the accident. One eyelid droopy, one arm wasting away, and only half the mouth moved.

"Momums has asked you not to talk like that," said Selina, never losing her smile. "Can we ask nicely?"

Pony's eyes fell closed for a moment. Then the right one fluttered half open. "Mom, kin yuh hev Vony to fathroom? Vlease?"

"Of course, dear." Unflagging, Selina helped Pony with the messy and disgusting business. Selina's arms had grown stronger in the two years since the accident; lifting Pony had done it, and shifting Harold to make his bed on the days when he refused to transfer to the wheelchair. Selina found the muscles in her arms unpleasant. Subconsciously she knew that Pony was dropping weight, and she welcomed the chance for the bulging muscles to dwindle into something more ladylike.

When she had settled Pony back in bed, the horrid withered legs swathed in sheets and out of sight, and even the left arm covered, Selina smiled at her daughter. "You want a special treat, sweetie? How about some Twinkies?"

Pony's face twisted into a scowl. It must be the pain of her injuries, Selina decided, feeling her smile lose a little of its power. "Sugar," Pony said, and closed her eyes.

Well, she could buy the Twinkies and surprise Pony later. Although the last time Pony had had Twinkies she had been a little sick afterward—could the two things be connected? Nonsense. Wholesome golden sponge cake with cream filling . . . Selina felt hungry herself.

Harold was asleep when Selina looked into his room. The television was droning on about a ball game; Harold's hand had relaxed around the remote control. Snores came from his open mouth. Selina wondered whether to wake him and tell him she was going out. Maybe he'd sleep until she returned; he was so much more pleasant while he was asleep.

As she climbed into the station wagon and inserted the key into the ignition, Selina found herself almost thinking about the accident. She could feel her thoughts creeping closer to the forbidden zone. Quickly she filled her mind with images of flowers instead. Lobelia—what a gorgeous blue! Although the leaves were a rather sickly purple. Dahlias. Dahlias were perfect, large as babies' heads, colorful as a child's painting, and the leaves an ideal green. Imagine daffodils spiking their way up through winter snow, bringing in the tide of spring.

She smiled and started the car, then scratched her ear. Under her fingernails—a struggling black corpus, an ant. A shudder shook her. She wanted to thrust her finger into the car's cigarette lighter and crisp the little beast. It seemed larger than the kitchen ants had. Had it been feeding on something her body secreted?

She drove to the store with less than her usual caution, feeling the need for ant poison as an ache in her stomach. If only one could trust God to rid the world of ants. Things would be much nicer without them.

She loaded her shopping cart with six bottles of ant poison and two spray cans of air freshener, one wild-rose scented, the other forest fresh. She thought about buying Pony some crackers, but Pony had trouble chewing; Twinkies were much easier for her to handle. She could break off small pieces with her good hand and let them melt in her mouth. Selina bought six packs of Twinkies.

As she stood in the checkout line, Selina felt a crawly sensation on her chest. She glanced down at the buttons on her frilly blouse, then looked up at the other customers. She had chosen the wrong time to come to the market. It was almost 5 P.M. and people were shopping for their dinners. The checkout lines were choked with customers.

The sensation of tiny feet scrabbling moved down into her bra.

Selina felt the blood prickling in her cheeks. No repeat of the incident from summer camp; she was a grown woman and would not tear off her shirt and run screaming from the store, pushing other customers to and fro. Her left hand closed into a fist around one of the bottles of ant poison. She wished she could bathe in the liquid it contained.

"Ma'am?" said the checker, whose name tag read Charlie. "You want to let go of your groceries?"

From somewhere inside, she retrieved a smile, though most of her attention was focused on the sensation inside her shirt. She put the bottle of poison on the check stand counter. The creature in her shirt was *moving.* Wedging itself in under the fabric of her bra. Forcing its way closer to . . .

The wait for the checker to ring up the total seemed interminable. She paid for her groceries, snatched them from the bag girl, and bolted from the store. She almost dropped the keys unlocking the car door. Flinging the groceries onto the passenger seat, she slumped behind the steering wheel, taking a precautionary peek to make sure no one was watching her. Then she unbuttoned her shirt and removed the squirming black animal. It was nearly the size of a kidney bean, and she had to step on it three times, twisting the toe of her black high-heel, before its legs stopped twitching. A summer ant?

She remembered as a child in sixth grade doing a report about ants: honeypot ants, which hung from the ceilings of ant nests. They functioned only as storage receptacles; other workers fed them. Their abdomens swelled until they were the size of peas, clear, translucently golden, ripe with food. In times of need they could regurgitate the food for the other ants . . . the horrible things had filled her nightmares for months. She remembered reading about some ants who tended their queen for years, licking and cleaning and feeding her.

She tried to think of roses, but the images of ants were too fresh. Taking a piece of tissue from her purse, she scooped the squashed ant from the rubber mat on the floor of the car and flung it out the window. A shower would be nice. Maybe she could put a little ant poison on her soap, and rub it over her skin. Give the little monsters a distaste for her.

Harold was screaming her name when she unlocked the door and reentered the house. Her first instinct was to run to him and discover what was wrong, but then she remembered how often he had screamed for her, for trivial reasons: to adjust the television—he was very picky about the contrast —or to move a curtain an inch to the side because the streak of sunlight across the ceiling bothered him. She frowned and set her paper bag on the kitchen table.

A river of ants crossed the floor, coming out from under the sink, obscuring a whole line of happy faces, and pouring into the hall. Selina screamed, reached into the bag and began throwing down bottles of ant poison as if they were grenades. Dark brown liquid splashed as the bottles broke, but even the ants in the path of the poison continued their determined march deeper into the house.

"Selina! Selina!" Harold screamed, despair in his voice replacing the usual whining annoyance. Then he began gurgling.

She darted across the floor, her high heels slipping in the poison and the ants. She stamped as she ran, and sobbed. The ants seemed as big as her thumb.

"Maaaah," Pony wailed.

The hall seemed very dark. She did not stop to switch on the hall light and missed the pink glow from the rose-shaped fixtures. The whole hall seemed floored with moving blackness.

She reached Harold's room first. All the lights were out. Curtains blew at his window, letting the evening sun in in meager splashes. The television screen had turned to buzzing snow. Selina gripped her elbows, hunching her shoulders, and waited for a clear vision to enlighten her.

With the suddenness of a glance in an unexpected mirror, she saw Harold, illuminated by sun. The black river climbed up the covers, up his bare, blond-furred chest, and into his mouth. His eyes were wider than she had ever seen them. Only strange small sounds came from his throat.

Ants. Thrifty scavengers. Suppose she just left this room . . . left this house . . . they had already found him. In a week, perhaps only his bones would be left.

As she stood in the doorway, the clarity of the sun seemed to strike through her mind, leaving her emotionally bereft. Shorn of her responsibilities to Harold and to Pony—for Pony, too, had fallen almost silent—she could take a new name, a new personality, and start over completely.

The way she had after the accident.

She looked toward her feet. The flow of ants, now almost an inch deep, parted cleanly around her shoes. Rapacious army ants—they could only have come from Africa. She had read of their dreadful marches, of how they ate everything that stood in their way. How was it that Harold stood in their way, and she did not?

The curtains blew up again. Harold's eyes stared at her. His hands made scrabbling motions in the covers. One lifted toward her and turned, palm up, its fingers outstretched.

What was she thinking? This was her husband, her child. She had already robbed them of their health, the use of their limbs, their freedom of motion, their hope for any future. She could not stand by and do nothing while they died.

As she walked, stiff-legged, into the room, the memory of the crash came and flooded her mind with darkness. The person she used to be—who went by her middle name, Marie—drove the car, biting down on bitterness because Pony and Harold had had such a good time at the party and she had stayed in a corner, alone and unappreciated. Pony and Harold were golden and charming. Everybody liked them. She, Marie, was the dark person, with the poison inside, a poison people seemed to sense. They always stayed away from her.

Selina began brushing at the ants in Harold's chest hair. They pincered themselves on, refusing to be brushed off. She tried to brush them away from his chin, but they clung there, lifting off tiny pieces of flesh when she succeeded in moving them. She sat somewhere in her head, detached, watching herself move in slow motion. Harold's eyes seemed to be drying in his head. Water, she thought. She walked to the bathroom and filled a glass from the tap. Went back, threw it on the ants. It did not unseat a single one.

How had Harold ever decided to marry Marie? She had heard people wonder about it. Her hearing was very acute. People like Harold's friends would never understand how a lonely, clever woman could bring pressure to bear on the most promising man in her freshman class. They didn't understand how, if one repeatedly abused a person like Harold, in a subtle way, eventually a person like Harold would have to decide he liked being abused, in order not to lose his good self-opinion. How could anything he didn't like keep happening to him? Eventually a person like Harold might decide he couldn't live without such abuse. And Marie had been the only person who could abuse him in just that fashion.

Selina thought of her cupboards full of cleaning products. Perhaps she should try anything—air freshener, furniture polish, spray cleaner, cleansing powder, bleach, detergent—something must stop these determined little horrors. She did not feel much hope. The damage the ants must have done to Harold already would certainly require another trip to the hospital emergency room, and she had barely been able to pay the medical expenses of the accident, at a time when they had had insurance. Her present salary as a librarian barely kept them all alive now.

Feet dragging, she walked to Pony's room and glanced in. Pony liked her curtains open. Her window faced north, so the sun never spent much time in her room, but she liked to look at the blue sky. She told Selina once she imagined she could fly.

Ants completely obscured Pony's pale face and hair. Selina sagged against the doorjamb and watched Pony's thin chest for a sign of life. There was no rise and fall in the rib cage.

Harold and Pony had always worn their seat belts. Marie had counted on that when the mad impulse spoke to her on the mountain road home after the party, saying, "End the misery. Drive the car over the edge and leap free." She had let the wheel pull her into a flimsy guard rail, let the door open, let herself fall out onto the steep slope as the car continued downward. She had hoped for an explosive Hollywood conflagration, some suitable mourning, and a new start. But the only person who died in the crash was Marie.

Faced with a staggering load of obligations, Marie had slipped into oblivion, and Selina Sunshine, the endlessly eager do-gooder character she had tried being in grade school, reawakened. Selina could cope with almost anything; when her thoughts darkened, she concentrated on flowers.

But flowers wouldn't save her now. Selina looked at Pony. A nice bath would no longer cure her. Selina turned into the darkness of the hall, staggered back through the ants to the kitchen, her favorite domain. The happy-face floor was no longer visible under the kinetic mosaic of ants.

She stood for a moment, watching them. Mother would disapprove; just their being here meant the house was dirty, as if they became the visible incarnation of Selina's inadequacy. Then again, Selina had never been able to satisfy mother. Marie had never wanted to.

Selina reached for visions of daisies and zinnias, but the ants were too real and black to be driven back with flowers, and she kept seeing Harold, and Pony. Selina closed her eyes.

Seelie-Marie opened her eyes. She knelt, placed her hand on the floor. The ants parted around it. They had lost interest in her. She moved slowly through them toward the refrigerator, kicking off her high heels as she went. Stupid shoes. And the pantyhose would have to go, too. She opened the refrigerator door and took out loaves of bread, then opened the plastic sacks, casting sliced bread upon the sea of ants.

"Always keep your house spotless, Seelie-Marie, and you'll never have problems with ants."

Seelie-Marie had never been a very obedient little girl.

Introduction

It's never easy for an adult to return home. Things are gone, things are smaller, things are shabbier. And things, in every sense of the word, are also a lot more dangerous.

Texan Ardath Mayhar's stories and novels have appeared with greater frequency over the past few years, much to the delight of all her fans, new and old.

NOR DISREGARD THE HUMBLEST VOICE

by Ardath Mayhar

It was November, and it looked every inch of it. Gray sky, gray grass, gray leaves that hadn't yet fallen from the trees made me feel just as gray as the rest of the landscape. That wasn't hard to do. The funeral of one's last living relative will do that for you, without any help from the weather.

Now I had to return to the silence of my grandmother's house, the empty and echoing rooms and hallways and attics that had held the most joyful times of my childhood. It seemed impossible that of all that band of rampageous cousins, I was the last lonely remnant.

There were, of course, old friends of the family—unbelievably old, most of them—who offered to stay with me, help with packing up those family mementoes I chose to keep, anything at all to comfort me. As gently as I could, I discouraged them all without making it too obvious that I was not ready to preside over any demise from sheer old age that might overtake one of their number at any given moment.

So I went back alone, up the wet gray cement of the walk, between the ranks of the frost-killed chrysanthemums, through the silent slab of oak door my great-grandfather Marsh had hung there a hundred and fifty years before. I had never entered that door in my life that a welcoming voice hadn't sung out cheerfully, or that hasty steps—more than one set, usually—hadn't come pattering from the kitchen, along the length of the dampish hall that could never be adequately heated. For years on end those pattering feet had belonged to my grandmother. Then to my aunt Annabelle. The last ones had been those of my cousin Rose . . . and it was to her funeral I had come.

I turned the huge key in the ponderous lock, pushed open the door. Silence. Of course. I hadn't expected anything else.

Sighing, I turned and relocked the door, pulled the antique bolts into place. When the Marshes had built this house there had been no thought of locking its doors against the neighbors in this quiet neighborhood. But now it was no longer a quiet neighborhood . . . it was one of screams in the night, gunshots beyond the tall stone wall. It was just as well that we were all gone, now, for our exclusive world had left first, leaving us orphaned in a hostile environment.

I went through the motions of eating, choosing from the tremendous number of casseroles my neighbors and old friends had provided for the sustenance of one single bachelor. I took a long, hot bath, trying to soak some of the chill gray out of my bones. Then I lay in my bed—the narrow one in the room beneath the eaves, where I had taken refuge when I was six and the world had flown apart as surely as had the plane on which my parents had been passengers.

Then, my grandmother had been there, a short, round rock of a woman, ready to warm away the mullygrubs from her firstborn grandchild. Though she must have been hurting terribly herself at the loss of her son and daughter-in-law, it had been years before that had ever occurred to me. All the pain had been mine, I'd thought at the time, and never by so much as a grimace had she shown me a glimpse of hers.

My eyes seemed locked on the Open position. The dull drip from the eaves just above, the dismal swooshing of the sodden evergreens below, all conspired to keep me awake. I tried conjuring the memory of Gramma as she had sat so many times on the foot of my bed, making up outrageous tales of her childhood for my amusement. A ridiculous pastime for a man past forty, you might say, and you'd be dead right. But somehow, on this terrible November evening, I felt orphaned all over again.

She'd told stories that her own grandmother had told to her in times so remote that they had less reality for me than the incidents in the book of historic tales I'd been given for Christmas. Odd stories out of their mutual past in rural East Texas were my favorites. Things about "scrinch owls" and bobcats squalling on night-bound rivers and catfish six feet long that sometimes ate the fishermen who came to catch them.

And now her voice, husky with age yet still young in tone, was almost there in the room with me. Her favorite philosophy, which she'd drummed into me all my life, came so vividly to my mental ear that my physical ears could almost detect it in the silence of that orphaned house.

"Listen to the critters, Jonathan. Hear the tame beasts and the wild ones, the voices in the wind and the words in the leaves. Don't ignore anything or disregard the smallest voice, for they're all there for you, like the Good Book says. We're all part and parcel of each other, and we weren't given dominion over the beasts just to hunt them and to eat them. We care for them, some of us, and they know, somehow. So they care for us. Even the mice in our attics and the beetles in our walls are a part of us, after all these years."

I thought about that, now, for the first time in years. She had claimed that just knowing the mice were there, chewing away in their mousy way, was company for her when she was alone. Now I wondered if it had all been inside her head, or if in some way generations of small beasties that had lived in this house and died here might actually have developed some feeling of kinship with the human beings living in such close proximity.

It was one of those wakeful-night notions that nobody in his sane senses would have entertained for even a moment in daylight. Now, in that disoriented state that comes with the loss of someone you love, in the dreary night, it didn't seem so outlandish. Still, if the little creatures did take interest in us, it wasn't of much help. It hadn't helped Rose, for instance.

Though what a bunch of mice and beetles and crickets could have done to a bunch of doped-up kids with murder and robbery on their minds I really cannot say. That thought made me shiver under the quilt that was a legacy from Great-grandma Marsh. I'd checked all the bolts, front and back and side. I'd made sure the big windows were secured as well as they could be— though that wasn't very comforting when I thought of the french windows onto the rear garden.

The police hadn't been surprised at all that the killers had been able to get into the house. They'd pointed out those wide expanses of glass, the multitude of smaller windows all along the first floor, and even the ornate Victorian porch posts, which had let climbers gain access to the window at the first-floor landing of the stairway.

Perhaps that was one reason for my wakefulness. It wasn't just the drippings and rustlings from outside—it was also my close attention to any sound inside the house that was keeping me so tense. Even with the most vulnerable windows boarded and the french windows barricaded with furniture, there were all too many places where a determined hooligan could make his entry.

But my remembered visit with Gramma seemed to calm me. I found myself growing drowsy, and somewhere between wondering whether I'd checked the basement (almost unheard of in East Texas) and how I was going to manage with packing up the accumulation of so many generations of Marshes, I fell into a troubled sleep.

When I woke it was still dark, broken only by fitful gleams from the streetlight beyond the garden wall. There was a sound. Shrill, small, pervasive. Like . . . squeaking?

I sat and listened hard. Something scurried across the floor of the room. Tiny sounds came to my ears. Cchhk! Cheee! Prrrk! But very small, almost inaudible to anyone who hadn't been taught to hear even the humblest voices. I clicked on the light and looked down. A mouse sat beside the nighttable, staring up at me.

"Skeee!" it said peremptorily.

I knew I was dreaming. My memory of Gramma's words had triggered this, it was obvious. But as I showed no sign of waking from the dream, I might as well go along with it. I pulled on a thick robe and scuffed my feet into slippers. Then I rose to follow the rodent as it fussed toward the door.

I turned on lights all the way downstairs. I didn't intend to go stalking around in this huge place in the dark. There was no guarantee that the murderers of poor Rose hadn't returned to finish off the family for good and all. There was no sign of anything amiss on the first floor.

My small guide had disappeared as soon as it was obvious that I was going to check out the place. Being up and either awake or sleepwalking, I thought that I might as well do a thorough job of it. I went through the downstairs painstakingly. There was nothing to find.

I felt certain that anything happening above the first floor would have caught my attention. That left the basement. A nasty thought. I'd never liked its dank depths. In this climate mildew was the lot of any enclosed space below ground, and our basement had a lot of that. But it did have two windows—too small, you'd think, to admit anyone larger than a child. Still, I knew I'd better check it out. That mouse just might come back to chew me out if I didn't.

The stair was still as narrow and precarious as I remembered it. The lightbulb was still a twenty-watt superdim one that made shadows look deep as ink. I felt my way down cautiously, holding up the tail of my robe so as to keep from tripping. I'd hate to lie at the bottom of the steps with something broken until such time as one of the ancient friends came looking for me.

I looked with suspicion at the bulk of the natural-gas furnace. It had always reminded me of a monster lying in wait for a small boy to come within pouncing distance. It hadn't changed a bit. The huge steamer trunks Great-aunt Felicia had taken on her trip to Europe still huddled in a corner like a herd of buffalo lying down for the night. The small window on the right glinted dully above a rickety table.

I turned to look behind me at the other window. There was a curious, lumpy shadow below it. I moved closer. It was a very solid shadow. Too solid. There was something lying there, half-concealed by a corner of the ancient dresser that had been too large to get up the attic stairs.

I moved forward with much caution. It was a person who lay there in an attitude that a living body isn't capable of assuming. I turned and sped up the steep stair, through the hallway to the kitchen, where I found a big flashlight. There was an extension of the telephone there, too, and I used it to call the police.

Then I went back down to see who it had been who had died in the Marsh cellar.

I know, it would have been more sensible to wait and go back with the police. I wanted to do that. But something inside demanded to know. To see. To understand what had happened to that intruder into my family's house. The Marsh tendencies run that way.

With the flash in hand I went again to bend over the still shape below the window. It was that of a young man, almost a boy. His pocket bulged with something that looked both hard and lethal, and I didn't disturb it. His hands were bloody—torn. Chewed? It looked that way.

The hands were clamped over the face, as if protecting it from something. I knew it was foolish to move them, but something inside me demanded to know what that face had looked like. I pulled them back a bit and turned the full glare of the flash onto the features.

That will haunt me as long as I live. For there were no features. Gleams of bloody bone shone through gnawed rags of flesh. Two ragged holes marked the places where eyes had been. And everything was marked, scored, raked with the imprints of tiny teeth. Mouse teeth?

The police never said what they thought about it. I never told them of my dream that wasn't a dream. Just said I'd waked in the night, uneasy, and checked things out. God knows, I had plenty of reason for that.

The boy was a known thief and junkie. They theorized that he'd wormed his way through that narrow window to try and pick up something salable out of the house. What happened after that was never mentioned in any detail. The newspapers assumed that he'd fallen crookedly and broken his neck on the cement floor of the cellar, and nobody ever corrected them.

As for me, I think it was Gramma's mice. They were nice, Marsh-trained mice, never suspecting that people hurt other people. When Rose was raped and bludgeoned to death it must have shocked them horribly. They didn't give that kind of thing the chance to happen again.

It probably says something very strange about me when I say that I understood the entire thing. And, God help me, I felt responsible for all those trusting, dedicated Marsh critters, there in the house I had intended to sell.

I haven't any family. Not anymore. The apartment in Dallas was just a place to store my gear, not a real home as this house has always been to me. Even now, I can hear small nibblings in the walls, tiny chirpings from the ancient woodwork. From time to time my watch-mouse comes out to keep me company.

I have a niggling feeling that they wouldn't let me leave, even if I wanted to. I have had good evidence that they could stop me, if I made it necessary. But I don't really mind it.

I'm too much of a Marsh to want to leave.

Introduction

The boundaries of horror—they are not only defined by what Man can do to Man, but also, and more horribly, by what people are willing to accept . . . when it suits them.

Janet Fox has appeared in Shadows *before, as well as in most of the major anthologies and magazines in the field. Poetry in all that she does is her hallmark, and few are able to equal it when that poetry is as dark as . . .*

THE SKINS YOU LOVE TO TOUCH

by Janet Fox

Ginger drove along the winding road, letting her thoughts drift. Beside her in the seat Madge, her mother-in-law, kept up a steady monologue that had to do, Ginger knew, with *her* views on almost any subject you could name. Ginger thought Madge's views all inutterably stupid, but since she never said so, she and her mother-in-law got on famously. So much so that Winston had sent them out together on this Sunday afternoon on an impromptu antique hunt.

Signs fairly bristled amid the lush foliage of the hillsides; it seemed that every other farmer had stopped cultivating the land to harvest the money of silly, antique-crazy rich women from town. "Only," she thought, reconsidering that idea, "*I*'m one of those women, too."

She'd always known Winston had money; it was just difficult to connect that with herself, even though she'd been married to him for almost a year.

"Look, look, stop here!" Madge's plump white hand, glittering with several rings, indicated a weathered sign almost hidden in the trees. Sharkey's, it said in letters rudely burned into the silvered board. Ginger braked the station wagon just in time to make the turn into the almost overgrown drive.

"Are you sure this is an antique shop?"

"In this area it couldn't be a massage parlor," said Madge with an earthy laugh. "Or could it?"

Light was cut off by overhanging branches, and the wagon bounced jerkily through iron ruts. There was something diseased-looking about the trees, Ginger thought; probably lack of sunlight. Fat ropy vines twined about trunks that showed patches of phosphorescent white beneath peeling bark. Madge was oblivious to the atmosphere, taking out her compact mirror to study her perfectly made up fiftyish face, the lacquered sweep of auburn-dyed hair.

The buildings were widely scattered in the forest growth—a house that seemed scarcely more than a shack, dilapidated outbuildings leaning to one side or with boards missing. A newer, larger structure of corrugated metal seemed to be the shop, if shop it was.

Madge didn't hesitate but pushed open the door.

Inside was an old-fashioned glass display case in which reposed several crude wood carvings, human and animal figures.

"Not much in here," said Ginger, poised nervously near the door. The place unnerved her with its echoing emptiness, cobwebs wagging from walls and ceiling in an unfelt breeze. A harsh chemical smell hung heavy on the air.

There was a clump, scuff, clump from a room beyond this one, and a man emerged from it, walking with a limp. One leg was obviously shorter than the other, making him list to one side, and he held his head at an awkward angle to compensate.

The grin that opened in his almost chinless face showed the jagged snags that were all that was left of his teeth and made Ginger think the name Sharkey was accurate, however he'd come by it. She noticed that his hands, toying with a chisel, were, unlike the rest of him, very clean.

"We were just looking at your, er, wares," said Madge. She had touched the dusty countertop and now wiped her fingertips with a tissue.

"Oh, that there's more like a hobby," he said and went to one side of the room. Dust covers obscured what were obviously chairs by their shapes. Sharkey pulled off one of the covers to display a chair covered in darkish beige leather. The legs and fronts of the armrests were intricately carved. Ginger had to move closer to see that they were fashioned in the shapes of human faces and hands.

"Ah, the craftsmanship," said Madge.

Ginger didn't like the designs; they were almost too lifelike, and the expressions weren't pleasant. As usual, she said nothing. Madge ran her hand along the top of one armrest and made a small sound of amazement under her breath. "This really is extraordinary work," she said.

"All done here, every bit," said Sharkey. "M'dad taught me to tan the hides and I sorta larned the whittlin' on m'own."

"Feel," said Madge, drawing Ginger's hand toward the fine-grained leather. Tentatively, she touched it, then let her fingers run along its length. It had really a strange texture, she thought, velvety smooth and it seemed almost to hold . . . warmth.

"Well, sit down in it. I can see you're intrigued," said Madge. "Can you picture it in your living room, across from the sofa? Divine!"

Ginger eased into the chair. There was no squeak of stiff new leather; smooth warmth slid along the backs of her thighs. The springs gave beneath her and she felt suddenly cradled, although there was something vaguely repellent about the feeling, too.

"I can tell it's so comfortable it's almost obscene," said Madge.

That was the word. Ginger struggled to rise and it was as if the chair clung to her caressingly a moment before releasing her.

"How much?" asked Madge.

"Two thousand," said Sharkey quickly, as if ready for the question as well as for the reaction to his response.

"What, for a chair? That's outrageous!"

"Yes, definitely too much," said Ginger, finding a voice as she rubbed briskly at the places on her arms that the chair had touched. "Let's go."

"But we've only just started to bargain," said Madge.

"Sharkey, telephone."

The slatternly woman had appeared in the doorway so quickly she gave an impression of being insubstantial—faded gray housedress, wispy mouse-colored hair.

"If you'll wait right hyer, ladies, we can talk about it some more," he said and went out with the woman, who must be his wife, Ginger thought with a shudder.

"I don't like this place," said Ginger. "Or Sharkey, for that matter."

"He's a little rough. But what a craftsman. I think you can talk him down on his price. I think he was afraid we were going to leave. With these people, bargaining is expected."

Ginger looked down and saw with embarrassment that her hands had found the back of the chair and were making subtle caressing movements. Quickly she pulled her hands away, buried them in the pockets of her jacket.

Sharkey had now been gone some time, and Madge paced the length of the room, pausing to peer through the back doorway. Then she went through the open door, into the back room.

"Madge—Mom," she corrected, though she had never said that second word with ease where Madge was concerned. She didn't have to imagine Madge as Winston's mother, though; they had the same steely stares, the same jutting chins. "That man will be back any minute."

There was silence from the back room, and when Ginger could stand the suspense no more, she rushed through the door, almost colliding with her mother-in-law. The room was dim, crowded with cluttered workbenches and low vats in which some vile-smelling liquid sat, topped with clots of greenish scum. Arcane tools lay scattered about, and the tiles of the floor were discolored with dark rustlike stains. Madge was standing as if paralyzed, and then Ginger saw she stared at a workbench on which lay a sheet-draped form.

A recognizably human form. Here and there on the sheet's surface were blotches of red. Madge's mouth was working without bringing forth anything very coherent. The color had washed from her face; the dots of rouge on her cheeks made her look like an aging rag doll.

"Shouldn't we just . . . look," said Ginger, touching the edges of the sheet. "Maybe it's not—"

"No." Madge half-screamed the word. "Can't you see he's taken the skin?" She made a half-stifled retching noise as Ginger dropped the sheet, visions of striated muscle tissue red with blood slipping past her mind's eye.

They both heard the opening of the door, the step, shuffle, step coming nearer; too late to pretend they'd seen nothing.

"Ahhh." Sharkey looked embarrassed, as if he'd been caught with his hand in a cookie jar, instead of this monstrousness. "I wish you ladies hadn't come in here. Now you know my little secret."

Ginger hung back, waiting for Madge to burst out with a tirade, but there was silence.

"There's really nuthin' like it, you know," said Sharkey. "Works up so easy, kinda with a life of its own. M'daddy gave me his secret formuler. Wears like iron, too."

"But these are people . . ." began Ginger.

"Only in a manner of speakin'. They swarm in the city like lice—junkies, bums, runaways. My cousin, Mort, he's smart about things like that. It ain't never anybody'd be missed. Nobody cares about 'em, y'know."

Madge began to nod dully. Color was working its way back into her face behind the masklike makeup. As they talked, Sharkey had somehow maneuvered them out of the dim workroom. Once out of the place, Ginger felt that it almost didn't exist. They stood in the cavernous showroom where the chair sat in a wedge of sunlight cast through a curtainless window—a piece of furniture, that was all, inert and harmless. Somehow she kept thinking of its smoothness. She felt almost an ache to run her fingers over its surface.

"I know the kind of people you mean," said Madge almost meekly.

"It makes the chairs, well, different like, I dunno . . ." said Sharkey.

"Unique," said Ginger, surprised at the firm tone of her own voice.

"Yeah," he agreed, "kinda gives the chair a soul, or that's the way I see it."

"Why, that's very poetic," said Madge, and then she fell silent as Ginger snapped open her purse and withdrew her checkbook.

Sharkey rewrapped the chair in the dust cover and with difficulty carried it out of the shop and loaded it into the back of the station wagon. "Mine," thought Ginger. She couldn't remember feeling this much at ease with herself or who she must become. She owned something that no one else could have at any price.

"You really should try and be a little more careful," she said to Sharkey as she sat in the station wagon, ready to drive away. Now very poised and in control, she could afford to be kind. "You should never leave customers alone like that."

A small gleam ignited in Sharkey's deep-set eyes. "Oh, I always let 'em catch me, ma'am."

"You *let* them catch you?"

"Sure, it always gets me my askin' price." He cleared his throat and turned his head to spit. "Ever' single time."

Introduction

A relationship between two people contains the best and the worst of what those people have to offer; and when things don't work out, when the going gets rough, the best and the worst aren't always easily distinguishable.

Craig Shaw Gardner, a Massachusetts resident, seldom disappoints when his talents work on the dark side of life; and when his talents take a skewed look at things, the giggles are guaranteed, as in A Malady of Magicks, *his first novel.*

WALK HOME ALONE

by Craig Shaw Gardner

There are things in our cities that we never see.

The headlights swept across the wall at the back of the alley. Trash can shadows danced along the brick.

"What was that?" Joan's fingers dug into my shoulder.

"Where?" I pulled the car into her parking space and turned to look at my wife.

"I thought I saw something moving back by the garbage cans." She stared past me, her eyes searching the alley wall we had swung past a moment before. I craned my head around. Maybe I could spot what had upset her so much.

Something too large to be a rat ran between the cans.

"There!" I whispered. My finger thumped against the glass as I pointed to the retreating animal.

"Oh." Joan frowned, as if she were unhappy that I had found it for her. "Was it a cat?"

I shook my head. "Did you see that striped tail? That's a raccoon."

"Raccoons?" Joan turned away from me to unsnap her seat belt. "In the city?"

I opened my door and climbed out of the car. "Well," I replied. "They have to live someplace."

Joan had managed to get out of the car before me. I got a great view of her back as she moved down the passageway that led to the front door of her new place. I started thinking again. When she was frightened a moment ago, she had actually touched me. More than that, she had reached for me. Sometimes, I guess, old habits die hard.

She paused on the front steps, waiting for me to catch up. I handed her the keys.

"Thanks a lot for the car, Frank. I don't think I could manage without it." Her voice was high and fast and cheerful, as if she were auditioning for some Saturday-morning cartoon show. She rested her hand on my shoulder. Her lips brushed my forehead, like a mother forgiving a naughty child. "Are you sure you don't want a lift?"

"Nah." I scuffed my feet in best naughty child fashion. "Like I said. It's a nice night, and it's all of six blocks. I'm old enough to walk home alone."

She showed me a genuine smile, gone the instant it covered her face. It still made me ache inside. Then the key clicked in the door lock, and she had disappeared, safe and sound, away from me. No suggestion of a nightcap, or a "Frank, let's talk things over." Well, maybe I didn't expect those things anymore. At least, not much.

I looked at my feet and told them to move. Another typical evening in the life of Joan and Frank: a dinner that had gone even more badly than the last time we had met, followed by one more of Joan's quick retreats. What else was left? Time to go home to an apartment that was one size too large.

But why did I care? I needed this walk to clear my head. I looked at the sky and took a deep breath. It was the kind of summer night they sing about, when the day's heat had cooled down to gentle breezes. There was no moon, but the sky was clear enough to see a dozen stars through the streetlight glare. Enough of dying relationships and disastrous dinners. I was better off without her.

Why was it so hard to let go? I concentrated on walking, counting the cracks I stepped on with my running shoes. It was time to do something else with my life.

There was a noise like muted thunder overhead. I looked up, startled by the sound. It wasn't thunder. It was more like a drumbeat, echoing off the surrounding buildings, something beating time, like the flapping of a great bird's wings. I realized then how still the night was. Everything else was so quiet; that's what made a single noise sound like thunder. Still, it must have been a large bird, its beating wings magnified by some trick of the night air. A hawk or some other predator, perhaps, lost in the city.

I smiled, pleased to have been startled from my reverie. Awfully good of nature to show me there was more to life than a sour relationship. More than ever, I realized it was time for a change.

I heard a call, far away in the night sky, a high, fierce cry, as loud as the beating wings. I shivered, which startled me more than the noise. I looked down the deserted street. Newspaper pages ruffled in a trash can. A traffic light in the distance went from red to green. There were no other pedestrians, not even a car for the last minute or two. I should probably walk more quickly. On a night as warm and quiet as this, there were probably more things than birds that I should worry about.

A couple emerged, arm in arm, from a corner bar just ahead of me. They walked my way, talking and laughing, and took away my monopoly on the night. I walked more quickly, passing them, eager to be away from all reminders of relationships. I kept up my new pace and was home in no time.

I had a couple of drinks and turned on the TV to keep me company. Eventually it was late enough that I could go to bed.

Sometimes the alcohol helps me sleep. That night, it didn't. Oh, I slept some. But I also dreamed.

I stood in front of Joan and I talked. I talked, but she wouldn't answer, no matter what I said. I screamed at her, but got no reaction. She simply stared at me, without any expression. "You will talk to me!" I shouted. Still she was silent, but her eyes reproached me. I grabbed her shoulders, but she would not move. I tried to pry her lips apart, but found that her face was made of stone.

I awoke with a start. Something had banged against the bedroom window. I shook my head, still not fully out of the dream. There was something scratching against the windowpane. A squirrel must have gotten itself caught on the ledge or something. I looked at the clock. It was a little after four, maybe an hour before dawn. The sound had stopped. I decided to get up and take a look.

When had we stopped talking? That was what my dream was all about, what so many of my dreams were about. When did our relationship fall apart? It was so hard to say. Nothing had ended between us, exactly. Instead, it had just sort of slipped away.

I tugged on the shade more forcefully than I meant to. It rolled up with a snap. The noise made me close my eyes for a second.

When I opened them, there was nothing on the ledge. The sky, so clear a few hours earlier, was now entirely covered by clouds. For a second, I thought I saw a dark shape flying before the clouds, but it was hard to tell, like looking at black on black. Maybe that was my late-night caller. It had to be a bird, close by the window. Unless it was something larger, much farther away.

I shook my head, marveling at my late-night fantasies, and went back to bed. To my surprise, I managed to fall back to sleep.

I woke late in the morning to rain. The clouds I had seen the night before had opened with a passion, and the water came down with force, a machine gun rat-tat-tat on the street below.

I listened to the rain and smiled. I discovered that I was genuinely hungry, and wandered into the kitchen to see what might still be edible. I found some bread that wasn't too stale, and some cheese that didn't have any mold on it yet, and set about making myself a grilled cheese sandwich and a pot of coffee. The smells mingled on the stove, making me hungrier still. I felt like I hadn't eaten in a week.

The phone rang just as I took my first bite.

"Hi there!" a bright voice said. I swallowed my food. It was Joan. She talked about how her morning had gone, how well she had accomplished her errands, how heavy the rain was falling. She asked me if she should bring the car by early that evening, before she went out. I told her to just park it on the street and leave the key in my mailbox. That was fine with her. She had to run. Goodbye.

I looked down at the remains of my sandwich, cold and yellow on the plate. I wasn't hungry anymore. I scraped the remains into the garbage.

I decided I couldn't stay inside, rain or no rain. It was Saturday. I'd go see an early show of a movie, before date night got into full swing.

It had stopped raining when I got out of the film, a nonstop action thing starring some over-the-hill kung-fu champion. The sky was clearing. It looked like it was going to be another nice night. I took a deep breath of the rain-washed air. The film had done me some good. I marveled at what a relief mindless violence can be.

Joan had found a parking space right in front of the building. The car keys were waiting for me in the mailbox. She hadn't left a note.

I stuck the keys in my pocket. I'd picked up a pizza and a six-pack on the way home, intent on having a good time. Maybe there was something good on television.

I threw the *TV Guide* across the room. If I had seen a single episode of some show, that was the one repeated tonight. I hadn't used to watch that much television. How could I have already seen everything worth watching?

The pizza sat at the bottom of my stomach. The pepperoni seemed to have transmogrified to lead. It had gotten dark outside, and the open window admitted a breeze. I usually ran the air conditioner in my bedroom, but tonight I decided to open all the other windows and let in some real air.

I moved to the second window in my bedroom and pulled up the shade. My hands reached for the bottom window, and stopped. The screen on the far side of the glass was torn, ripped diagonally from edge to edge.

When had that happened? Lately I had liked to keep my bedroom dark, hadn't even thought of opening up the place. The screen could have been like that for weeks and I wouldn't have known. I tried to remember—this was the window I had looked out of last night at 4 A.M. But it had been so dark, and my eyes had quickly glanced up at something flying away.

I thought of the noise out there, the scratching sounds, and the thump against the glass. Could something have torn the screen last night? What would have wanted to get in so badly?

I left the bedroom window closed. I'd have to find a hardware store on Monday and get a replacement screen. Of course, I could always wait for the landlord to do it. But I wanted the screen before I started to collect social security.

I looked out again at the beautiful night. The walk I had taken last evening had done a lot to clear my head. Maybe I was being told to get out of this place again. After all, if the fates controlled anything, it would surely be television reruns.

So I took a walk. A lot of other people seemed to have had the same idea, and the streets were crowded with strollers. There is a hill behind my apartment. It is quite a steep climb, but once you get to the top it gives you a spectacular view of the city. I decided it was just the sort of thing I needed.

Something rustled in the hedges as I passed. The breeze brought the faint odor of a skunk, thankfully still at some distance. The scent of summer roses soon drove both skunk and city smells away. It seemed nature was out in full force tonight.

As I strode up the hill, apartment buildings gave way to multifamily houses, then single-family houses, and finally a small park at the summit. There were a couple of lovers busy on one of the benches, but, besides them, I had the place to myself.

I spent a good two minutes looking at the city before I thought of Joan. Last summer we used to come up here, hand in hand—I stopped myself before I went any further. There had to be places for me, by myself, without memories of Joan coming in to muck everything up. Joan wasn't coming back. I had to live for myself. I could sit in the park and breathe and think and talk and laugh and who knows what else, just for Frank and nobody else.

I closed my eyes against the lights of the city. That cold feeling was back at the bottom of my stomach. I realized what I had just told myself.

Joan wasn't coming back.

I had known that, but it was the first time I had ever really admitted it to myself in so many words. Furthermore, when I thought about our last year together, I didn't want Joan back. At least a big part of me didn't. Not the way we had ended things.

Something crashed in the trees above my head. I looked up and yelled. I jumped off the park bench and fell on all fours, rolling in the grass. I lay there for a moment. Nothing fell on me from above. Nothing attacked. I felt nothing but the night breeze.

"Hey, man." The male half of the couple on the other bench had temporarily disengaged himself. "You all right? What's the matter?"

I shook my head. I wasn't even quite sure what I had seen. It had looked pretty big, and I had thought I saw a pair of wings.

"Sounds like a bat to me, man," the other man replied to my confused explanation. "They get them up here, you know."

"Joey?" the other half of the couple called from the park bench. "You didn't tell me there were bats up here!"

Joey turned back to his partner. "Well, there aren't many bats—"

The young woman shivered. "Joey, let's go back to my place!"

Joey threw his hands up to the sky. "But your mother—" he began. He threw me a look of one who knew he'd lost an argument before it had begun, a state of things I was all too familiar with. He walked back to his girlfriend, and they left me on the hill.

I stood there for a moment, alone again.

So I had been startled by a bat. Until I reacted that way, I didn't realize I was so jumpy. I decided I might have had enough of my back-to-nature feeling. Right about now, nature was getting too close for comfort.

It was a bat. Somehow, that didn't seem right. Bats weren't the size of the thing I had seen. What else could it have been. A cat? A bird? All I could think about was a pair of great wings. I half wanted to make a joke about Count Dracula.

The trees rustled in the wind. At least there was a little bit of a breeze, enough to move some leaves. I looked up to where I thought I'd seen something. I decided I wanted to get out of there.

On my way downhill, I kept looking at the sky. I kept expecting something to jump out at me from nowhere. It was stupid, really. I couldn't even say what it was I had seen. For all I knew, I could have seen nothing more than moving leaves. The way I had been reacting to things the last few weeks, I wouldn't trust anything at first glance.

I felt better when I got back inside. But even as I sank down on my couch in relief, worry came right behind. I couldn't help but feel that whole thing in the park was nothing more than another overreaction, another way for my mind to deal with the loss of Joan. Depression wasn't enough. My psyche wanted to throw fear in for good measure. Well, I'd win out over these feelings, too. I didn't want my separation turning me into a recluse.

I fell asleep that night with the television on.

I dreamed I was back in the park, or maybe I was in a forest somewhere. I was surrounded by trees. And although I couldn't see them, I knew the trees were full of living things.

Someone was walking toward me, out of the distance. It was a woman. Sometimes she looked like Joan, but she was too far away to tell. I wanted to call to her, but I was afraid. There were too many things watching me, waiting for me to act. There was no noise here but the footsteps of the approaching woman. I could not break the silence.

There were more footsteps. The woman was not alone. Someone spoke to her in a deep voice. The woman laughed Joan's laugh.

"No!" The scream came from deep inside, from my feet and hands and chest and groin; all of me cried out to the night. And my cry made the forest come alive.

Things took to the air from the trees overhead, great shapes swirling about the branches high overhead. I threw my arms over my head to fend off attack, but the things kept their distance. There was too little light to see them clearly. All I could see was their great dark wings etched against the stars. The night was full now of their beating wings and their strange, piercing cries. I felt, somehow, that they were calling to me.

I ran blindly out from under the trees, into a clearing.

A hundred feet from me, one of the things landed. It was the size of a man. It folded its great wings behind it, and walked toward me on powerful legs.

I wanted to run away, but found I couldn't. Instead, I was walking toward the thing, my arms opened wide as if I might embrace it. I had to turn away, to look somewhere else, but I had stared into the creature's eyes. It was impossible to look away. I began to run. The thing smiled as I rushed to meet it, showing its long and pointed teeth.

I awoke with a start. Something was at the window.

It had woken me from the dream. I distinctly heard the bang of something against the glass. I pulled the sweat-drenched sheet away from me and jumped from bed. This time I would not miss what waited for me. I thought I heard the screen tear again, and a sound like claws scrabbling on stone.

I ripped the shade away and pressed my face against the glass.

The thing screamed at me with a mouth that covered the lower half of its face. I pushed back from the window, rushing even faster away from something that in my panic I had wanted to meet. I got one final glimpse of the thing as it, too, pushed away, its wings like gray leather, lifting it into the sky.

I realized, when it was gone, that I was screaming too.

I stood in the middle of the room, trying to control my breathing, to keep myself from screaming any more. I stared at the shade, torn in my mad rush to confront whatever it was that wanted me.

I began to shake. I managed to quiet my legs and sit back on the bed. Then I began to cry.

After a while, I stopped. I was all alone. There was no one here to comfort me. I didn't want to call Joan. I became oddly calm. What had it been? For all my fear, it had not harmed me in any way. In fact, it had fled from me as I had backed away from it. I shut my eyes, but I was too tired to sleep.

I sat on the bed the rest of the night, and waited. But it did not return.

I found myself oddly disappointed to see light creeping into the sky. I knew I wouldn't see my visitor again after dawn. I slept at last.

It was Sunday, and I knew nothing would be open before noon. I rose around eleven, took a shower, and went downtown to the library.

I found a parking space just up the street. The day was relentlessly sunny. There were no dark shapes flying overhead now, just pigeons and the occasional sea gull. I even saw a cardinal perched on a time-temperature clock. I felt for a moment that I might be forced to cheer up.

The doors to the library had been propped open to admit the summer air. I walked over to the information desk and had them direct me to the reference room. I hung my jacket over a chair and went in search of a picture or two. I quickly pulled a half-dozen books to take back to my desk.

I turned and found that an attractive young woman blocked my way back. She scratched at one blond temple and looked quizzically at the stack of books in my arms.

"A little light reading?" she asked.

I smiled back at her. I was feeling a little giddy, probably some sort of reaction to last night's crying jag. "Encyclopedias are my passion!" I hefted the volumes with a grunt. "And much cheaper than health clubs."

The young woman arched an eyebrow at my display. "Not to mention much more intelligent. I'd rather have a conversation with an encyclopedia any day."

"Indeed. If you will excuse me." I decided I needed to deposit my load of books before I developed a hernia. They crashed on a table with rather more noise than I would have liked. I looked up and shrugged at the young woman. She smiled and walked over to a desk on the far side of the room.

I'm afraid I exclaimed out loud when I saw the photograph. It was just what I wanted. The thing I had seen in the window had been a gargoyle. The teeth were there, and the deep-set eyes, and the wings spread to either side.

It had horns, too, which I didn't remember. Then again, it might not have been my gargoyle.

The text, however, wasn't as helpful. *Gargoyle* came from the Latin for "gutter," they were used as ornamental drain spouts on Gothic churches, there was no such thing as a real gargoyle.

But I had seen one.

I found a short passage in a dictionary of folklore. Two lines that said that, for someone, gargoyles did exist:

"The exact function remains in doubt. It is said to typify evil forced to serve God, to act as a talisman to terrify the devil."

But what did that mean? I swore softly to myself.

"Young man." A woman's voice said over my shoulder. "If you can't keep quiet, I'm afraid you'll be in trouble."

"Oh," I replied. I looked up again at the attractive young woman. "Are you the librarian?"

"Thank heavens, no." She smiled. "What are you looking at?"

"I'm afraid I get too enthusiastic about things sometimes." I showed her the picture of the stone gargoyle.

"They're architectural, aren't they? Water spouts and such?"

I nodded my head. Supposedly, that's what they were.

She nodded back at me and smiled. "I always liked those myself. They seem to show a very fierce imagination. You know, Gothic architecture had a resurgence about a hundred years ago. There's half a dozen buildings with beautiful examples right downtown."

Really? Somehow, that seemed significant. As farfetched as this whole thing was, I very much wanted to see these things. I asked her to give me directions.

"Good luck," she said as I stuffed the directions into my pocket and turned to leave. "If you need any more help, I'm here most every Sunday."

"I need all the help I can get," I said in my best Groucho Marx leer. As bad a joke as it was, she still smiled. I added, "The library isn't such a bad place to come on Sundays."

"The most fun you can have for free," she added. "At least in public."

I smiled back at her and headed for the door. I never realized books could be so enlightening.

It was starting to get hot outside. I tied my coat around my waist and set out to see the gargoyles. I wanted to look at what had scared me so.

I pulled out the directions the young woman had given me. She had drawn me a map. I noticed that on the bottom of it she had written her name, and a phone number.

I turned onto the broad avenue and looked for the first gargoyle. It wasn't quite what I had expected, little more than a leering stone face halfway up an ancient church facade. I began to feel foolish. What was I doing this for? Who was I to see gargoyles?

The second ones were small, but more what I was looking for—a pair of green demons snarling above a brick town house. Gargoyles, I realized, were always posed in the midst of action, as if, perhaps, they were about to attack. And the looks on their faces told you that whatever they attacked, they would fully enjoy ripping it to shreds.

I had seen the third one on the map before. It was perched over a little outdoor neighborhood café. It stared at me knowingly. Our eyes had met before. It was fully the size of a man, its large mouth open as if in greeting.

Small points of ice danced within my chest. What did it want from me? I wanted to call out to it, but I was in the middle of the city, in broad daylight. I would feel foolish screaming at a stone.

Why did it stare at me? Why had it brought me here?

I heard Joan's laugh.

My eyes shifted from the creature to the tables below. It hadn't been my imagination. It was Joan, holding the hand of someone I knew, a good friend of the family, first-name basis, over to dinner a dozen times. What did it mean? Should it mean anything?

The two of them kissed.

I found myself shaking as much as when I had seen the face in the window. I turned away, forcing myself not to call out. Not in the city. Not in broad daylight.

Somehow, I got myself home. Everything that had happened between Joan and myself seemed to be thrown in my face. All the feelings, all the grief, all the misunderstandings played themselves over and over again in my mind as if they were trapped there, spinning forever.

I fell asleep again in late afternoon.

The gargoyle came for me in dreams. He stepped past Joan, who sat and talked to a dozen faceless men. I could see him clearly now, his demon grin wide and deep. His mouth opened, then opened more, until it was large enough to fit a man.

I was awake. A weight slammed against the window with such force that I was sure that it would break. I had slept until dark. I found I was shaking again, my head still full of Joan. The banging redoubled against the glass.

I couldn't do this anymore. If it wanted me, I would come to it. I jumped from bed in a rush, flinging myself at the window.

"Here!" I screamed. I swung my arm above my head and down through the glass to meet my devourer.

The pain brought me to my senses. Fine lines of blood trickled down my arm. I looked at my hand through what was left of the window. There was nothing else out there now but the warm summer wind.

The window had shattered when I pushed my fist through it. My knuckles were covered with hairline cuts. I glanced idly at them in the weak moonlight, looking at the red paths in my skin as one might look at the map of a foreign country. I knew all of them would heal.

I stared out into the darkness. I might have seen wings in the distance, flying against the new moon. Far away, I heard a high cry of longing, but then that, too, was lost in the silence of the night.

Introduction

When one is a child, a house is peopled by gods who know all and cure all; when one begins to attain experience, and that experience translates into wisdom, the gods don't die, they just become something different.
T. L. Parkinson, who lives and works in San Francisco, is no ordinary writer. He's demanding, and rightly so, because too often these days spoon-fed is equaled to the best. On the other hand, he seldom pulls his punches.

THE FATHER FIGURE

by T. L. Parkinson

I can't remember the exact moment I realized my father wasn't human.

Two men in dark uniforms stood in the doorway. They asked to see him. I called for him down the cavernous hallway. He entered in a blast of light thrown by the opening kitchen door. The men drew him like magnets. He ran, hastily pulling on his coat. He tousled my hair as he whirled past. Hopelessly I straightened my hair, as the nearest officer reached for me. I ducked.

They climbed into a blue car with a flashing red light that made the elm tree in the front yard look like Christmas. As they pulled away, I waved madly into the air. The tree lost its holiday feeling. I went back inside to finish breakfast.

That night the house was achingly empty. Father had not returned. Mother wept in her bed. I wept also, feeling her pain sweeping through the thin walls.

I waited at the window. Wind whipped the trees into frantic motion; then it was still. My tears flowed, and I could not see; then I was dry as bone.

I got into bed. The quilt was unbearably heavy. I threw it on the floor. Lying in my imprint, I tried to imagine how much space I would occupy when the tree that now threatened the window was a few seasons older. I would be as big as Father; bigger, if my imagination came true.

I fell into a cold sleep. I woke in a sweat, a dark figure in a dripping coat standing at the foot of my bed.

Bathed in the ghostly blue light of the TV screen, he played solitaire. He and Mother had not spoken since his hurried departure two nights before. I was giving him the silent treatment too.

I gathered it was all over some dangerous assignment that he had under-taken. I watched him through the crack in the door, which even then I was widening with the penknife he had given to me on my last birthday. He looked untouchable, solid as stone. I wondered what could possibly harm him, and what Mother was in such a state about.

He turned infrequently in his chair; a quick sharp movement, then a card thrown down. The TV droned; the room flickered silver and black, daytime furniture now ominous and cold.

I fell asleep against the door. In my dreams, there were footsteps, then a knock at the door. He came in without waiting for an answer. Strong arms picked me up, as though I were nothing, and carried me to bed. Under covers, still dreaming, I felt the heat of breath on my neck.

I turned to him, but his features were swimming dark lines; I tried to piece them together, but they did not fit.

"It's warm inside," he said. "I am so cold."

When I woke, my head still pressed against the door, Father stood up, pulling off his shirt to reveal a conditioned torso. He ran his hands down the gray-blue chest, tenderly, and reached to turn off the TV.

He hesitated. I recognized the movie. It was a favorite of ours, *Invasion of the Body Snatchers.*

His hand hesitated above the switch. Something was wrong. The harder I looked, the less human his hand seemed: too solid to be flesh, greenish in color, with faint moss sprouting from the fingers.

I fell onto my back and rocked.

Real footsteps approached. I scrambled into bed and pretended to sleep.

His good-night kiss left a saliva trail on my cheek. I rubbed it furiously as the door closed.

I closed my eyes so tightly I saw stars. Then I passed out.

I was sick the next day. I had a fever, or so I told Mother. She took my temperature; it was normal. Well, maybe an invisible fever. Something real, and awful, is making me ache. Wait; you'll see.

By mid-afternoon, I had worked myself into a temperature of 99.2. Mother said she was impressed. My son, your imagination has gotten the better of me once again.

Father came home early. I heard him put the gun in the drawer and lock it. Then he locked the bedroom door.

They made strange muffled noises. The toilet flushed. A window opened. I opened my window and saw the cigarette smoke he blew into the yard.

I closed the window, turned up the volume on the TV. I sat in my straightbacked thinking chair, but could not get comfortable. This body was awkward: too many limbs, and too big. I was from another planet.

The detective was Barnaby Jones. Despite his wrinkled, doglike face, he betrayed no emotion. I watched him intently, waiting for him to make a mistake and show his true colors.

Father knocked on my door, then peered in. Eagle profile, gray eyes that women found alluring, pouty lower lip, sneering upper lip that indicates character. The day-old beard framing his face like carefully applied makeup. How you doing, old chum, etc. I nodded sagely, giggled.

I hoped he would not pummel me. He checked the program I was watching, smiled, and withdrew.

I got up, slipping on the polished floor. My diary and I feel headlong onto the rug, which smelled like cat.

I knew boys weren't supposed to keep diaries. Father didn't know about this one. I began to write.

"Something is wrong in this house, but I can't put my finger on it. Mother cries too much. I dream all the time. And Father is—" I fell asleep before I could finish.

The farm was roughly twenty acres. In the morning, before the school bus came to wind me away from my uneasy security, I would stand on the front porch as the sun set the purple fields on fire; the cows, the horses, the birds stirred.

Sanctified, I felt better able to face the coming day.

Father sometimes joined me and together we stared into the spacious, bright land.

One weekend, Father took me riding in the distant hills, government-owned land that was seldom visited.

He showed me a trench where a body had been found. This desolate place was a favorite dumping ground for various types of garbage, some human, some otherwise. There were chalk lines in the shallow grave, where the woman had been thrown like a bag of dirty laundry.

Father coolly described the scene, the uncovering of the grave, the stench of the decomposing body, the worms that crawled out through her nose, the drawing of the lines.

I listened until the bile ran up my throat. Then I spurred my horse into a gallop, Father's voice, still narrating, fading into the distance.

He did not follow immediately; a bad sign. When he caught up, he pulled in front of me, like the Lone Ranger stopping a criminal. He sat between me and the sun; the aureole blackened him, stripped away his features.

I pulled to his side, although frightened. He looked—unfinished, alien, his face still fixed in the same blank expression he had had when looming over the grave.

He led the way, silently, into the hills. His silence was killing me. The sun beat on our necks, on the snakes stretched across rocks. In the low brush, in the distant trees, insects chattered.

We stayed out all afternoon. Occasionally I glimpsed our house, green in the distance, and Mother's ghostly form on the porch.

My neck was sunburned when he finally brought us home: my punishment for lack of attention.

I opened the front door. His larger hand, like the shadow of my own, grasped the door, pulling it closed.

The ceiling fan hissed like burning cicadas; but here inside it was dim and somber, and I felt suddenly sleepy.

I barely made it to bed.

In my diary I recorded a dream.

We vacationed in Hawaii. Hawaii was a disappointment—crowds of pink-and-white-striped tourists, hostile natives, and the azure water seemed painted.

The lagoons where I wanted to snorkel were filled with more tourists, whose heads bobbed like apples. An old woman was bitten by an eel. I giggled; a Samoan policeman looked like he was going to arrest me.

Father rescued me, showing the officer his badge.

In a green and black jeep, we drove directly to the airport. Father did not say where we were going. When I closed my eyes, I could see the vision of the airfield, as though Father and I shared the same brain.

We boarded a small jet, which Father flew. I had never imagined Father could fly; I stifled my protests.

During the long flight, I occupied myself by reading a science fiction novel in which a young man discovers that he is the last real human being in a world of tumor people, cloned from cancerous tissue.

We arrived in the Philippines. Father piloted the plane onto an immense sickle of white beach. The ocean was blindingly blue, as clear as glass.

I stepped onto the warm sand. The ocean sounded like the ceiling fan in our living room. I knew we were somewhere very familiar. I looked at Father. He had a pained expression on his face. He stared inland, where a dense jungle formed a barrier to sight.

We made a double set of footprints that paralleled the curve of the water-line. A large black dog walked beside me, nuzzling my hand.

We walked down the beach for hours. The sand pulled at my feet. We were getting nowhere. Father's face reddened, like heated metal; his hands clenched.

He grabbed my arm. The dog growled lowly, but I restrained him.

We turned into the jungle, taking a path that Father seemed familiar with.

Ahead, there was a gate of flowers, and a dark tunnel beyond. I felt as if I were entering a familiar garden, or falling quietly to sleep.

The jungle shielded us from the bright sky, for this path wound under a roof of leaves. Animals jumped from branch to branch, but moved so quickly I could not see them.

A snake fell in front of us, like a dead hand dangling from a hidden corpse.

Father brushed it aside, as easily as he would a spider's web. I winced. The snake obediently twined itself around the tree, frightening down leaves as it ascended.

We came to a road, unpaved but well tended. The road curved constantly, so it was impossible to see more than a hundred feet or so at a time.

Father's anger had vanished. In its place was a frozen mask of pain. His skin had assumed the greenish tinge of the jungle.

The road frightened me. I thought that the jungle resented our passage through. There were few sounds, as though the animals were silently scrutinizing us.

Finally we came to a clearing. Father now sighed as he walked, like a dreaming woman.

The empty village lay in a hollow beyond the clearing, above a small muddy stream. There were barracks, whose roofs of corrugated metal were like frozen waves, and small grass huts whose roofs had caved in. Black vines with brilliant flowers twined about the ruins.

In the center of the village, which formed a circle, like a wagon train in distress, there was a stone hearth, either for cooking or for religious ceremonies.

Father sat on the lichen-covered base of the hearth. He placed his hand on a roughly shaped heart carved in the stone.

At first I thought it was the murmuring of the jungle. But it wasn't. Father had begun to cry, softly at first, then in thunderous heaves.

The dog whined. I looked at the crying man, the stranger.

The dog nuzzled my hand. I don't know why, but that gave me strength. I sat down next to Father. I was too small; his face was above me. I moved to the next step. He seemed to shrink with the loss of tears; soon, he would be gone. I grew larger.

I pulled his head to my shoulder. He did not try to pull away. He cried until we both were wet. The sun disappeared into the trees.

As the sky darkened, the jungle turned from green to black, blacker than the sky. We began to walk. I was again the small boy at Father's side, taking two steps to his one.

We took a shortcut back to the plane. The path was narrow, but my fear had disappeared.

Father stopped once, to show me a marker on a grave, on which nothing was written.

"That's where they buried me," he said.

Suddenly I knew where I was. Father had spent five lost years here during the war; had sketched native faces; had seen his friends die and rot in the dripping jungle. He had had a dog that lived with him in the trenches.

When we reached the beach, the plane was gone.

There was a fugitive in the hills. Mother tried to restrain us. Father brushed away her hand. She moved into the dimness behind the screen door.

"I'm taking him with me, to show him what you're afraid of," he said, his back to her. He might as well have said it to the sky, for the response he got. I felt mildly embarrassed, and withdrew into the yard.

It was close in the police car: hot breath, cigarette smoke, and something unstated hanging in the air. I watched the rushing, smoke-colored trees through the tinted glass.

One of the officers spoke to me. I looked at him blankly. He munched on a smelly cigar, the end of which was wet. I thought of jungle rot.

Father seemed nervous. He glanced at me occasionally with eyes steely, yet afraid. He put a hand on my knee, squeezed too hard. I said nothing.

We wound up a slight hill; coasted down the other side, pursued by our own siren, stalked by the flashing red light.

I wondered where I was going. Father had mumbled something to me, one evening when he had found me examining his gun, that if I was curious about his work, I should watch him work. I thought he had gone to a movie.

Lucky he hadn't gotten back earlier. I had just crawled out from under the porch, where I was looking for pods.

We passed near the location of the young woman's grave. Father pointed, reminding me. One of the officers, who had a thin neck and thick arms, gave Father a nasty look.

"No need to push too hard. Everything in its time."

I didn't like the sound of that. How could he know what was in store for me? We were strangers.

We spent the afternoon combing the faint hills. The sun was hard and bright. I wore a long-sleeve shirt, the green one that brings me luck. My hands got sunburned.

At home that evening, I removed my shirt to reveal white arms and hands that looked like red gloves.

Faint hair sprouted on the backs of my hands, in the spaces between the knuckles.

I put my hands under the pillow and went to sleep.

In my dreams, a grave waited. I stared up into a patch of blue sky, as a man who looked like me started to shovel in the dirt.

I wrestled with the covers. Something was there with me. I bolted upright. It had sprung from the dark window, and now stalked me under the blanket. It was a long slinky rodent, a snake, a man's arm. I leapt from bed, startling the cat.

I searched the room. No sign of the intruder in the light. I got carefully back into bed. When I finally relaxed, it came again, swelling the covers with its movement.

I leapt out again, putting on the light, feeling a little foolish. Now convinced I was awake, I saw a hollow in the covers as though something had passed through. I reached in with my arm, more afraid of not knowing than of anything I would find. The hollow ended in a wall of blanket. The creature had escaped me once again.

Sadly, I crawled back into bed, quite alone.

"We're going hunting." He had the retriever by his side, a blue rifle in his left hand.

I pulled on my coat. The dog looked nonplussed, too old for this kind of thing. He would rather sleep all day long; so would I.

We were after birds.

It rained. The brown puddles held rushing clouds. I thought of myself miserably standing in the soggy forest, watching lead-filled birds fall from the sky.

It was much the way I imagined it. Father barely said ten words to me. I shivered in my black slicker, diverting myself by watching my feet destroy images in puddles, reflections of my own face.

I hoped this time we would not see any deer. Father often took potshots at them, even though it was not the season. He had an alien coldness in his eyes, more dangerous than a bullet, as he watched the white tails disappear into the underbrush.

Near the end of the day, after seeing no deer, and killing about ten birds, Father looked at me like that.

I nervously helped him put away the gun. I figured if I touched the gun myself, I might discharge my fear of his menacing eyes.

We tore out of there as though a demon chased us, throwing a stream of mud into the air that made backward vision impossible.

Father gripped the wheel tightly. He cleared his throat. We rounded a bend, into a squall of rain.

For a moment I could not see outside; the rain furiously hammered the windows. When the rain let up, the land had changed. We were in the jungle of my dream. I remembered the grave with the blank headstone. A dead man drove the truck.

"How long have you known?" he asked.

I said nothing, but shook my head to try to clear it of the confusing images.

Vague suspicions had flickered, like ghosts that dragged themselves down the halls of thought, but vanished when I turned to face them.

"I don't know," I said. My voice sounded small and insignificant against the roar of the wheels and the pelting rain.

I glanced at him shyly, trying to bring tears to my eyes. Tears would not come. I tried blurring my vision, but his image would not blur, as though it were fixed inside me. Green skin, arms like dead tree limbs, legs like exposed roots; a plant, not a man, a replacement for my father, something hollow inside and not-quite-alive.

He reached for me.

Memories flooded me, as though the windshield had broken and the storm reached inside.

I felt the sudden urge to vomit. There was no place but my own lap, so I held it back.

He breathed in my face, his eyes glassy and cold, squirrel eyes peering out of a dark hole. I squirmed away from him, but the cab of the truck was small. In the back the dog had begun to bark. Father's breath smelled of cold earth. The dog threw himself furiously against the glass.

Father grabbed my hand, placing it on his forearm.

"Just like you," he said. I felt the blood course, the evidence of a heart. "I died on that island. Ask your mother; she knows what I was like when I came home. I was—changed. I told you this story at night, so you'd know who I am, who we both are."

The windows had steamed over, from my panting moist breath. I could not see the road, but heard the beating rain, the tires humming. I did not know what was out there—the path home or the jungle trail leading to the grave.

I pulled my hand from his arm. He reached for me. I slammed against the door, knocking it open. For one dreamlike moment, I flew through the air. Then I sank in a soft sticky mixture of mud and pine needles.

The nights we shared, the dreams, something unspoken between us. The truck skidded to a halt. The father figure tore through curtains of rain. I crawled into a ravine, found a deep hole next to a blank, rain-shiny rock: a headstone for my grave or a tablet on which to inscribe my life. I closed my eyes, pretending I was not there.

Eventually, however, he found me.

Introduction

Every town has a place like this. It's the house you were dared to go into when you were a kid, and the one that fascinates you when you're an adult. You didn't go when you were a kid because you knew better; you don't as an adult because you think you're above all that kid stuff. Which one is the wiser?

Joseph Payne Brennan. The best news I've had in years was the news of his retirement from his Yale Library job. It means, for all of us, more from the typewriter that has produced more classics in the field than any other.

AN ORDINARY BRICK HOUSE

by Joseph Payne Brennan

I'm addicted to long walks around Arborvale. Nothing much to see. A declining and largely bypassed New England coastal city, a few marginal factories, a fair-size shopping center, a "better part of town" reserved for the owner-manager element, and streets of the working poor deluding themselves that they are lower middle class.

A depressing milieu, but I never minded—I guess because I'd grown up in the place and gotten used to it. I convinced myself that the dingy streets and dilapidated houses had a sort of picturesque appeal. Sometimes I even wished I were a young artist instead of a retired hardware dealer.

One afternoon in late March I walked to the far end of Maple Street. Impelled by some obscure impulse, instead of turning back, I trudged past the last square of cracked pavement onto a rough dirt road. The adjacent ditches were littered with rusting cans, smashed bottles, and water-soaked cartons. Weeds and a few scrub apple trees straggled alongside the ditches. The last scattered structures were weatherbeaten empty shacks surrounded by burdock and plantain.

I plodded along in spite of the unpromising surroundings. After a mile or so, as I was finally about to retrace my steps, I noticed an isolated brick house off the road to the left.

As I came abreast of it, stopped, and surveyed it, I was gradually engulfed by a sense of utter desolation and hopelessness. I could not account for it. It was an ordinary-looking two-story brick house. It appeared empty, but the windows were intact, the hedge in front had been trimmed, and there were no weeds sprouting along a flagstone path leading to the front door. Certainly a solidly built, no-nonsense sort of house.

I stared at it in the swiftly descending twilight. Why should such a house induce a feeling of despair? I had no explanation. But even as I shrugged and walked away, the feeling persisted.

I assured myself later that anyone might feel depressed by the sight of an empty house, seen at twilight, in the midst of weedy, abandoned acres bisected by a neglected dirt road. But I could not convince myself that this was the case. Inevitably, of course, I returned for another look at the brick house.

It was mid-morning. The sun was up; skunk cabbages were starting up in the watery ditches; a few tentative blades of grass were showing. After I reached the brick house and stood looking at it for a few moments, however, I again experienced a sense of acute dejection and despondency. This mood lingered after I was well away from the place, back in the main streets of Arborvale.

Unfortunately, I've seldom been able to shrug things off. I usually want to delve to the root of the matter at hand.

I began walking down the seldom-used dirt road, past the forlorn fields, to the brick house, several times a week. The intensity of the emotion varied, but I never came away without feeling inexplicably depressed.

One afternoon, near dusk, I was briefly frightened. As I turned to leave, I thought I glimpsed a huge, ungainly-looking dog run behind the hedge in front of the house. It gave me a nasty start. I like dogs, but this one looked threatening and unusually ugly.

At length, one day as I again stood watching the house, I was astounded when the front door opened and a woman walked slowly toward me.

I had assumed the house was untenanted. I remained as if frozen in position—although I'm afraid my mouth may have dropped open!

The woman was middle-aged, well dressed, with a care-worn but not unfriendly face. She appeared both alert and intelligent.

Stopping only a few feet away, she looked straight at me. "I have seen you watching this house several times. May I inquire why?"

I hesitated. I was tempted to make up some excuse—that I was not really watching the house but merely resting before turning back, or that the simple architecture intrigued me. But there was that about her gaze, so open and direct, which seemed to preclude evasion.

Although I feared my reply might anger her—might even infuriate her—I blurted it out. "There is something about the house, something intangible, which unaccountably depresses me. And the cause of this interests me."

She looked startled but not angry. She stood staring at me as if she were at a loss for words. I had an impression that she surveyed me with sudden interest.

" 'Unaccountably depresses,' " she quoted. "Is it possible for you to be more specific?"

"Well, I sense—acute grief, despair."

She nodded. "I see." She glanced at her watch; almost within seconds a large black limousine pulled up nearby.

She started toward it, stopped, and turned. "The house is not uninhabited, as you may have thought." It was in no sense a warning or a reprimand. It was a simple statement of fact.

She continued on to the car and was driven away.

After one final scrutiny of the brick house, I hurried off—even though my curiosity was cresting. Perhaps, I reasoned, her last remark did imply that loitering near the house was not appreciated.

I stayed away for over a week, but curiosity gnawed at me. At length I convinced myself that no one could object if I merely strolled *past* the place.

It was a warm spring afternoon, and I walked slowly. The soft green of early buds was showing; the air seemed pregnant with promise.

As I approached the brick house, I saw that the woman I had previously encountered was waiting in front—for her ride, I presumed.

I bid her good afternoon and she replied pleasantly enough. Soon we were chatting about the marvelous weather. The limousine was late. Before it finally arrived, we had talked for nearly a half-hour. By the time she was driven away, we had introduced ourselves and I felt that we were friends.

Although we spoke largely of inconsequential matters, I learned that her name was Mrs. Romiss and that she was a widow. She worked as a sort of companion-housekeeper to a handicapped woman who lived in the brick house. The place looked empty because living quarters had been established in four rear rooms not visible from the front. The rest of the building was now unoccupied and nearly unfurnished.

As the weeks passed, I continued my strolls past the brick house, timing them so that I often encountered Mrs. Romiss. She did not appear to object. We became such good friends, in fact, that she finally accepted my invitation to dine out one evening.

I took her to the Emerald Room at The Palisades, Arborvale's only first-rate restaurant. After a leisurely lobster dinner, I ordered cognac and she told me the tragic story of the woman who employed her, Mrs. Ruth Kestelling.

Born Ruth Monroe, of parents in comfortable but by no means opulent circumstances, she met Kenneth Kestelling, millionaire, sports enthusiast, and big-game hunter, at a carnival ball. In less than a month she married him. She was eighteen, Kestelling forty.

About a year later she accompanied him on a hunting trip in Kenya. Three weeks into the bush, he was accidentally shot and killed by one of the gun bearers. Not surprisingly, everything went wrong afterward. Some of the native guides deserted; others went about their tasks with reluctance. The only white man left with the expedition, a Mr. Sellmer, Kestelling's friend, stayed drunk most of the time.

Equipment was neglected; meals were slapdash; routine precautions were largely ignored. One night when the demoralized party was scarcely halfway out of the bush, Mrs. Kestelling, weak and exhausted, collapsed into her bedroll without waiting for her tent to be erected.

Sometime during the night, a prowling hyena, slipping noiselessly into the sleeping camp, bit off half her face.

In spite of blood loss, infection, and shock, by some miracle she survived a nightmare trip to the coast and a chartered flight to a hospital in the States. Although her life was saved, very little could be done to restore her face. The disfigurement was too massive. Grafts were inadequate. Synthetic flesh was rejected. Eventually a mask was fitted over the remnant of face but it was so uncomfortable Mrs. Kestelling usually wore a heavy veil instead.

"How extensive was the injury?" I asked.

Mrs. Romiss poured herself another glass of cognac. "The entire right cheek was ripped off, along with nearly all the nose, the lips and part of the jaw. A grown hyena's bite has the tearing, crushing power of a steel trap."

"Was her mind affected?"

"For some months she was—highly irrational. But she recovered enough to handle Kestelling estate matters and to take care of most personal needs. Of course, she demands strict privacy. That is why she purchased a house on that rundown dirt road on the far outskirts of Arborvale. Aside from an estate attorney and a doctor—and myself—she sees no one. She is permanently depressed and she has intervals of almost suicidal despair."

I nodded. "I suppose that is what I sensed. An aura of despair seems to imbue the very air around the house!"

"There are times when I think I can stand no more of it," Mrs. Romiss commented. "But the pay is excellent and at my age it would not be easy to find another situation."

"Is the work very difficult?"

"Ordinarily, no. I prepare meals, keep the rooms in order, read aloud sometimes, gossip to keep her amused. The—wound—affected her speech and she seldom speaks. I have never heard her laugh."

"She wears a veil all the time?"

"Day and night. I have seen her without it only once and that was by accident. I hope never to see her without it again."

Less than a week after my dinner with Mrs. Romiss, I picked up the morning paper to read that Mrs. Ruth Kestelling, reclusive widow of the late Kenneth Kestelling, millionaire sportsman tragically killed in a hunting accident seventeen years before, had been found dead in her home in suburban Arborvale. A heart attack was given as the probable cause. No mention was made of her disfigurement.

Mrs. Romiss called to say goodbye about a month later. She had been left a substantial legacy by Mrs. Kestelling and had decided to settle in England, where she had relatives. I never saw her again.

I thought that was the end of the matter, but I was mistaken. Less than two weeks after Mrs. Romiss left for England, the papers reported a bizarre confession. An aged black in Kenya, a former gun bearer for Kenneth Kestelling, revealed on his deathbed that the millionaire's demise had not been accidental. The dying man swore that Mrs. Kestelling had paid him a thousand dollars to shoot her husband and make it appear that he had been accidentally killed.

I assumed that Mrs. Romiss learned of the confession, but I had no further word from her.

I left Arborvale early that summer for a driving trip, which I had looked forward to for several years. It proved so rewarding I didn't return until nearly September.

The matter of Kestelling's murder and the tragic aftermath had pretty much receded from my mind. The tabloids had played it for all it was worth and a bit more. It was no longer news.

As I resumed my walks about Arborvale, however, my recollection of the brick house returned. Curiosity finally prevailed, as it usually does.

Late one overcast September afternoon I found myself once again walking down Maple Street toward the neglected dirt road that led past the Kestelling house. As I approached, I judged that it had not yet been sold or rented. The hedge looked ragged; tufts of grass and weeds were showing along the flagstone path.

Traffic along the road was light and I noticed no one in the area. As I stood musing in front of the place, I recalled the huge gaunt dog that I had glimpsed running behind the hedge months before. With a start I suddenly realized that what I had briefly seen might easily have been a large hyena!— or the hideous image of one, possibly created by the brooding thoughts of the disfigured woman within. I began trying to recall what I had read about thought forms becoming visible, projected, as it were, by the sheer obsessive power of a haunted mind.

I impatiently shook off these thoughts. Nonsense, I told myself. To show my contempt for such speculations, I walked up the path to the front of the house and boldly peered into a ground-floor window.

I have regretted it to this day.

It is true—dusk was approaching, and the imagination can perform strange tricks. But the thing I saw was not a configuration created by nerves abetted by late-afternoon shadows.

Looking through the window, I saw a veiled face directly in front of my own. My impulse was to pull back quickly, but I was so startled, I froze instead.

As I stood, the figure inside lifted the veil. The words to describe what I saw do not exist in my vocabulary. It was the hideous caricature of a face, half skull, blood-smeared and partially splintered, as if the hyena's teeth had bitten into it only moments before. In the remnant of mutilated countenance, yellowish eyes glowed with malignancy.

While I stared, petrified with horror, the thing laughed. It was a long, low chuckle that chilled my blood almost more than the sight of the monstrous mangled face from which it issued.

I suppose, in retrospect, that I stared at the nightmare thing for only seconds—but it seemed at the time that long minutes passed before I managed to pull away from the window, turn, and rush down the path to the road.

Shaken and appalled, I hastened home, determined never to go near the house again.

I had nightmares about the mangled face. Sometimes I awoke suddenly, sure that I had heard that mirthless, chilling chuckle again. But after a few weeks, the nightmares became less frequent and less intense.

One evening, however, as I was returning from a walk—far from Maple Street—I experienced an abrupt, unaccountable conviction that I was being followed.

I turned swiftly, in time to glimpse the half-shadowed silhouette of a large, ugly-looking dog before it darted out of sight behind a yew hedge.

I waited, but it did not reappear. Scowling, I continued on. Nerves, I told myself. My experience at the brick house had left me badly unstrung—more so than I had previously realized.

I reached home without incident, but before closing my front door, I glanced down the flagged path to the sidewalk.

The big, bony head of a dog with oversize jaws was just visible beyond the pathway gate.

Pretending I saw nothing, I stepped inside, softly closed the door, ran into my study, opened a drawer, and drew out my .38 automatic. Hurrying back, I flung open the front door and literally bounded down the path to the sidewalk.

The dog was no longer near the gate, but as I looked along the walk, I saw two glowing eyes halfway down the block, near a large elm tree.

As I raised the .38, the eyes disappeared.

I did not sleep that night and I have not slept well since. The damned thing keeps stalking me—mostly at dusk. I never seem able to see it clearly, or close up. I am not sure that I want to.

Of course it is nothing more than a lingering thought form summoned up by a mind saturated with guilt and grief. When that mind is no longer earthbound, I am sure that its creation, in turn, will disappear.

Thus I reassure myself. But what if the dog thing has achieved a separate existence of its own? Suppose it is no longer dependent on a haunted mind to maintain its tangible shape?

God forbid it has now attached itself to me for its own obscene and evil reasons. Perhaps because I know its origin?

I no longer dare think along these lines. I remain confident that it will fade away in time. But I have stopped taking evening walks and I double-check all locks.

Every now and then I still have to go out in the evening—and whenever I do, I am always aware that the hideous thing is somewhere nearby.

I refer to it, and try to think of it, as a dog—but of course I know what it really is . . .

Introduction

The people in your neighborhood that you know the best are your neighbors; and the people you know the least are the same, because, unless you're the fly on the wall, all you see are the faces they want you to see. The rest of the time is shadow.

Lou Fisher lives in New York State, works for IBM, and has at last decided that he'd rather do more writing for himself, and for us, than for Big Blue.

OVERNIGHT

by Lou Fisher

It occurred to Bill Grady as his heart beat faster that the pale glow of the doorbell button might be the only light on the whole street. He pressed it with a finger that wouldn't quite hold still, and on the second attempt he heard the chimes go off inside. Waiting, trying to whistle softly, he half turned on the top step so that he could take another look at the neighborhood. It almost wasn't there. Through the clouds, the moon gave him the shape of a few houses, though for the most part you could only see the peaks of roofs and the top fingers of trees.

"It's about time you got here." It was Stan Wossack's voice, barely audible, recognizably husky but maybe a little more strained. Bill leaned in. From the doorway he could not make out Wossack's face in detail. He had to recall it from memory: heavy, jowly, with eyes not exactly crooked but somewhat out of kilter, as if Wossack was always in remote thought. "Ah," came the rest of the complaint, "where the hell have you been?"

Bill held up the paper bag and shook it. "I had a lot of stops to make." Lowering the bag, he touched Wossack's shoulder with his free hand. "Hey, Stan, I'm here now. Let me in."

The door opened wider.

He squeezed by Wossack and heard the door close quickly behind him. He moved no further.

"Can't we have a light?"

"No," said Wossack. "And keep your voice down."

For a few moments he tried to remember how the living room was arranged, and when he had it in mind, he felt his way to a soft chair. As he sat, he dropped the bag to the floor at his side, then leaned his shoulders back into the cushion. From there he watched a shadowlike Wossack cross in front of him and sit, too, on something or other; you could assume it was the new brown couch. Bill faced the spot.

"I don't exactly like this," he said.

Wossack grunted. "Too bad. I live here—you don't."

"Sure, but you said . . . you told me this was a safe place to be."

"It is," Wossack said firmly, but still so quietly that it couldn't have been heard from any further than the few feet of space between them. "Look around, Bill. And listen. Ah, whoever they are, they won't even know we're here."

Resting his hands in his lap, Bill lowered his head to consider the environment. Zero. Blank. You could imagine you were buried.

Deep dark in the ground.

But that wasn't true. It was just that every house was so dark that even the TV sets must have been off. In fact, all you could hear coming up the street were the strums of music from someone's radio, and they were so faint that the sound was broken into unmelodic fragments. So dark and so quiet. And how did they keep the dogs from barking? By the time he raised his head he had another question. "Stan, where's your family?"

"In the back."

"Joyce? The kids?"

"Yeah, all of them," Wossack whispered. "They're together in the big bedroom, and that's where they're staying till morning." He paused for a moment. You could hear his foot rub on the carpet. "And you and me, Bill, we're staying out here. Waiting and watching. Did you bring everything I wanted?"

Bill slapped the paper bag to show that it was there. "You can try what you want to try, but if you ask me—"

"I didn't ask you anything," said Wossack.

"Well, you asked me to buy the junk, to bring it here."

"Maybe it's junk," said Wossack. "But you'd better be like me, and pray that it works."

Bill didn't pray much, ever, and in fact until he walked down this street tonight, he hadn't considered himself in any need of prayer. Luck, maybe. You always needed luck. But even now the odds were plenty against anything happening to him here or anywhere. And his eyes were getting used to the dark. Wossack, he could tell, was moving from his seat, a careful step at a time, possibly to look out the picture window.

"Well, we've done it, haven't we?" Wossack said. He moved further on, circling the room, and, finally, as far as Bill could make out, he returned to the same end of the couch. "Stayed out of their way, turned off the lights and the sounds, and made ourselves invisible. Ah, but you think it's a bad idea."

That was exactly what he thought. And what he felt. Maybe it was just because he was sitting in the dark.

Anyway, he had some advice for Wossack. "It doesn't work, Stan. It just calls attention to your street and makes it easy to hit. Like a target." He waved a hand around the room, though he doubted that his friend could see it. "You should've gone about your business, watching TV, grilling hamburgers, whatever it is you usually do on a summer night."

"You really think so?"

"That's what I'd have done, Stan."

Wossack grunted. "Well, not me. I don't plan to die while I'm waiting for the charcoal to get ready. I feel safer with the lights out. Besides, it wasn't just me; that's what everybody thought."

Bill shifted in the chair, touching his watch. If it was past ten, then the worst could be coming soon. If it was past eleven, then maybe it was all over for the night, somewhere else, on some other quiet street. You could feel, though, that it was still early. And anything could happen. Before he spoke again, he peered into the darkness to make sure Wossack was there.

Then he told him, "Well, I'm not going to argue one way or another. But no one has figured out why a particular street is chosen—or not chosen—or who the hell is doing it."

"Or *why*," said Wossack. He might have leaned closer. You could feel his breath; you could hear it, too, between the words. "Ah, I think I know something, though. The cops, the Guard, the newspapers, they don't know anything—but I might know."

"Sure, Stan, you're so smart. Okay, tell me."

For a moment there was no answer. Then Wossack stood up.

"Wait—later. Let's get ready for them first."

"I don't know why I listen to you," Bill said. He picked up the paper bag and rattled it again for Wossack's benefit. "All right, you wanted this stuff, so let's do something with it." Reaching inside, he put his fingers around a plastic-wrapped package and lifted it out toward Wossack. "Here—whew!— here's the garlic."

"It doesn't smell till you peel it," Wossack said. He came over to take the package; you could hear him breaking it apart. "I want one piece at each windowsill and a big hunk outside the front door."

Although Bill had an opinion about the value of garlic, he decided not to discuss it. But he wasn't going to put up with the smell. He reached back into the bag. "Well, you do that part yourself, and I'll handle the silver cross," he said. "If you tell me what to do with it."

"You sure it's silver?"

"Plated, probably."

"How big is it?"

Big weighed it in his hand. The hand was trembling, and he squeezed it on the cross to stop it. "Ten inches, I'd say."

"Ah, you could've done better . . . Let's hang it in the vestibule, where you came in, right down from the chandelier."

Bill nodded his head in the dark. You could never change Wossack's mind about anything; you could only shrug your shoulders and get to work. And by the time he had found the chandelier in the front hallway and suspended the cross from it and returned to the living room, Wossack was back, apparently having distributed the cloves, window by window.

"Just let me put this last piece on the door," Wossack said, and when he returned in a minute or two he wanted to know, "What else did you bring?"

"Exactly what you asked for," Bill told him, going back to where he had set down the paper bag, next to the chair. "First the garlic, then the silver cross, and now what's left are four bottles of bleach. You wanted them, you got them. Four bottles of bleach, medium size. You sure do come up with crazy ideas."

"Keep your voice down," said Wossack.

You never knew for sure about Stan Wossack's ideas.

In April, as in every April, they had been up north in the Adirondacks, fishing.

And they had been at the stream for two full days, crawling into the tent for short naps or brief escapes from the sun, but most of the time holding the shiny poles out over the flow of white-tipped blue water, not catching anything, nothing at all, just waiting, and griping, and hoping. All of which Wossack seemed to be involved in when Bill emerged from the tent and unwrapped a sandwich.

"What are you eating?" said Wossack.

Bill refused to feel guilty. "Well, it's half of the last sandwich. I saved the other half for you."

"Peanut butter?" asked Wossack. When Bill nodded, Wossack stood up and pulled the line out of the water. "Let me have a dab of it with a small piece of bread."

Bill pinched off a portion and handed it over. "You're not going to use peanut butter as *bait?*" he said, laughing.

Wossack set his chin. "Nothing else has worked, has it?"

About five minutes later a fair-size trout was wriggling on the hook, and Wossack smiled just a little as he held it up for Bill to see. "Ah, my crazy ideas are better than starving, right?"

Bill nodded. Sometimes you didn't have much choice but to go along with Wossack and either win or lose.

Dark out, dark in, the moon was no help, and Bill counted to four, out loud, but not too loud, as he pulled the bottles out of the bag. He set them a few inches apart on the end table in front of the lamp that wasn't lit.

"Let's get the caps off." Wossack was whispering, with his hands on the first bottle. "The bleach is for throwing in their eyes if they try to get us."

Unconvinced, Bill grabbed the neck of a bottle and twisted off the cap. You could smell the bleach immediately: clean, chlorine, antiseptic. At least better than garlic. Sniffing, he set it down. "Stan," he said, "some people have had loaded guns, and fired them, and still ended up with their heads half off or their stomachs in their hands. We don't even know what kind of creatures are doing all this—what the hell good is bleach going to do?"

"Throw it in their eyes," Wossack said again. "Guns don't work—we'll try what I want to try." There were a few breaks in his voice, and it grew more hoarse as he went on. "I said I knew about them."

"You can't know anything. Nobody knows."

"Do you want me to tell you or not?"

Bill uncapped the last bottle of bleach, put it back on the end table, and poked his hand to the bottom of the bag to make sure he'd taken everything out. A bag full of junk. Not much against what was happening. House by house, this one and that one, picked out somehow by whoever they were— then throats slit and bodies gutted and floors covered with blood. The strongest men and everyone else: grandparents, mothers and daughters, babysitters, all mutilated and tossed aside; evident attempts at self-defense proving to be of no defense at all. You could go to any of those streets right afterward, as fast as the cops could get there, and find every person left dead, with no witnesses, with no clues as to the identity of the terrorists. Then some night a week later . . . You could try to figure it out, or you could try not to think about it.

There was an ache across his shoulder blades.

He folded up the bag. "Do you think they're from hell or someplace? The garlic, the silver cross . . . is that why we put this stuff all over your house?"

"When I tell you what I think, I want you to take it seriously."

"Stan, there's nothing about this business that I don't take seriously. But you haven't told me anything yet."

Wossack rearranged the four open bottles on the table, coughing a bit as he did it, and he drifted off to the center of the room. "They're coming back," he said finally, his raspy voice rising just for that statement, then returning to a whisper, "from the dead."

Bill sought the chair, crossed his legs, and wondered what time it was.

Wossack sat, too.

"If you remember," he went on, "this all started a month ago. The first street was Teawood—you knew a guy there, didn't you? Harry. Harry what's-his-name. And that lady he lived with. But listen, I want you to remember more . . ." He stopped for a few seconds, as if to recall it for himself. "Remember, Bill, just a couple of days before that, when the truck driver went nuts and shot up the country music bar from one end to the other—wasn't that just a few blocks from Teawood? And he knocked off the whole band, didn't he? Blasted 'em. Now I'm going to tell you, I think those five guys in the band, and the two girls who sang with them . . . That night at the bar, they were murdered, for nothing, I mean for *nothing*, and they're coming back to get even."

"They're dead," said Bill. This was insane. The darkness, the junk, and now this. "Nobody comes back from the dead."

"You got a better idea?"

"I don't even want ideas like that."

"C'mon, Bill, it could be them."

No, it couldn't, he thought. If you were murdered, you were stuck with it. You could want revenge and deserve it, too, but how much would it take to bring you back from the dead? Could you need it so badly . . . ? "Look," he said to Wossack, "just because one thing followed another—"

"But right after. I mean just a couple of days after. And close to Teawood, too."

"Yeah, I hear you," Bill said, leaning forward. "Still, how can you even think such a thing?"

Wossack rose up from the chair again, moving to the window; you could hear the rustle of curtains as they were pushed aside.

"Well," he said from that spot, "there's a lot of deep feelings in country music, and when people play it night after night. . . ."

When you knew Stan Wossack, you knew about deep feelings.

Bill drove him back from the hospital after Brian had been hit by a car. The boy, who had been picked up on the front bumper and flipped over the trunk, was still alive, just barely, and the doctors had expressed their doubts about future activities like seeing and walking.

"He'll be all right," Bill kept saying on the way home. You could try all you wanted to comfort Wossack, but you could tell by his ever-scattered eyes that something was ready to burst out.

But Wossack said nothing.

"You know, little kids are strong," Bill insisted as he parked in Wossack's driveway. Right there, just that morning, the car had come tearing through, careening onto the sidewalk. "And Brian's a real fighter."

Wossack said nothing.

Climbing out of the car, he looked up and down the street as if he expected the hit-and-run driver to return at full speed. Then he walked straight back to his garage, pulled up the wide door, went inside, and came out with both hands on a shovel. The look on his face made Bill back off.

"Hey, you can't . . ."

But Wossack stormed forward down the driveway.

"Ah, I'll get every car I can find," he mumbled, and went to work on Bill's Civic. Arms and shovel outstretched, he broke the headlights first and then the windshield, which shattered with an awful sound, and then the side windows and the rear hatchback window going right down to the taillights, and with one more swing he knocked off the side-view mirror, which bounced twice toward the street before it and Wossack came to a stop. Bill watched from well up near the steps to the front door. The two of them had been friends for a long time; when Wossack got started, you stayed out of his way.

But from that distance he said, "It's not as bad as you think. Brian'll be okay, I tell you. Take it easy now."

It was as if Wossack couldn't hear. Running back to the garage, he started to attack his own station wagon, hitting every smashable object on it and yelling at God and stamping his feet and ramming his shoulder against the door trying to overturn what was left of the car; until finally, after a last vicious swing through the empty air and another expectant look up the street, he tossed the shovel aside and sat down on the grass at the edge of the driveway.

"I've done enough," he said. He looked over to Bill. "I'm sorry about your car."

Bill was sorry, too, but he nodded, shrugged, and went over to sit next to his friend for a few minutes.

"Well, even if it is that group from the bar," Bill said, "they would have had enough by now. More than enough. How much does it take to make up for seven useless killings?"

"A lot, I'd say," offered Wossack. "Tough people play in country music bands." A shadowy figure, he walked back to the chair and fell into it, facing Bill again. "Ah, but you think it's just another crazy idea. I can tell."

"No, it could be, who knows?" Bill said, only to save the trouble of disagreeing. The idea was junk, like all the stuff in the bag; except that some group was killing a lot of people, overnight, any night. You could hide, you could run, you could speculate about who they were. He said, "I wish I knew what time it was. Stan, I have to get out of here. I think you've just called attention to this street, with all the lights out, and so quiet, and I don't want to wait around to get my throat cut."

"Keep your voice down."

Bill covered his mouth with his hand. His breath was warm, and he could feel the sweat on his lip. He wiped it off with two fingers. "I have to get out of here."

"Ah, do whatever you want. Me, I ought to go back and check on the wife and the kids."

Bill had a picture of them in his mind. Joyce was a small dynamic blonde and it was hard to imagine her not coming out to say hello and give him a hug, and those two curly-haired boys never stood still for a minute, especially when "Uncle Bill" was around. "How's Brian been doing?"

"Coming along," said Wossack. "A lot of swimming now. Builds him up."

"I told you he'd be okay." Bill edged forward in the chair. You could leave now, he thought, or you could stay another minute. Well, no more than another minute. "Good kids," he went on. "I tell you, they're sure being quiet back there."

"They're supposed to be. That's what we're all doing. We're just being quiet and staying out of the way. And we're going to do it every night until—"

A scream, from somewhere, stopped his talking.

"Was that glass?" Bill asked.

"What?"

"I thought I heard something break."

It came again. You could hear the splinters falling.

"A window," said Wossack, with a quick draw of breath. "In the bedroom . . . God!"

They stood together and bumped shoulders, each groping for the end table and the nearest bottle of bleach. "C'mon!" yelled Wossack, starting immediately toward the back of the house, and Bill took a step to follow; but he stopped—he knew that the dark street had been a mistake, you could know that in one quick look, just another crazy idea . . . He opened his fingers and dropped the bottle to the floor, and when he heard it hit, he turned and ran through the darkness under the silver cross out the front door past the garlic clove down the two front steps and right into their knives and their broken guitars.

Introduction

If the boundaries of horror are to include the past, as they must, how far back do they go? And what happens when the past, the present, and an unpleasant part of the future blur those boundaries into shadows that make the whole argument academic?

Galad Elflandsson again, proof in some way that winters in Ottawa may be beautiful, but they do strange things to even stranger minds.

THE LAST TIME I SAW HARRIS

by Galad Elflandsson

The last time I saw Harris Frazier was in June of 1972, about a week after our graduation ceremonies at Cornell University. After four years of raising all sorts of hell on campus, in Ithaca, and all over the Finger Lakes region of upstate New York, we had stayed on in the apartment we had shared, unwilling and, in some strange way, unable to just pack up and leave like the rest of the graduating class. Harris and I had done everything together, from our first hits of LSD right on through to swapping lies and half-truths about our "exploits" with the girls we dated. We went to Woodstock, marched on Washington, burned our draft cards with discreet defiance, and shared just about everything two young men could possibly share . . . except Jessie Manchester. I made love to her once, about four weeks after she and Harris started seeing each other—on a night when we both knew he would be hours doing some research in the library—but it was something I was never proud of, an act motivated (*rationalized* perhaps is a better word, seeing as I didn't try very hard to keep Jessica from undoing my belt buckle) by lust, a spurious concern for what I thought was a bout of depression on her part, and not a small amount of jealousy on mine.

Jessica was, in the vernacular of the era, a *fox*, five feet six inches of deeply tanned flesh from head to toe—there were dozens of places where you could get an all-over suntan without outraging any of the locals—with large black eyes, a finely chiseled nose, and a mane of jet black hair that fell to her waist. With her clothes off she looked about thirteen going on puberty, but from the moment Harris and I first laid eyes on her we both agreed there was something about her, an *aura* (a very cosmic word in those days) that was any and all things but innocent . . . and Jessie proved it I don't know how many times with Harris, and that one time with me. Her lips, which were full and a tiny bit too large for the rest of her face, seemed to be a constant invitation to *anything* that moved on two legs—one very drunken night Harris let slip that she went both ways—and when she took up with my good pal and buddy, about a month into our sophomore year, I was simply the first in a long line of disgruntled young bucks (not to mention the gay ladies) who looked on their relationship with ill-managed grace and very poorly disguised envy.

But on that last day, when finally we had decided it was time to leave Ithaca and move on to bigger and better things for the summer, Harris dragged me into the small tavern on the street leading up to the main gates of the university—would you believe I can't remember the name of the street or the tavern?—and thumped a pair of chilled mugs of draft down onto the scarred wooden table in front of us.

"I guess this is the end of the line, Edward old boy," he said, pouring a dash of salt into his beer. "The bags are packed, the bank accounts are empty, and the last of our stash is smoked, eaten, or otherwise ingested. It's time to indulge in one last cold one, shake hands, and bid each other a fond farewell and godspeed."

I shook my head and took a healthy slug from my beer.

"Bull," I said with a grin. "You know damn well we're not turning our backs and walking off into our respective psychedelic sunsets. Not after all the shit we've been through together. Besides, I've got your address for the summer and you've got mine; and we're both gonna be back here in September, so don't try to tell me we're not gonna stay in touch, Harris."

I had never called him anything but Harris—maybe that was why we became such close friends—but those who called him Harry did so only once and in peril of their lives thereafter. He had a decadent sort of dignity about him that demanded it, yet Jessica was the only person I ever knew who did not respect it without suffering his quiet but implacable anger. She got away with an awful lot where Harris was concerned, but he never seemed to take notice of it. I looked at him sitting there beside me at the table, with a small, almost foolish smile on his face, and sensed that Jessie was about to become the cause of the unthinkable.

"I can't promise you that anymore, O faithful partner in druggery," he said quietly. "There's been a slight change in plans . . ."

"What're you talkin' about?" I sneered, but my stomach already was doing a slow sink into my boots. "We'll both be back here for postgrad in the fall and—"

"No." He smiled. "You'll be back here for postgrad in the fall, Edward.

I've decided this old horse needs a bit of a rest from hallowed halls and the Ivy League—"

"You mean Jessie's decided it for you!" I shot back.

For a moment, I saw a rare flash of anger contort his usually placid features, but it was gone almost in the same breath, and his quiet smile back in place.

"We're taking off to find America, Edward me lad. Pooling our assets, both liquid and otherwise, buying a van, and heading out for the high country."

"Harris, you're bullshitting me . . ." I said, knowing full well he wasn't. Somehow, from the instant Jessica Manchester had taken a fancy to my good friend Harris Frazier, I had known she eventually would take him away from me. "You can't be serious," I said, still hoping I was wrong. "Harris, all this— our four years here, I mean—has been great fun, but neither of us ever believed it was the real world. We just had a good time while it was there to be had . . . but now we've got fifty-plus years of *real* life in front of us. We're too smart to blow it."

Harris shook his head apologetically, but the silly smile came back on his face and it never wavered.

"Me and Jessie are taking off, Edward," he said softly. "It's what we want to do. I'll try to keep in touch, but it might not work."

"I don't believe I'm hearing this from you, Harris."

He looked at me long and hard for almost a minute, with a very odd expression on his face; then he shrugged and emptied his mug of draft in one long swallow.

"Gotta go, Edward," he said, getting up from the table and offering me his right hand. "You take care of yourself. Maybe we'll send you some postcards along the way."

I sat there, staring up at him in a daze and shaking his hand mechanically. Then he turned and walked toward the door of the tavern, and I saw Jessie looking in through the plate-glass window, staring at both of us with a satisfied smile on her tiny-bit-too-large-for-her-face lips, waiting to collect my friend. And that was the last time I saw Harris.

I had never told him about Jessie and me, the night he was at the library and we had undressed in the hallway outside his bedroom door. Shame at my betrayal of him was one reason, but the other had been something I had never admitted to myself until I saw her waiting for him outside the tavern. Jessica Manchester had frightened me that night. In the middle of what should have been pure mindless passion, a part of me had stood back from our naked, perspiration-soaked bodies and looked on with something that approached absolute terror.

I thought a lot about Harris in the first year or so, especially when I went back to Cornell in the fall. The two postcards I did receive from him—one that summer, from somewhere in Ohio, and another just after I got back to Ithaca, from western Colorado—were read with a mixture of bitterness and longing, and, without even realizing it at the time, a fresh surge of jealousy for what he was doing and who he was doing it with. But after a while, when it became clear I probably would never hear from him again, I let the vast amount of study and postgraduate work swallow me. I stopped thinking about Harris and went after my degrees in engineering, planning a career as a consultant.

I made a great deal of money, at the same time traveling most of North America on other people's expense accounts. I never felt that I had sold out to the Establishment—traded in the high ideals of my college days for a three-piece suit and an affluent life-style—because I pretty much went on living them, but with a practical notion that all the ideals in the world would not feed me or keep a roof over my head. I did the best I could and all the good I could manage, within the framework of my existence.

As the years went by, I built a dam in Idaho, designed an eighty-story office tower for a Denver-based corporation and a rather unique residence for an aging rock star whose records had filled hundreds of drug-hazed hours during my undergraduate years at Cornell. I breezed through all of it, making a name for myself and my work, forever on the lookout for new challenges and projects that would keep me face forward, so I would never look back long enough to really feel the vague discontent—or the fear—that still flickered somewhere inside me. Only once in the thirteen years that followed did I ever slip back into the past, and then it was a memory of Jessica that rose to haunt me.

I had designed and overseen the construction of a bridge in North Dakota when it happened. The last of the workers and machinery had been cleared out of the area in anticipation of the official opening of the bridge to traffic the next day; the party thrown by the money men of the project had been going on since lunchtime, and when the whole thing had gotten a bit too smoky and liquor-crazed for my tastes, I decided to drive out to the bridge and have a last look at the product of my talents.

I parked my car at one end of the bridge and walked out to the middle of it, just as the sun was going down in a blaze of crimson and gold, and the fifty-foot drop from the surface of the roadbed began to fill with purple shadows. There had been a smaller-scaled version of it on the Cornell campus, a place simply called the Gorge, and one November evening, on my way back from classes, I had noticed Jessica standing at the railing, looking down at the rocks and the dark rushing water below.

"Hi, Jess," I said to her. "What's happenin'?"

She turned to me, slightly startled, a rustle of night-black hair and a faint waft of some musky perfume, and smiled with her inviting lips. It was just after she and Harris had fallen in with each other, just before the night we had gotten into each other's pants.

"Oh . . . hello . . . Edward . . ." she said, very softly, a purring whisper. "What are you doing here?" She fastened her eyes on mine and I saw a slow dance of laughter shine in their depths. "Have you been following me?"

"Why would I do that, Jess?" I said quickly, perhaps too quickly, because the laughter in her eyes got brighter. "I had a late class. You comin' back to the apartment?"

"Not right away," she said, turning back to the railing so that her face was a mass of shadows in the waning light. "Maybe later. It's so sad about that boy . . ."

"The guy that jumped?" I said. "Yeah . . . it's a downer, all right. I wonder why he did it."

She was quiet for a while, staring down with her long-fingered hands on the top bar of the railing, utterly still except for the wind that stirred the heavy mass of her hair.

"Who knows why people decide to kill themselves," she said in a fierce whisper. "I can't understand it, not when there's so much life to be lived."

"Did you know the guy, Jess?" I asked softly, and she turned back to me for just a moment, her face gone pale and ghostly and devoid of any expression at all.

"As a matter of fact, I did, Edward . . . a little bit . . . not much . . . not enough to understand why."

"Well . . . I guess I'll see ya later then," I said, walking away slowly.

"Yeah, I'll see you later," she said, and it almost sounded as if she was angry . . .

To this day I don't know why I took the job that sent me to the backwoods of Maine—to the shores of Chamberlain Lake, at least a million miles from the middle of nowhere in particular. I guess I was tired of the concrete-and-steel set, looking for some way to find a bit of peace and quiet without giving up the distraction of work. The lumber company flew me to Bangor at the beginning of May, and from there, on into the hinterlands by light plane, where I and the company engineer—a tall strapping fellow named Carl

Lacroix—settled into a small cabin on the site of an old lumber camp, along with a handful of other company people.

Spring was a long time coming in that part of the country. Most of our first days there were grim gray overcasts, broken by odd flurries of snow and a chill wind off the lake that seemed to spring up only at night, whistling through the chinks in the cabin walls and making sleep something of a chore. That was when I started thinking about Harris again, somehow linking the desolation of my surroundings with the sense of desolation I had felt when he had walked out of the tavern in Ithaca . . . and out of my life as well.

Lacroix and I spent our days going over the terrain, speculating on the hows and wheres of the projected pulp mill, but one night toward the end of May, when the weather finally showed signs of turning toward warmth and leaves started showing on the trees, we sat out on the cabin porch and cracked a bottle of Johnnie Walker. There was a light breeze coming off the lake, whispering through the dense pine forests on the north side, and as we drank and the sun went down off to our left, we started talking about the things we had done, the places we had seen, the people we had known. For the first time, I actually spoke of Harris to another human being, let the whole story—except for the night I had made love to Jessica—come tumbling out in a gush of maudlin intoxication. Lacroix listened patiently while I rambled on, shaking his somewhat balding head of brown hair and making sympathetic noises as I told him of my friend's desertion. When I was finished, he poured us another pair of whiskeys and looked at me with a pair of slightly bloodshot eyes.

"Things like that happen," he said with a New England drawl, and suddenly I was sorry I had mentioned Harris at all, "but I've heard about women like the one you were talkin' about." He was referring to Jessica, of course. "They're a real strange breed, somethin' apart from most women you'll meet. I guess the best way t'describe 'em is hungry, but the appetite they've got for men goes a lot further than just droppin' drawers and rollin' in the hay. It's like they got to own each man, body and soul, for as long as they're with him, and the poor guy takes up with one of 'em is like a rabbit caught in a snare, wishin' like hell it could get away but held fast by the cord round its leg."

He got up from his chair and paced back and forth across the porch while I looked down into my glass and mulled over what he had said.

"It wasn't like that with Harris," I said finally, lighting a cigarette. "At least, if it was I never saw that in him. I don't know where, when, or how he changed, or our friendship stopped being the fierce thing that it was, but one day I looked up from us being thick as thieves and I realized it didn't matter to him anymore; that Jessie had become the most important thing in his life, and he wanted it that way."

Lacroix stopped pacing and nodded at me soberly, which was ludicrous because we were getting to where we were anything but sober.

"Sometimes it's like that," he said, "when the woman's so damned intense that her will becomes his will. Listen, Ed, your friend Harris, was he a big man, tall, strong, like you or me?"

"Yes, he was," I said, puzzled. "Actually, he was taller than me by a few inches, and heavier by about fifteen pounds. Hell! We had to be strong, or all the stuff we were into at the time would've killed us. But why do you ask?"

Carl didn't answer right away, but suggested we go inside before the wind picked up and things got downright cold. He set a match to the kerosene heater and stood awhile in front of it, wringing the chill out of his hands.

"Reason I asked about your friend was because I would've been real surprised if he hadn't been made the way he was. They only want the strong ones, and full of whatever it is they're hungry for."

"Jessica was hungry all right," I said, sitting at the plank table in the center of the single room we shared.

"And I'll bet she wasn't all that good-lookin' either," said Lacroix, "but she had all the boys lined up stiff-legged anyway."

I thought about that for a moment or two before I replied, realizing he was right—Jessica had *not* been beautiful, or even as pretty as dozens of other coeds Harris and I had chased after as freshmen. Yet there had been that indefinable something, that aura about her, that had made her maddeningly desirable.

"How did you know that, Carl?" I asked him, more puzzled than ever.

He turned to face me and I saw the light of intoxication we had been cultivating so assiduously start to fade from his eyes. He seemed to debate some question in his mind, stood unmoving before the kerosene heater for almost five minutes while he did so, and then he nodded to himself as he walked to his bed and stretched out on the top sheets.

"I was lyin' to you when I said I'd heard about women like your Jessica, Ed," he said, staring up at the ceiling. "The truth is that I knew one . . . and same as what happened t'you, she ran off with the best damned friend I ever had . . .

"Her name was Jenny Lynn Stratton, and just lookin' at her was like gettin' it every night of the week and twice on Sunday morning. Me and Steve rolled into U-Maine together, just like we'd been from kindergarten on up, and we were so much like brothers by then that we could tell what the other one was thinkin' just by lookin' at his face. So I found out real quick how Steve was feelin' about Jenny Lynn, just like he knew I was feelin' the same thing. We met her in a bar one Friday night, stepped on up to her, from different directions, in the same breath . . . and we took turns dancin' with her, sat down the three of us at the same table and spent that whole night just starin' at her . . ."

Lacroix smiled faintly, still looking up at the ceiling, as if he were conjuring images of the past on its cracked, white-plastered surface. Finally he sighed, and went on.

"We never talked about her when we were together," he said in a whisper, "but I think that was because we were afraid to, because we knew she was gonna come between us eventually and make an end to our friendship. There were nights when he'd tell me he was goin' out t'do this, that, or some other thing, but I knew it was bullshit and he was goin' off to see Jenny Lynn because the next night I'd be slingin' him the same bullshit back, for the same reason. After spendin' a night with her I'd come staggerin' home in the early hours and have to wipe the shit-eatin' grin off my face before I ran into Steve, and I don't doubt he did the same his nights . . . and we went on like that for almost two months before Jenny Lynn decided it was Steve she wanted instead of me.

"Soon after that, he moved out of the apartment we were sharin' and moved in with her, and would you believe I never saw him again—except in passin' or in classes we happened to share—for almost a full two years!"

"God," I murmured, "that must have been pretty hellish. What did you say to each other?"

He smiled again and shook his head.

"I don't remember a word of it, Ed," he said. "It was like bein' in the middle of your worst nightmare. The Steve I had known was tall and healthy as a goddamn horse, with an easy laugh to match . . . but he looked like hell that day, seemed old and tired like he didn't give a hot one for anyone or anything, until I mentioned *her* name. Whatever I said, it made him madder'n hell. He turned his back on me and walked away. I didn't see him again for another four months—I went home for the summer, but he stayed on with her—and then it was for the last time, before he died."

"Carl, are you sure you want to tell me this?" I said quickly. He sat up on the bed and motioned for me to fill his glass again.

"You bet your sweet ass I wanna tell you, Ed," he said hoarsely. "I've been waitin' years t'tell it to someone, just like you've been waitin' . . . but I'm tellin' you because I don't think you realize just how lucky you've been."

"Lucky?" I said incredulously. "I lost the best friend I ever had and you're telling me I was lucky?"

Lacroix's head moved up and down in the shadows that had begun to fill the cabin.

"That's exactly what I'm tellin' you, Ed. When your friend Harris ran off with that babe, whether he knew it or not, he was doin' you the biggest favor of your life!"

"You're crazy, Carl . . . or too drunk to hear yourself talking."

He took the glass I offered him and held up his other hand as if to tell me to be patient, to let him finish his story. Then he downed the contents of the glass in one long swallow.

"Don't you bullshit me, Ed," he snapped. "I could see from the way you talked about her that Jessica scared you shitless. Jenny Lynn did the same thing t'me, but I kept on wantin' her anyway because I was too damned stupid t'see it . . .

"Anyway, the last time I saw Steve was three days after I got back to U-Maine for my junior year, and he stood at the door of my apartment for half an hour, beggin' me to let him in. It wasn't until I heard him start to cry that I opened the door. He looked worse than hell, all shrunk in on himself, and he was so weak I had to half-carry him across my living room to a chair.

"For a long time he just sat there, starin' down at his hands and lettin' the tears run down his cheeks. And then he started to tell me about the time he had spent with Jenny Lynn, with all the details. The things they had done together, how they made love to each other, and what she had to say about this, that, and the other. Halfway through it he started grinnin' at me, a dumb-ass shit-eating grin, but he never stopped cryin' the whole time he was grinnin'. I thought he was tryin' to rile me, rub my nose into the fact he'd gotten Jenny Lynn and I hadn't . . . but I looked closer and I saw he was bitter, and real scared.

"Ed, he looked me straight in the eyes and told me he was gonna kill Jenny Lynn and then he was gonna kill himself; that he couldn't stand any more of it, that she was evil . . . 'Not evil like she knows what she's doin', Carl,' he said to me, 'but evil just the same. I gotta end it now, before it's too late.' "

"Christ!" I interrupted him. "Didn't you try to talk him out of it?"

Lacroix got off the bed and lit a cigarette from my pack.

"Of course I tried to talk him out of it!" he snapped at me. "I told him he was bein' crazy, that he was sick and needed a doctor to check him out. And when I asked him why didn't he just up and walk out on her, he got this real pained look in his eyes and said he could never do that . . . and that the only way out was for him to kill her.

"After a while he staggered out of the apartment and went back to her. Next day all hell broke loose when someone in the place they were livin' heard a gunshot and called the police. Steve had shot himself in the head, but before doin' that he had killed Jenny Lynn with a carving knife, cut off her head and stuffed her mouth full o' wild garlic."

I stared at Lacroix in horror.

"That's it?" I cried. "You just let him go ahead and never tried to stop him?"

He dragged heavily on his cigarette and met my stare without flinching.

"No, that's not it, Ed," he said quietly, "but I did let him go, and I never tried to stop him because before he left my apartment, Steve had a few more things to say to me, things I wouldn't have believed from anybody else but him."

"Like what?" I demanded. "What the hell could he have said to make you turn your back on him like that?"

I could barely see Lacroix's face now; it was nothing more than a muddle of shadows, but his eyes were bright in the glow from the kerosene heater.

"He told me about Jenny Lynn, the things she whispered when he was in bed with her, and the more I listened to him tellin' me what she had said, the more scared I got. The last thing he said, just as he was goin' out the door, was, 'Don't you understand, Carl?'"

I groped blindly for the bottle of Johnnie Walker and thought back to the last time I had seen Harris, and how wrong I had been in thinking Jessica had made his decision to leave school for him. I remembered the odd expression on his face before he had walked out of the tavern, and finally recognized that it was the same terror I had felt once . . . on the night he had been at the library.

Harris had known. Maybe Jessica had told him. Either way, he had walked out on me because it was the only way he knew to protect me. And I began to wonder if he had done the same thing Steve had done . . . or if he was still out there, somewhere . . . with her . . . trying to stay alive long enough and strong enough to keep Jessie from coming back for me. He seemed awfully strong, the last time I saw Harris . . .

Introduction

Facing facts is what we're told to do when we're faced with a problem that threatens to overwhelm us. Face facts, bite the bullet, stiff upper lip. But facts, like shadows, aren't always what they seem.

Peter Tremayne's latest novel, Angelus, *may at this writing be available in this country. If it isn't, it ought to be. And if you can find it—or any of his others—you're definitely the richer for it.*

TAVESHER

by Peter Tremayne

Cnoc na Bhrón is one of those comfortless, unfrequented, and isolated places that still exist in the wild landscape of the bare Kerry mountains of Ireland. It is a gloomy solitude, high among the barren peaks that are among the tallest in the country. In English Cnoc na Bhrón means "The Hill of Sorrow," but this is an area where English is seldom heard, where the people cling to the ancient language of the country and traditions that were millennia old before the coming of Christianity. Cnoc na Bhrón is a desolate spot, wreathed in brooding melancholia and grieving friendlessness.

Perhaps I am getting ahead of my narrative. I ought to tell you what brought me, Kurt Wolfe of Houston, Texas, to that wild spot thousands of miles from my home. It is a simple story. I work as a surveyor for a mining corporation that decided it was worth the risk of undertaking a prospecting survey of some of the old, deserted copper mines of southwest Ireland. A century ago there were many such mines operating quite profitably. In those days Ireland had been ruled from England, so when England found it cheaper to extract its copper from Australia, the Irish mines found it impossible to compete and gradually, one by one, they were forced to close. My company was concerned with the viability of opening some of those mines once more.

I had made preliminary surveys of several mines in the region and was heading for the village of Ballyvourney. Here, according to my map, I would find a road that would lead me into the Derrysaggart Mountains to one particular peak, Cnoc na Bhrón. On the slopes of Cnoc na Bhrón stood an old mine called Pollroo, which I learned was a corruption of the Irish *An Pholl Rua*, which meant "The Red Hole" and doubtless had something to do with the fact that red copper was mined there. My notes showed that Pollroo was one of the last mines to be worked in the country and had not been entirely deserted until the turn of the century.

I found the village of Ballyvourney easily enough, but although I had a large-scale map of the district, I had difficulty finding the road to Cnoc na Bhrón. I was lucky enough to spot a police car parked in the village and drew up behind it. Two policemen, members of the *Gárda Síochána*, as the Irish police are called, sat inside, and I approached them to inquire the way.

"You'd be an American, I'm thinking," said the moon-faced driver morosely, in response to my question.

I nodded.

"There's nothing up at Cnoc na Bhrón," the second man said.

I explained the purpose of my visit. The men exchanged glances with raised eyebrows.

" 'Tis dangerous up at Pollroo; the mine has been deserted since the turn of the century. No one goes there these days."

I suppressed my impatience and said, "If you could point out the way to Cnoc na Bhrón . . . ?"

After a further exchange of inconsequential conversation, they finally pointed me through a maze of farm lanes onto a small dirt track that I would have had no hope of finding if I had been left to my own devices. It was a small, narrow track that had once been paved with stones but was now overgrown. It twisted and climbed high into the mountains, passing many deserted stone crofts; ancient, roofless cottages.

In spite of the bleak aspect of the higher reaches of the mountains, the weather was surprisingly mild and the fact that this was usual was reflected in the wide variety of subtropical plants that occurred in the area. Predominant across the broad lower slopes was the purple mist of heather; fuchsias were also common and so, too, was the arbutus or strawberry tree, which grew in amazing profusion. It is an evergreen, flowering in the autumn and winter, and it has an edible fruit that, at first, reminds one of wild strawberries although the flavor is a trifle bitter.

I was lulled into a pleasant, warm feeling as I drove through this gentle, sunlit vista.

It came as something of a surprise, therefore, to turn my car across the shoulder of the mountain and come abruptly on a flat of land that constituted a plateau and a valley at one and the same time. It was as if a hand had suddenly been stretched across the face of the sun; I went from lightness into darkness. The area appeared as if some giant had scooped a large hole in the side of the mountain. The plateau was surrounded on three sides by a protective semicircle of black granite cliffs. The actual width of the plateau was probably a mile across and the same distance in depth. I could see a tarn, a small mountain lake, and the ruins of an old house. Beyond the house were ruined outhouses and buildings that I easily recognized as the deserted mine workings. The sun did not seem to penetrate onto the plateau, and there was a peculiar stillness and rawness; a penetrating chill permeated the area.

I drove my car along the uneven track that skirted the tarn and halted it before the ancient, decaying house. According to the map I had, it was called Rath Rua and it appeared like so many of the stately houses of a bygone age that you find littered through the countryside of Ireland. It had once been the prosperous habitat of the mine owner and his family. A century of decay and neglect and the incursions of nature, insidious creeping weeds and hungry, devouring ivy, now disguised the once-grand aspect of the place. I climbed out of my car and stood staring up at its eyeless windows, its dark frowning exterior. Its great stones had obviously been quarried from the black granite from the surrounding circle of cliffs.

The atmosphere seemed damp here and I caught the whiff of bittersweet decomposition as a cold breeze blew its chill breath against me. I turned toward the tarn. It was quiet and still and very black. The water was obviously stagnant and on its surface were strange green stains. It took me a moment to realize that this was caused by copper ore permeating the lake, presumably from the disused mine. The realization lightened my heart. If the ore was still staining the tarn, then there must surely be copper deposits left in the workings.

I glanced at my watch. It was midday and there was plenty of time to take some initial samples. Obviously, I did not mean to make a thorough survey there and then. In fact, I knew that I would have to get plans of the old mine workings and perhaps a local guide in order to get to the copper veins in order to see if they could be reworked.

Behind the house were the remains of an overgrown path that led directly to the base of the black granite cliffs and the entrance to the mine. Its black, gaping mouth was nearly obscured by undergrowth. I returned to my car and pulled out a small haversack in which I carried the tools of my profession. I took out a flashlight, slung the haversack on my back, and made my way carefully over the path.

If it was cold at the house, it was even colder here. Brooding blackness stretched out to envelop me. I switched on my flashlight and turned the beam along the walls, which had been hewn by the hand of man into that thick granite. The walls were damp and oozed with water. It was obviously seepage from the mountain draining through the innumerable cracks and crevices. From farther along the tunnel came the sound of gushing water making a noisy, echoing music.

I moved forward cautiously, swinging the beam to right and left. It was not long before I noticed that the tunnel was growing narrow; the roof began lowering over my head. The walls glittered with green-stained water and the floor was slippery with the slime of disuse. In fact, I had barely started along the tunnel when I slipped, struck out wildly for support, and fetched my head a crack against an overhanging thrust of granite. It stunned me for a moment but I retained my footing, rubbed my forehead ruefully and moved on—this time a little more carefully.

However, the conditions began to worsen. My mind was just forming the notion that the place was too treacherous to proceed further on my own when my feet slipped from under me again. This time my feet seemed to slide away from me. The torch fell from my hand and I cried aloud. I tried to catch hold of some object to save myself, but my forward momentum was unimpeded. Then I was falling; falling into utter blackness. I felt sharp rocks jabbing at me, scraping my flesh, tearing my clothes. Something cracked against my head but this time it was no mere stunning impact. For one terrible moment I felt fear; complete, heart-stopping fear stabbing like a knife in my chest as I realized that I was falling down a vertical shaft. I hit the bottom with a vague feeling of impact and then . . . nothing. A deep, silent, black void enveloped me.

When I opened my eyes, the first thing that I became aware of was the cheerful, crackling fire roaring away in a rather ornate hearth. I blinked and frowned, trying to bring my surroundings into focus. I was apparently lying on a couch; the couch was in front of a large arabesque marble fireplace in which the vigorous fire played with logs of sweet-smelling pine. My gaze expanded to take in a large room, decorated in somber burgundy and gold, a touch too old-fashioned for my taste. Numerous prints and drawings covered the walls, and there were some exquisite pieces of period furniture about.

"Relax," said a voice close to me. "You're all right."

I turned my head slightly to see a tall man with pleasant features standing at the head of the couch. I made to sit up but groaned at the dull ache in my head.

"Steady," admonished the man in a gentle tone.

"What happened?" I mumbled, raising a hand to massage my temple.

"You've had a fall, old fellow," replied the man, moving around to stand in front of me. He reached forward and took my wrist between his finger and thumb in a most professional manner. His gray, deep-set eyes peered into mine and then turned to examine my forehead.

"A slight contusion, but you'll be fine enough."

"What happened?" I demanded again.

"You fell down a shaft in the old mine," he replied.

The memory came flooding back.

"There was a damned stupid thing to do," I said ruefully.

"Very stupid. My name is O'Brien. Dr. Phelim O'Brien."

I told him my name and asked, "Where am I?"

"Mothair Pholl Rua; it's a house close to the mine."

"I thought this spot was more or less deserted," I replied, lying back. "Have I been out a long while?" I asked, realizing that the curtains were pulled and night had apparently fallen.

The doctor nodded.

"Is this your house?"

"More or less," O'Brien replied in a tone that roused my curiosity.

"How did I get here?"

"I brought you here."

"From the mine shaft?" I raised my eyebrows in astonishment.

"I happened to be nearby when you fell," he replied shortly, turning to the mantelpiece and picking up a pipe. He slipped into an armchair at the side of the fire and proceeded to light the pipe, all the while regarding me thoughtfully.

"You are an American."

"Guilty." I smiled. "And are you the local doctor?"

"No, no." He shook his head. "My practice was in Cork City. But that was years ago now."

"What brought you to these wilds then?" I asked. I suppose I was simply making conversation, because I was actually wondering whether I was well enough to drive back down to Ballyvourney to look for a hotel for the night.

"Oh, I came here a long time ago . . ."

As he was not much more than forty years old, I remarked that it could not have been so long. He replied with a wry smile.

"When you live here, here in the midst of these mountains, so close to nature, time ceases to have any practical meaning."

"What made you give up a city practice for the remoteness of these mountains?" I asked, my curiosity now overcoming my initial diffidence.

"In the first place—a woman."

He stared disgustedly at his pipe, poked at it, relit it, and tried a few experimental puffs.

"I was engaged to a girl at that time. It was she who wanted a taste of the country life. In those days there were quite a few great country estates on the market; places that had fallen into a state of dereliction and that one could purchase for a song."

"So you decided to buy one?" I nodded.

"That was the idea," he agreed. "I learned from an estate agent that this house Mothair Pholl Rua was for sale. I didn't tell my fiancée because I wanted to inspect the place first. One Sunday I climbed into my car—I had one of those new Fords—and drove out to Ballyvourney."

"And so you decided to settle here?"

"No."

I stared at him in surprise. "But here you are," I said.

"I did not want to stay." He frowned at me abruptly. "To be honest, Mr. Wolfe, it is a tale that takes some believing."

It was plain that O'Brien wanted to tell the story, and I gave him full credit for the way he was catching my interest.

"Have you ever heard country people hereabouts speak of the *taibhse?*"

"Tavesher?" I echoed, trying to pronounce the Irish word with English phonetics. "What is that?"

"A *taibhse* is a phantom," he said solemnly. "Do you believe in such things?"

"Good Lord, no!" I smiled broadly.

"Neither did I . . . until the day I came to Cnoc na Bhrón."

I glanced at him to see whether he was joking, but his face seemed solemn enough.

I sighed. "Tell me your story," I invited.

He stoked up his pipe and sat back. "Well, as I said, I drove to Ballyvourney and then found the road for Cnoc na Bhrón. It was a pleasant enough day and I was driving along without a care in the world. The road was deserted and so I was driving at a cracking pace without a thought of meeting anything on the road. It happened very suddenly. I swung around a bend of the mountain road and, out of nowhere, an ass stood in my path. I didn't have a chance to halt in time and so I swung the wheel to avoid the creature. Now if I had swung to the right I would have gone straight off the side of the mountain and careened down into the valley below. So left I swung and went into a ditch that bordered the road. Down went the hood of the car and, as it ceased its forward motion, I was propelled into the windshield and fetched my head a crack.

"I must have lost consciousness for a moment, for when I came to the damnable beast had ambled off. The car was so positioned in the ditch that I knew it would be futile to attempt to move it. So I decided to walk up to the house—Mothair Pholl Rua—which I could see in the distance. I half-hoped that there might be a telephone still working in the house from which I could ring down to the village and save myself a long walk. Well, there was no telephone . . . but I am getting in advance of my tale.

"I walked up the mountain track toward the imposing edifice of the house. I knew enough, even from a distance, to say that it was not my sort of place. It was a solitary, isolated spot. You may think it ridiculous, perhaps, but I felt that there was something strange about the house. After all, what is a house but a lump of stones, wood, and glass, thrown together by the ingenuity of man? A house is only an inanimate object, a lifeless, inorganic, abeyant structure. In spite of that knowledge I felt that there was something about it that threatened me.

"As I came to the stone wall that marked the borders of what had presumably been its gardens, I suddenly noticed a small boy sitting on the top of it. He was staring into space and whittling at a piece of wood.

" 'Hello!' I called. To my astonishment the boy ignored me. I wondered if he was deaf. I walked toward him and called again. I swear that he raised his head and stared at me . . . no, stared through me as if I had no existence. Then, calmly as you please, he threw away the stick, put his clasp knife into his pocket, jumped down from the wall, cast a glance around him, and was bounding down the mountainside. He neither uttered a word nor looked back in my direction."

"Children can be strange at times," I volunteered, interrupting O'Brien's narrative.

The doctor looked thoughtfully at me and inclined his head in agreement. "So I thought at the time. Well, I continued on to the house and peered through the darkened windows. The estate agent had given me the key, and feeling rather ridiculous at my initial reaction to the house, I let myself in. The feeling returned even as I was dismissing my former reaction. The house was somehow unfriendly and forbidding. I felt cold and nervous. If that house had ever been filled with love, love had long since fled. I soon realized that my faint hope of finding a telephone still connected was to be dashed. I made up my mind to start walking down to the village. It would be a long walk, but I set off with a confident stride. I felt quite relaxed and well."

He paused and stared at me. "I emphasize the point because of what happened next. I had walked back as far as my car and proceeded not more than fifty yards further on when I was overtaken by the weirdest sensation."

"What sort of sensation?" I intervened.

"I felt sick; so sick and dizzy that I thought I was going to pass out. The attack, or whatever it was, was so acute that I was forced to sit down by the side of the road. My body seemed to grow ice cold, and an odd blackness hung before my eyes as if it were evening twilight . . . yet I knew the time to be little after midday. I realized that in such a condition I could not continue down the mountain. Somehow, I thought, I would have to try to crawl back to the house and rest there.

"I did so, straining every limb. Imagine my astonishment, Mr. Wolfe, when, as soon as I was but a few yards away from my car, I began to feel better. I pause, if I felt well enough perhaps I had recovered from whatever the attack was. I turned over the symptoms in my mind. The only thing I could think of was that it was a case of delayed shock arising from my accident. But I felt well enough now. I shrugged, turned, and started to walk down the mountain again.

"No sooner was I but fifty yards down the track when the same thing happened. In all my years as a doctor I had never experienced or heard the like of the sickness that I suffered. Eventually I made my way back to the house, let myself in, and crawled to the very couch you now lie upon. This time it took me a little longer to recover, but recover I did."

He paused for a moment and stared into the fire. The dancing flames were reflected in his somber grey eyes.

I shivered. It occurred to me that in spite of the brightness and zestful play of the fire, I felt oddly cold.

Doctor O'Brien saw me shiver. His lip drooped, and he made no comment.

"I lay on that couch for quite a while. It was dusk when I finally gathered myself together and decided to make a third attempt to walk down the mountain. It was then that I noticed a small fire burning outside the house.

"I peered through the window and saw that it was a campfire blazing away before a tent. From the light this campfire sent flickering into the darkness of the night, I saw a young man and a girl seated before it and cooking something over it. Now we get a lot of hikers and campers in these mountains and it was obvious that while I had been lying down, these two had chosen to make camp for the night within the garden of the old house. Well, I was delighted. Here was company and I could get something to eat and drink from them. I went out of the house and across the wild tangle that had once been the lawn.

" 'Hello!' I cried, well before I reached their friendly campfire. I took pains not to frighten them by a sudden appearance.

"They made no move to look up, though they surely heard my call. Instead, they bent to their food, chuckling and whispering to each other.

"I reached their campfire and stood before them.

" 'Hello,' said I. 'Sorry to disturb you but I've had an accident down the road.'

"They ignored me.

"Then it was that I was swept by a sudden coldness. I noticed that while the fire leapt and crackled, it cast no warmth. The figures of the boy and girl seemed to have an odd ethereal quality about them, a silver flickering sheen. Their features, when I looked closely, were pale, so near transparent it seemed as if I could stare right through them.

" 'What's the matter?' I cried, trying to keep the fear from my throat. 'Don't you hear me?'

"They continued talking—talking about the tramp across the mountains to Kenmare that they were planning for the next day.

"A sudden anger seized me. I reached forward to shake the boy by the shoulder.

"*A Dhia na bhfeart!* My hand—my hand went right through the shoulder. The boy had no corporal existence. His only reaction was to shiver slightly and turn to his companion and say, 'There's a chill wind up here.'

"I stepped back in horror.

"Was I having a nightmare vision? Of course, the old people often talked of seeing the *taibhse*—phantoms—shadows without any tangibility. I backed cautiously away from these ghostly campers, expecting that at any minute they would simply vanish from my gaze. They did not. I was sweating . . . yet at the same time I was cold with fear. I did not know whether to start immediately down the mountain path into the darkness or go back to the house and wait until dawn brought a friendly light to the scene.

"A hollow cough behind me made me spin around, wondering what new danger could threaten me.

"A man sat on the low stone wall of the garden border. He was old; his face was deeply etched. I could see his graven lines clearly, for he held a storm lantern in one hand. His dark eyes stared solemnly at me.

" 'God between me and all evil!' I cried in Irish, for a terrible fear was upon me.

" 'Amen to that,' replied the man.

"The relief flooded my body. 'You can hear me?'

" 'I can.'

" 'You can see me?'

" 'I can again.'

" '*Buíochas le Dia!* Thanks be to God,' I said with a sigh. Then I turned my head. The wraiths were still seated at their ghostly campfire. 'Yet can you see those?'

"Again the man nodded.

" 'But they can neither see nor hear me,' I cried in exasperation.

"The old man raised a shoulder in a shrug.

" 'But that is the way of it.'

" 'How do you mean?'

" '*Mo bhuachaill,*' he said, adopting a kindly attitude. 'My young man, you must know that they be phantoms. Up here in the mountains we dwell close to nature, seeing many things that those who dwell in the cities think are strange. But we do be all part of one universe, one world, where nature and supernature are two sides of one coin. There is no "natural" and no "unnatural," only what is and what is, do be.'

"If I had been told that I would be talking about higher philosophy with an old peasant high in the Derrysaggart Mountains in the middle of the night while staring at a phenomenon I believed impossible, I would have thought the person who dared propose the idea to be insane.

" 'Truly,' I asked the old man, 'you say that they are phantoms?'

" '*Ceart go leor.* Right enough,' he replied. 'They be *taibhse.*'

"I stared at him, seeing the truth of the matter reflected in his solemn gaze. I reached up a hand and wiped the sweat from my brow. Then I brought my mind to more pressing matters.

" 'Can you direct me to where I might rent a bed for the night?'

" 'I would willing give you a bed but my cottage do be five miles walk from here and I must be at work. Try at the house. Miss Áine will be there right enough.'

"He turned and walked rapidly away. I called after him, protesting that the house was deserted, but he vanished into the night. I cast a shuddering glance at the ghostly campers and decided that the only thing to do was take shelter in the house for the night.

"I went in through the door and halted. Whereas before the house had seemed cold, unfriendly, and forbidding, I was aware that it had grown warm, a soft friendly warmth. Whereas before the dust and cobwebs predominated, everything now seemed clean, as if someone had suddenly brushed, polished, and tidied the place. Even the cold furniture, which I had thought rough, damp, and near decay, was almost new and had a comfortable, lived-in feeling.

"I felt that I had had enough shocks for the day and was turning away when I heard the faint rustle of silk skirts. The door to the living room opened abruptly and there stood a girl. *Dia linn!* She was beautiful. A slim slip of a girl with red-gold hair and grave green eyes. She looked like some goddess standing in the half-light of the lamp that she held in one hand. She did not seem in the least perturbed by my presence.

"I stumbled for the right words: 'I'm terribly sorry,' I said. 'I had no idea that the house was still occupied. The estate agent said that it had been deserted before the Great War.'

"The girl frowned, drawing her brows together gently as if perplexed. 'I'm sorry, sir,' she replied. 'I do not know what you mean.'

"I plunged on desperately: 'The estate agent told me that this house Mothair Pholl Rua was for sale and I—'

"She interrupted me with a smile. 'But this house is Rath Rua, sir.'

" 'Then I am in the wrong house and have made a terrible mistake.'

"The girl smiled, but the frown did not leave her pretty face.

" 'The house you are looking for is called Mothair Pholl Rua?' She asked, with a shake of her red-gold hair. 'But I have never heard of such a house and I have lived here all my life. My name is Áine FitzGerald. The estate and the mine belong to my father, Lord Cauley FitzGerald.'

"I introduced myself and told her that I regretted not having heard of her father. In turn, she invited me into the living room and we sat before the fire and spent some time in idle chatter. I did not mention my experience with the ghostly campers, for fear of frightening my lovely companion. I did wonder why she appeared alone in the house.

"It was about then that I noticed the gray cold light of dawn creeping in at the window and I realized that I had not been to sleep. Strangely, I felt alert and refreshed. I began to apologize for my thoughtlessness in keeping the girl talking all through the night.

"She smiled softly at me and chuckled. 'Do not trouble yourself, doctor,' she said sweetly. 'No one bothers with sleep here.'

"I frowned, thinking that I had misheard her. 'I should be on my way back to the village,' I said.

"A sad expression came on her pretty features. 'Alas, it is futile for you to try to walk back to the village.'

" 'How so?' I demanded, suddenly feeling uneasy.

" 'Ah, my poor doctor. Don't you know? I would have thought that a man of your intelligence would have been able to work it out.'

"I tell you, Mr. Wolfe, a terrible cold fear began to creep upon me.

" 'Work what out?' I demanded.

" 'Why, you will not be able to get beyond the point where your car crashed. You see . . . you were killed there.' "

O'Brien paused, sighed, and kicked at the fire with the toe of his boot.

I gazed at him for a long time, wondering whether to laugh.

"The girl continued. 'The ghosts you thought you saw last night? They were living people. It is you who is dead.'

"Well, Mr. Wolfe, I was shocked, I can tell you. In fact, it took me a long while to realize that the girl was right. And here I have been in this house ever since that day . . . I remember it well. May twelfth, 1929."

He sat back indifferently and began to rekindle his pipe.

I stared at the man for a moment and then snorted in disgust. "I do not find this a very amusing story, doctor," I said, tight-lipped.

His grey eyes twinkled at mine. "It was not meant to be merely amusing, Mr. Wolfe."

He turned and glanced at the curtains.

"But here is the first glimpse of dawn," he said, rising and going across to pull aside the heavy velvet curtains with a swish.

It was true; the cold gray light of dawn was filling the tall glass windows. I stood and shook my head. Dr. O'Brien either had a bizarre sense of humor or else he was a little touched in the head.

From a distance came the purr of a motor car engine.

"If I am not mistaken, Mr. Wolfe"—O'Brien's voice was genial—"that sounds like a search party coming to look for you."

I joined him at the window. Across the mountain there was a good view of the old roadway, and in spite of the neutral effect of the gray early morning light, I could pick out the bright flash of the headlights of a car sweeping this way and that as it twisted and turned its way up toward us.

"Well, at least they can give me a lift to where I parked my car," I said. "Is the old ruined house near the copper mine far from here?"

O'Brien smiled broadly. "Your car is outside this house where you parked it."

My jaw gaped. "But I parked it outside the ruin, the old house called Rath Rua. What game are you playing, doctor? Besides, you said that this place was called Mothair Pholl Rua."

"Rath Rua was the name of the house when it was young and alive. You should have learned that in Irish *mothair* means a ruin, Mr. Wolfe. That is what people call Rath Rua now."

I snorted with indignation. I had seen the ruins of Rath Rua last night and this place was well kept. It was certainly no ruin.

The car halted outside. I looked through the window and saw that it had a blue flashing light on its roof and the sign *Gárda* on it. The Irish police. Here was some sanity at last.

"I'd better go out and tell them that I am all right," I said distantly.

O'Brien smiled softly but did not say anything.

I turned from the living room and walked through the hallway and opened the massive doors. They led onto a large sweep of half a dozen steps to the driveway outside.

Directly below, at the foot of the steps, stood my car illuminated clearly by the lights of the police car and the pale gray of early morning. My mouth opened in astonishment. A number of thoughts raced through my mind, concluding with the thought that O'Brien himself must have driven the car here from the ruins where I had left it.

A car door banged and a moon-faced policeman strode up to my car and peered inside. His companion was leaning against the side of the police car with the door opened and a microphone in his hand.

" 'Tis the American's car right enough," called the moon-faced officer.

He had evidently not seen me and so I started down the steps with a grin on my face. "It's all right, officer," I called.

To my astonishment, they both ignored me.

"We'd best look through the old ruin first, but if he isn't there then I'm thinking we'll have to look in the mine next. Didn't I warn him it was dangerous up here?"

"You did, John-Joe," replied his partner.

"Now wait a moment," I demanded, growing slightly angry.

I stood in front of the moon-faced policeman as he turned from my car. Staring me straight in the eyes, the man took a step forward and walked right through me!

O'Brien's peal of near-maniacal laughter slowly roused me from the shock of it.

I turned to stare up at him as he stood on the steps of the house. "What— what's happened?" My voice was a shocked whisper.

"Don't you see?" O'Brien paused to wipe the tears of laughter from his eyes. "Don't you understand yet, you poor fool? You are just as much a *taibhse* as I am. You broke your neck when you fell down that shaft in the old copper mine. You are dead!"

I uttered a cry of disbelief, of terror. Never had I felt such a surge of blind panic. I turned down the steps of the house into the welcome light of that early morning; I turned to flee from this dark brooding place. As I did so, I lost my balance on the step, tumbled, and fell heavily. The jarring shock knocked the senses from my head.

I regained them but a moment later; I had merely been stunned.

Yet it was cold and dark. Brooding blackness enveloped me. I found I held a flashlight in my hand and switched it on. Its beam reflected along the wall that had been hewn by the hand of man out of the thick granite. The walls were deep and oozed with water. It was obviously seepage from the mountain draining through the innumerable cracks and crevices. From farther along the tunnel came the sound of gushing water making a noisy, echoing music.

I stood bewildered for a moment, raising my hand to massage my aching head, feeling the smarting abrasion on my temple.

Then I felt a sudden desire to shout with laughter. I was in the old copper mine. As I entered, I had slipped and fetched my head a crack on the overhanging granite, which must have stunned me momentarily—*momentarily*—but in that moment what a strange fantasy had sped through my mind. I shuddered and then smiled ruefully to myself. The countryside with its countless legends and ghosts must be having more of an effect on me than I would have admitted. Well, I was recovered now. I hesitated a moment about pushing on into the mine; it was rather dangerous. Still, I ought to see all I could before starting back.

I moved forward cautiously, swinging the beam of my torch to right and left. It was not long before I realized that the tunnel was narrowing, the roof lowering over my head. The walls glittered with green streaks of water and the floor increased its slipperiness with the slime of disuse.

My mind was just forming the notion that the place was too treacherous to proceed further on my own when my feet slipped from under me again. This time my feet seemed to slide away from me. The torch fell from my hand and I cried aloud. I tried to catch hold of some object to save myself, but my forward momentum was unimpeded. I was falling; falling into utter blackness. I felt sharp rocks jabbing at me, scraping my flesh, tearing my clothes. Something cracked against my head but this time it was no mere stunning impact. For one terrible moment I felt fear; complete, heart-stopping fear stabbing like a knife into my chest as I realized that I was falling down a vertical shaft. I hit the bottom with a vague feeling of impact and then . . .

Nothing.

Introduction

*If boundaries imply describing the traditional as well as the experimental,
they're going to have to be constructed as a damned high wall. What seems to
be traditional has a delightful habit of casting multiple shadows, and some of
them are definitely not what we expect.*

*Steve Rasnic Tem, from Colorado, has appeared here before, and this, I
guarantee you, is both a sample of his traditional work and proof that he
refuses to allow himself to be categorized. As should we all.*

BLOODWOLF

by Steve Rasnic Tem

Deadfall Hotel. A curtain of gnarled, skeletal oak and pine hides it from the
California coast. The hotel is not well lit, there is no sign, and night comes
early here. The main highway bypassed its access road nearly half a century
ago.

From the air (and a few private pilots still venture over out of curiosity) the
hotel appears to follow the jumbled line of a train wreck, cars thrown out at
all angles and yet still attached in sequence. New levels have been added
haphazardly over the years, with varying degrees of success, and paid differing
attention as to repair. From the back, facing the water, various boarded up
windows, doors, even entire discarded sections can be seen, coated in slightly
different shades of paint, constructed of varying materials and in a range of
styles. But the owners have always tried to maintain a uniform appearance in
the front of the hotel, facing the road, even to the point of establishing film-
set-like facades over some sections of the structure.

Although the hotel has over three hundred rooms, fewer than a third are
serviceable on any given date. The staff has always been kept small, and the
repairs are too many. Systematic repair schedules have been attempted, but
time seems to work its destruction at varying rates throughout the rooms,
favoring some and wreaking vengeance on others, so that projections on the
decline of any one part are virtually impossible. To walk here is to become
disoriented as to time, place, even spatial relationships. Unless one has a
guide. Unless one is of the right frame of mind, or species.

The current owner will not bother you; he will try to respect your solitude and, besides, he will have too much else on his mind. Once again, the previous owner has stayed on as caretaker.

The hotel takes its name from the grove. Those who stay here often complain of the trees in their dreams—long, snakelike, involved limbs they imagine must mirror the trees' root systems. Limbs you feel compelled to follow, in and out of shadowed hollows where branches disappear, where newly inhabited and ancient abandoned nests alike are hidden. In parts of these trees the branches are so interlocked—within individual trees and among members of a group—the strongest coastal wind won't free them.

Yet when the time comes, and only the grove itself seems to know the secret of this timing (certainly no natural thing; past owners have allowed botanists to study the grove, and all have been at a loss to explain its peculiar physics), the branches, the deadfall, drop away like dried web, to join the decades-old clutter layering the floor of the grove.

Running such a hotel requires a special calling, or need. There are visitors coming, guests who have nowhere else to go.

Spring was a time of pests: small animals nesting in the rooms, insects prowling over the walls and chewing into hand-carved woodwork and flocked wallpaper. Except for their occasional forays into the realm of human anxiety (a peripheral glimpse of a few silverfish might effectively highlight the mood of one of the hotel's more paranoid guests), most of these tenants remained hidden until their deaths, and then their bodies would be discovered behind furniture or in hollow sarcophagi eaten out of the hotel's decaying structure with the creatures' final, instinctive meals. It was a time of grass that grew too quickly to mow, and in nooks and crannies too out of the way to trim. And it was a time of blood. Richard's daughter was becoming a woman.

But not overnight, much to his relief. He found the early and sudden maturities of so many children saddening, and occult in their implications. It pleased him that there still remained so much of the little girl in Serena's dress and fantasies. Even now he could hear her in the great side yard, debating loudly with the squirrels concerning some new infraction, perhaps their appetite for doll blankets or their continued abuse of the trees. Serena had her own theories about the fantastic jumble of deadfall left lying under the grove every year—she said it was the squirrels, gnawing and hacking and fighting in the trees. She claimed to have seen one one time with front teeth some three inches long, and marked by body-length running sores. "A real fighter of a squirrel, Daddy," she had said. Serena hadn't left him yet.

Addie used to complain that Richard would do his best to keep Serena a child, that he'd never quite let her go, that he'd keep her his little girl forever if he could. It was one of the few things they'd argued about. Maybe one of the few things they'd needed to.

She'd been right, of course, as she had been right about so many other things. He sometimes wondered what would have happened if he hadn't encouraged Serena's long childhood, if he hadn't tried to breathe life back into every ghost of her infancy, with the tickling, the stories, and the almost mad play. Maybe she'd be with him even now. Or maybe she'd be as lost to him as her mother was.

Addie had never understood Richard's need to hang on to his daughter's past, to keep things forever the way they had been, frozen. Just as she had never understood the true nature of hauntings, how the past is forever our world and when we breathe we breathe memory. All knowing was a haunting, all living. He wondered if she had perhaps, at last, experienced what he meant by that.

Richard and Jacob were stationed at one of the gradual corners made by the seaward wall of the hotel as it traveled over the harder rock of the cliff top. Here the foundation was so old it was sometimes difficult to tell where it left off and ancient bedrock began. Some of the masonry was obviously in trouble, heavily pocked and missing stones. Jacob was waist-deep in a cavity, blue coveralls turning white with rock dust.

"See anything?" Richard couldn't; the old man made an efficient plug.

"Oh I see lots o' things, you betcha."

The man's obvious tease irritated Richard. He had stopped pushing for the details of Jacob's knowledge some time ago. This former owner knew much more about Deadfall Hotel than he ever let on. But Richard knew better than to ask—Jacob distributed information only as it suited him, only when he thought Richard really needed it.

"Got it!"

Suddenly the blue coveralls were backing out, Jacob's shoulders scrubbing frantically against the crumbling stone. He moved fast enough to startle Richard, used to only patient and leisurely movements from this man. He got out of his way.

Jacob came out with scraped moss and root material sliming his shoulders, powder and cobwebs and dark brown bugs in his gray hair. Something long and many-legged danced around a blue shoulder blade, then dropped into tall grass and disappeared. Jacob's shoulder blades did their own dance beneath the coveralls. Then he turned around.

Jacob held out something—all black fur and squeal, with ridged, membranous ears and a rotted apricot for a snout. No tail. Richard stepped back further. The creature's relatively small mouth had suddenly filled with teeth some two inches long.

"Jesus! What is it?"

Jacob had already stuffed the little furred terror into a steel mesh bag, whose sides now warped furiously with the thing's struggles. Richard no longer wondered at Jacob's purpose for such an unusual container.

"Find one of these things every now and then. A long time ago, years before I came here, one of the guests left 'em behind. Guess they've been living and breeding somewhere inside the Deadfall ever since. Tell you more about 'em someday when I have the time."

Richard filed that bit of information away. Of course, Jacob never would have the time. A couple of weeks earlier Richard had observed as Jacob removed yard after yard of a slick and grayish ropelike fungus from around the foundation stones on the north side. The fungus had been remarkably tenacious—at one point a chunk of stone had come away with the growth—and Jacob had worn heavy gloves for the task. But the old man had neglected as yet to fill Richard in on the nature or origins of that particular fungus, or whether any cautionary measures were in order for the future. It had become quite apparent that he and this previous owner—now caretaker—had very different ideas about training. He was being trained, wasn't he? But for what?

"That daughter of yours, Serena, she be interested in the boys pretty soon, I'd say. She'll be ten, right?"

"Right. Her birthday's this weekend. Sunday."

"And there'll be a party?"

"I thought the three of us might get together, if you'd like to come. And maybe we could invite Gena Rutledge, the new cook's daughter. She's about her age."

"Well now, a party is the thing to have, I'd say. Her getting to be a young woman and all."

Richard chuckled uneasily. "She'll only be ten, Jacob. She's just a little girl yet."

"A girl in ways. A woman in ways. That's how it usually happens. My mama was all of fourteen when she had me. You'll be talking to her soon about her period, I suppose."

Richard just nodded in awkward silence.

Jacob looked at Richard over the pipe he'd brought out for lighting. "Or are you going to have the Rutledge woman, Sandy, talk to the girl?"

"I don't know . . . that might be the best thing."

"Hard being a single daddy sometimes. And when your daughter is first in her menses . . . ." He gestured vaguely.

Richard nodded.

"I'll speak to the Rutledge woman," Jacob said. "I've known her a time."
And with that he walked away, the steel mesh sack bouncing under its own
power above his shoulder.

Richard paced, angry with himself. Once again Jacob had taken over,
made him feel incompetent; but what was worse, this time it concerned his
own daughter. Jacob usually succeeded, intentionally or not, in making him
feel like a child himself.

He'd felt like a child more and more often since Addie died.

He leaned over and examined the hole in the foundation from which Jacob
had removed the furry pest. The darkness within seemed to vary in grada-
tions, in texture, in smell. When it began to move, Richard backed away. He
wondered how long it would take him to become a competent caretaker of
such a place.

Serena was still chattering amiably with the squirrels, who appeared
strangely drawn to her the past few weeks. There seemed to be a faint
coppery scent in the air. From a distance his blonde daughter looked older
than she was. For an anxious moment she looked like his dead wife. This
shadowed place by the hotel was too cool for him; he walked away from the
walls into the sun.

Dinner was lasagna that night. Richard was impressed; Serena had made it
all by herself. Ms. Rutledge had been teaching her for several weeks, and
once a week left early so that Serena could serve a late dinner in the main
dining room for whoever was around.

Tonight they were alone, dining by candlelight. There were only a few
guests in the hotel, and those were the not-atypical sort who kept largely to
themselves and had their meals in their rooms. Jacob was off attending to his
own mysterious affairs. He seldom indicated in advance whether he was
going to show up for a particular meal.

"I'm kind of glad Jacob isn't here tonight," Serena said. She cut her
lasagna expertly, holding the next portion daintily speared on her fork.

"I thought maybe you'd be disappointed," Richard said. "He should have
been here for your first try at lasagna." He stuffed his mouth with a huge
portion. "Mmm . . . and isn't it delicious!"

Serena laughed. "Where's your manners, Daddy?" She took a careful bite.
"Sometimes it's nice to have dinner with just the two of us. Makes it kind of
special. Besides, Jacob's weird sometimes."

"Well, I can't argue with that. But we couldn't do much without him
around."

"Daddy?"

"Mmm . . ." Richard's mouth was full again.

"I know what'd be good for my birthday."

"A new car, I suppose."

"Not this year. I thought maybe a razor. For my legs."

Richard looked at her. He was aware that his face must be showing surprise, but he'd actually been expecting this. "At your age . . ."

"Daddy! I've got hair . . ."

"I know, but it's not that much."

"It's embarrassing."

Richard knew she'd been wearing knee-high socks, and tights, even on very warm days. He'd asked her if she wasn't burning up. He should have known. Now that he thought about it, she hadn't shown her bare legs in months. "I understand, sweetie. I'll see what I can do."

Serena smiled broadly, then returned serious concentration to her meal. She straightened in her chair and raised her chin. In the candlelight she seemed to have aged several years. Richard took a deep breath and tried to finish his meal.

That night Serena was too excited to sleep, and he did let her stay up for a couple of hours past her bedtime. She'd insisted on watching a romantic comedy on TV with him, and again he couldn't refuse her. She'd tried to be very grown-up about it, laughing just slightly after the times he laughed, and furrowing her brow in concentrated study of the parts of the movie outside her immediate experience, which was roughly fifty percent of the time. She'd stopped watching any kind of cartoon several months before, saying they were for little kids.

He'd been touched by all this, of course, but it also frightened him. He felt in over his head. He was relieved when she asked him to read a fairy tale for bedtime and tuck her in.

His wife would have known what to do, what to say. She wouldn't have needed Jacob to prod her into doing the right thing.

Richard had always liked the nights spent in the Deadfall Hotel the best. He hadn't expected to—when he first arrived the thought of spending the hours of darkness within those chaotic walls had filled him with a dread he hadn't felt since childhood. The first few mornings he'd awakened with the covers pulled up over his head.

But after a time the night had become a comfort to him. After dark, the vast sprawl of the hotel began to disappear, the various wings and rooms falling asleep one by one until only the immediate suite of rooms, or the front lobby, were awake and part of the real world. At that time he seldom ventured into the other parts of the hotel, save for a few well-lit corridors where the current guests resided (unless they specified that their particular section of the complex be kept dark). It would feel too much like sleepwalking, or stepping into someone else's dream.

He could imagine that he still lived in a small house somewhere, with nothing to bother him outside his few comfortable rooms.

Addie had always wanted a house like that. She'd never have been happy living in the hotel.

So why was she here now, somewhere? It was a question Richard had avoided most of his stay in the hotel. That first winter in the Deadfall he'd thought of her as a hallucination brought upon by his intense grief. But obviously she was much more than that. Jacob himself had confirmed it for him just the other day. Richard had come up behind the old man in an upstairs hallway, standing before one of the rooms with the door open. Richard didn't think Jacob knew he was there, although he certainly never could be sure. Jacob had been closing the door to the room when he uttered just the one short sentence into the darkness: "There now, Addie, you rest now."

He wondered at first if Serena might have seen her mother, but he knew she would have told him—she wouldn't have been able to stop herself. He hoped she wouldn't see her. He wouldn't know what to say.

He was sitting in one of the huge overstuffed chairs in the front lobby, the floor lamp by the chair illuminating his lap, the book there, and a little bit beyond his feet. He'd been daydreaming about married life, and the last time he'd made love to his wife. He'd made love to no one since that time, and sometimes he wondered if that part of his life was over. He felt no real desire for women anymore—just a memory of such feelings, like a ghost of lust.

Sometimes in his dreams there was more—he'd wake up in the morning drenched, twisted up in his bedclothes, with no clear memory of the dreams of the night before. Except the vague idea that a beast had come out of his dreams, someone he did not recognize, and drowned him in its blood. What scared him the most was that he could not remember—or had suppressed—most of the dream. Forgetting increased its power over him.

The chair faced the broad staircase rising to the second story. A small antique lamp affixed to the wall illuminated the top landing. Most of the steps remained in darkness.

He'd have to do something about that, he thought. One night someone was going to try to come down those stairs in the middle of the night and he was going to break his neck.

And as he thought that, someone paused on the landing.

"Serena, it's way past bedtime."

There was no answer. The figure wavered on the landing, then bent forward as if to whisper something.

"Serena?"

Then the figure was falling.

"Serena!"

Richard jumped out of his chair and bounded up the stairs. When he reached the landing no one was there. He searched the steps frantically. They were dark and empty.

That night his dreams were so sharp edged that each transition of scene was like a raw scrape across the surface of the brain. Something with teeth had broken into the hidden suite of rooms he shared with his daughter, something with a high-pitched squeal and sharp smell and rough edges. But he could not see it. He held his daughter close to him, her flannel pajamas sweet-smelling against his face, and saw nothing even as the creature's wail increased in volume and her soft pajamas filled with red. He could do nothing, even as the pajamas he embraced so fiercely began to empty, until finally all he was holding was rags.

Serena came to him later that night, sobbing from a terrible dream. He should have asked her about it. Addie would have. He should have asked her about it, talked it through with her. But he was afraid. He hushed his daughter, told her it was just a bad dream, and held her close as she cried herself to sleep.

Shortly after two o'clock the next day a new guest arrived at the Deadfall. It was the hottest part of the hottest spring day Richard had experienced in some years, and Jacob vowed he'd never seen the like in this area of the country. Serena overcame her embarrassment over hairy legs and showed up downstairs shortly after noon in a bathing suit.

The fact that this new guest arrived in a fur coat gave Richard pause.

An ancient white Cadillac that looked meticulously cared for pulled up. A set of silver antlers ornamented the hood. The driver—a tall, skinny woman with long red hair—strode around the car and stood by the right rear door. She glanced around her with a studied casualness, but Richard could see the anxiety betray itself in the set of her mouth, the quick dart of her eyes. She wore a dark brown leather suit that in its cut was almost uniformlike. After a few seconds she bent over awkwardly and opened the door.

An elderly man slipped out of the car, his head low to the pavement. Richard thought he might be quite infirm, but, although he appeared bowed, there was something of a tenseness, a crouch, in his posture. And once he was fully out of the car the old man suddenly went electrically erect, as if he were being pulled up on tiptoes by something beyond his control.

And he was wearing that thick fur coat, like some hypothermic. Richard couldn't recognize the species of the pelt. It was a reddish brown, but with highlights of silver, yellow, and black.

The woman opened the hotel door with one hand. She obviously was far stronger than she'd first appeared.

Richard opened the registry as they approached the desk. The old man stopped and stared at him, his eyes wide and pinkish beneath bushy eyebrows. Deep creases runneled his face, leaving long, rough pouches of flesh between the lines. Every now and then there would be a slight tic, a shiver in the flesh. The skin on the man's face was slightly pale, chilled. His hair was brown, streaked with gray, and very thick.

"I'm not accustomed to signing." The man's voice was old, yet unusually strong. Richard thought of an actor's voice.

Richard closed the book. "We don't require it. Jacob says . . ."

"I will pay you when I decide to terminate my stay. I require a key," the man said.

"Of course." Richard started to turn as the woman began removing the fur coat. He stopped. The old man wore a three-piece black suit underneath. Wool. Some two feet of thick, luxurious red hair billowed out over his shoulders when she pulled the coat away.

The man stretched his arms, his shoulders straining under the tight seams of his suit. His head fell back slightly; he sniffed the Deadfall air with a narrow-stemmed nose that broadened into two nostrils opening like flowers.

Once the woman took the key from him, the pair moved quickly toward the stairs. The old man's stride did not falter as they headed up the steps.

"I see Arthur is back with us again." Jacob came around the corner and leaned on the desk.

"I don't know—he didn't want to sign his name. I take it he's been here before?"

"Old Arthur's a regular. Arthur Lovelace. Been coming here more years than you'd believe." He paused. "I see he has a new driver. Never seen him with the same one two years in a row, and they're always women. Tall ones. Did he say how long he was staying?"

"No, just that he'd pay me when he decides to leave."

Jacob gave a little snort. Then his voice became soft, almost sad. "Keep Serena away from him, Richard."

Startled, Richard touched the old caretaker's sleeve. "Why? What's wrong here, Jacob?"

Jacob wouldn't look at him. "Just do what I say. You just have to be careful sometimes, running this place. You know that. Just keep Serena away from him."

"If she's going to be in danger then he'll have to leave!"

Jacob looked at him sharply. "You know that's not an option. We don't turn guests away from the Deadfall. No exceptions. You knew that when you came here; that was the deal. She's safe, we're all safe as long as we stay careful. And most of our guests understand the protocols involved in staying here. A few, like Arthur Lovelace, we have to be careful about. More because he's getting old than because of what he is. Sometimes as they get older they get less predictable. Trust me, Richard. Just keep Serena away from him. She's on her way to being a woman now."

"What does that have to do with it?"

Jacob just shook his head. "I'll watch him, Richard. I won't let anything happen. I'm fond of that child of yours."

Richard wanted more—he was always wanting more from Jacob—but Jacob ended the conversation by walking away.

He could hear Serena playing right outside the front door. He'd have to watch her. He'd keep her inside all day, have her sit right next to him, if it took that. He stared at the Cadillac parked by the front door. The glare of sun obscured its lines, so that all he could really see was the grille, sharp edged and shining.

Richard and Serena sat out in the front lobby that night, talking, reading to each other. Serena would ask him to read her some article in one of the news magazines he'd been perusing, then in return she'd read him a passage from C. S. Lewis or E. B. White. It made her feel grown-up, and Richard usually enjoyed it immensely, although sometimes it went on too long for his taste—some nights Serena's tolerance for these readings seemed boundless.

Richard glanced at the staircase, where a shadow slipped down the carpeted steps.

"Serena, it's bedtime."

"Daddy . . ."

The shadow raised up and turned its head.

"Serena, it's time to go to bed."

"Daddy! It's only eight o'clock!"

"Serena . . ."

She stood and flounced away to their quarters behind the desk.

Arthur Lovelace eased off the last two steps and entered the enclosed circle of lobby furniture.

"A lovely child," he said, almost softly.

Richard stiffened. The old man sat down across from him. Backlighting filtered through his hair cast reddish shadows along the skin pouches that hid his cheekbones. The eyes were dark pits in the burning skin. "Thank you," Richard murmured.

"The young ones break your heart, do they not? I suppose it is because you know they won't remain young. All too soon they . . . mature, I suppose. They change, into young men, young women. Their bodies become unfamiliar things to you, and to themselves. Chameleonlike, the boy arises into manhood. And even more mysteriously, a tide of blood erases a young girl's face, and a woman's features are suddenly detectable beneath the coagulation."

Lovelace frightened him; he was suddenly afraid to make any sudden movement—as if he were in the presence of a snake. Richard could see a redness in the man's shadowed face as he spoke. Pinkish gums and a redder lining of the mouth cavity and an even redder tongue as Lovelace stretched his lips too widely in the articulation of each word, so that Richard was seeing far too much for comfort of the man's oral workings.

"A lovely child, a lovely child," the red mouth said.

"Yes, yes she is. Thank you very much." Richard felt giddy with anxiety.

"Do you suppose I might have something to drink this evening?" Lovelace said almost coquettishly. "Perhaps some sherry? My tongue becomes rather dry in spring. The climate, I suppose."

"Of course . . . I'll bring you some sherry."

"No water for me, thank you. It seems to irritate my throat."

"Of course, of course." Richard wondered why Lovelace felt the need to make the point.

"Makes me a bit irritable, as well." Lovelace chuckled dryly. Richard decided he'd get the sherry right away, to wet that dry chuckle.

He stood and started for the bar by the dining room. He staggered slightly, as if exhausted or drunk.

"Such a good child," Lovelace said, a little louder, as if calling after him.

Richard turned around. He could see the old man's eyes now, suddenly pushed out of the shadows. As if on wheels, he thought crazily. The eyes looked almost too human, exaggerated, like mannikin's eyes.

"Such a good child," the mouth said again.

Good enough to eat, Richard thought, hating himself for it. He turned and almost ran to get the man's sherry, feeling crazed and sick with himself. Addie would have known what to do. She always knew how to take care of things.

The next day Richard donned his Deadfall Recreation Director's cap. A baseball-style cap, it was crimson with black script lettering. The sweat band was cracked and stained with the sweat from every proprietor of the hotel since the early forties. The brim was too large and too soft to be stylish.

The accompanying T-shirt—with the same lettering style and similar, though not identical, color scheme—was newer, and Jacob's innovation when he'd been in charge. Richard was thankful Jacob hadn't insisted that he wear his hand-me-down but had a little shop in one of the coastal towns make up a new one.

In fact, there really wasn't that much recreation to be had on the grounds of the Deadfall, and in any case not many hotel guests were interested in such activities.

Two old women, draped like unused furniture in dark cloth, swatted at a shuttlecock out on the badminton courts. Black silk scarves hooded their heads so that Richard couldn't see their faces. He stood at the edge of the close-clipped grass and watched them for a while, his arms folded across his chest (he felt silly in his gaudy T-shirt and pseudo–sports cap in the presence of these dark-clothed, grim players). They didn't so much play, actually, as participate in some predefined ritual. He'd seen them out here before— apparently they were the closest thing the Deadfall had to permanent residents. Jacob said they had moved in sometime before his tenure. They were amazingly accurate in their volley, never missing over the short distance that separated them. They stood stockstill, monklike, their heads contemplating the flight of the shuttlecock.

Then one of the women let the shuttlecock fall to the court, and they turned and left together, the long-stemmed racquets held delicately upright, as they had every other time Richard had watched them. The fallen shuttlecock was forgotten—they used a different one every day. Richard wondered where they got them; they'd never asked him for one. In fact, like most of the guests, they made him feel fairly useless as a recreation director.

Few of those who came here were at all interested in recreation, at least of the sort the hotel sponsored in an official capacity. There was the occasional jogger (even their particular clientele wasn't immune to fad), sometimes a swimmer, and once an old, hunchbacked man who shot baskets most of every afternoon. But none who really needed any sort of director.

Jacob told him once that they used to have large tennis tournaments here, but after enough incidents of strangeness (nothing specific, no crimes committed, mostly just the uncomfortable charge of the atmosphere as hotel guests watched locals and locals stared in return), the local people stopped coming, and the tournament died.

The low branches hanging just over the courts stirred, birds flew, something dropped at the far end of the manicured grass and burst through the underbrush, and was soon moving aggressively through the trees beyond.

Richard trotted to the side of the courts and circled around the trees. In the distant green pasture that lapped the hotel grounds from the north, a figure was running, breakneck, charging. A long flag of red-brown hair flew behind his shoulders.

Again, something came into his dreams. Something faster than thought, swift and lean for all the rage it contained. He'd been dreaming of Addie, but the thing swallowed her whole, leaving only a fine red mist where the memories of her had been. Something slipped through the dark corridors of the Deadfall Hotel, which had become the secret paths through Richard's dreams, and, though it could not be seen, it could be felt. It made the dark air electric. It left the belly ill. It made the nerves and muscles dance. Richard tried to shout in his dream, tried to cry warning, but the thing had already stolen his breath away. He was suddenly empty and hopelessly inadequate. A fool. The thing's swift dance through his dream became playful, a light chuckle.

Serena's party was to be held on the old gazebo—just the thing for a small, intimate affair. Jacob had been working on it since early that morning. Richard found him there just after lunch, hard at work on the roof.

"You're going to have a heart attack, working so hard!" Richard called. Jacob just snorted. Richard knew well that the old man was much healthier than he was. It touched him that Jacob would expend so much effort on Serena's behalf.

"Ga-zeebo hasn't been used since I can't remember," Jacob said. "Terrible shape! Had to replace half of the floor supports—wouldn't support a five-year-old, much less Serena and the rest of us."

Richard nodded, walking around the bright white and red structure. The red looked fresh-painted. Jacob was doing a good job—the gazebo didn't look ill used in the least.

The gazebo was one of the first things Richard had noticed when he moved into the Deadfall, after the suicide cascade of tree limbs. It had seemed poorly proportioned, the pointed gray roof too high for the diameter of its base, and the side rails too high up on its eight support members. It was placed off-center within the surrounding group of tall, narrow trees and conical bushes, and it leaned, far enough to appear to have been moved aside by some giant hand. The boards had been warped, cracking with age and damp. It couldn't have been used in years.

Considering all that, what Jacob had been able to accomplish was amazing. The gazebo looked almost new with its white and red paint and new beams. There remained only a trace of the off-centeredness, the lean, and a faint scent of decay beneath the new colors.

Richard walked around and around the gazebo somewhat self-consciously as Jacob worked. He knew he was really looking for flaws, some excuse for Serena not to have her party here, even though that was what she wanted so badly and it was hard to deny her. And he knew Jacob must have known exactly what he was doing.

"Read the paper lately?" Jacob leaned over the railing so far it made Richard stare. He really *had* strengthened those members.

"Which paper?" Actually the question surprised him. Jacob knew Richard hadn't bought a paper since he moved into the Deadfall.

"The Winston *Daily*. Murders. Two of 'em in two days." He handed down a heavily creased clipping. Richard read the story with rising anxiety. They were, brutal, bloody killings. Although the paper didn't really spell it out, he could surmise that some dismemberment had been involved. "Young 'uns," Jacob said. "Teenagers. Wonder if Arthur has gone crazy enough, or desperate enough, to break the rules."

Richard stared at him. "He wouldn't . . ."

"Some have. You know that. I told you."

"We can't let this . . ."

"Hold on, now; we don't know if this is him. We have to be fair about this. I just wanted you to be aware, so we can keep a lookout. If this *is* him we'll be doing something, I just don't know exactly what yet. Arthur may be old, but he's a wild one, a bad one, always has been. He's not to be played with."

Jacob took back his clipping, stuck it into his back pocket, and with his usual lack of transition returned to work.

Something rustled the dried vegetation beneath the gazebo. Richard leaned over and peered past the latticework around the gazebo's base. Cold stared out at him. Cold blinked its eyes, then went away before Richard could decide exactly what had been there.

Richard straightened and looked around. He could see Serena out in the field, sitting up on an outcropping of black rock. Richard looked around for the running figure with the long red hair, the loping old man, but didn't see him. He began striding briskly in Serena's direction.

He was almost at her side when he saw the blood spot on her bright yellow shorts. Her face was washed out, pained-looking. He felt a sudden panic, reached for her shoulder, started to say something, then realized where the blood came from. He was embarrassed. He drew his hand back, and then was ashamed of himself.

"It hurts, Daddy."

Richard eased up on the rock beside her. "I know, sweetie. It's . . ." He gestured awkwardly. "It's what happens to you when you become a woman." He felt terribly stupid.

"And that old man scared me."

He stared at her, examined her carefully with his eyes. "What old man?" he asked as softly as he could.

"That old man. He ran right past me, and I didn't even hear him coming. Like a wind or something."

Richard followed her gesture. Lovelace was running near the trees. At that distance his stride looked impossibly long. "Did he touch you?"

"What?"

"Did he *touch* you?"

Serena looked up at him, startled. "No, Daddy." Her voice quavered.

Richard hugged her to him, feeling bestial and ridiculous. He could smell the faint scent of Serena's blood in the air and tried to ignore it.

In the distance he could see Arthur Lovelace standing against the backdrop of dark trees, watching them, his blood-colored hair billowing in the wind.

"This is my eighteenth—no, twentieth year here. I imagine it must feel odd at times, Mr.—oh, may I call you Richard?" Richard nodded his assent. "Very good. I was saying, Richard—I do prefer referring to the Deadfall's various proprietors by their first names—it must feel odd to have guests who know far more about the Deadfall than you may ever be privy to."

Lovelace had taken the chair next to him so quietly that Richard had at first thought him an apparition, since he'd been obsessing about the creature so. Certainly in his formal smoke-gray suit, his long hair blown out like a copper-color cloud, he appeared nothing less than that. Sandy Rutledge had just placed a cup of tea on his lap. Escape would have been awkward.

"It does feel strange at times, yes. But Jacob has shown me a great deal, Mr. Lovelace. A great deal."

Lovelace looked at him quizzically, then let a mild chuckle slip. Richard felt foolish, a bragging boy caught in his bravado.

It was about that time that Richard let himself think the word he had been avoiding. An outrageous, comic strip word. *Werewolf.*

Ms. Rutledge brought Lovelace a cup of tea. Her face seemed transformed by a vague disgust. Richard wondered if she knew what Lovelace was. Lovelace had wanted the tea strong, "undiluted by condiments." As Lovelace drank the tea, in surprisingly delicate sips, Richard noted subtle changes in the man. The cheeks grew even more flushed, as if the mere sensation of liquid in his mouth were exciting him. The nostrils flared to an almost grotesque width. Lovelace's head eased back and his mouth fell open, as if he had fallen asleep, although Richard knew he was wide awake—the body appeared tense, expectant. Richard looked across the lobby. Serena was poised at the front desk, her elbow draped casually on the counter, watching. Lovelace was watching her, his nostrils expanding even wider. Smelling her.

Richard leaned forward slightly and tried to see Lovelace's teeth. They weren't unduly long, but the surfaces seemed to have more sharp edges than was common—he could imagine them scratching the inside of their own mouth. They appeared to be meticulously cared for.

And then Lovelace was speaking to him again. "The first time I stayed here, it was a Mr. Grant, the manager then. A quiet, dark man, that one, said almost nothing. As 'other' as his guests. That one didn't die, I believe. He was simply lost on a midnight's journey to the lavatory. Perhaps he booked himself into a room." Lovelace's chuckle made no sound this time.

Richard remained silent for a long time. His tea was cold when he began drinking it again. Then, "Why do you come here, Mr. Lovelace?"

Lovelace turned his head and stared at Richard—a rotation seemingly independent of the rest of his body. "A manager has never asked me that before. I'm not even sure if it would be considered bad manners." He tilted his head slightly. The mouth grew redder. "I can be myself here, young man. I do not normally have that luxury. Surely you can understand that much?"

"I can. But are you trying to tell me you never show yourself away from this hotel? That you don't follow your nature? I'd find that hard to believe."

"I'm an old man. There is little I can do."

"Come now. I've seen you run."

He grinned. His lips seemed too loose, too mobile. "I *do* enjoy my running. But I'm an old man. Where else could I run so freely and fail to attract attention? Away from here I am the old man again—I keep my hair tight under a wig. My cheeks fall inward. I am wound tight. I can hardly move, I am so—inside myself. Away from here I am a *safe* old man."

"But you have to—*feed.*" Richard tried to keep his voice under control.

The old man's, the old werewolf's, face grew flat, impassive. "I am old now. I feed as you do. My flesh does not touch another's blood. I promise you this."

Richard imagined Lovelace running through the woods, his face glowing, hair flowing, his mouth working nervously in preparation for the feeding frenzy to come. Richard imagined a ravager with tooth and claw, a shark on land. "I find that hard . . ."

"I swear," Lovelace insisted. "The flesh of my hands, the flesh of my lips, my solid teeth . . . they do not mar another. Never."

Richard found himself believing the man, and yet that night it was still Lovelace's face in his dreams, Lovelace's teeth in his thoughts.

"Let's have your party in town." It was obvious from the frustrated looks he was getting that Richard was making no headway with his daughter.

"But I want the party here, Daddy. In the gazebo. I've always wanted it here. And you promised I could."

"I could hire out an entire restaurant. An entire restaurant just for *you.*" He sounded foolish even to himself. He wondered if he could even get that much money; Serena must know he didn't have it.

"I don't understand why we just can't have it *here.*"

"Maybe Jacob won't have the gazebo finished in time. You did want the gazebo."

"He's almost finished. You *know* he's almost finished."

"He's pretty busy. I haven't seen him at all the last two days." Richard hesitated. He didn't know what more to say. He wasn't going to convince her, and he didn't feel quite justified in ordering her. Besides, Jacob usually knew what he was doing.

He felt something cool against his hand. He stiffened, and looked down at the small hand that had reached inside his own. "It's okay, Daddy," she said. "I'm older now. I like it here."

Something had been bothering Richard all night, worrying its way through the shadowed regions of his dreams, gnawing at the edges of the visual frame. He woke, sat straight up in bed, and found he could *hear* the gnawing. "Jesus Christ," he whispered, then wished he hadn't spoken. The gnawing suddenly stopped, as if the hungry thing were waiting, listening.

Something hard and dark dropped onto his bed. He went rigid, holding a frightened release of breath so that it throbbed painfully against his rib cage. The thing started moving up the covers.

He could feel its claws through the sheets.

He'd been holding his head stiffly to one side. He was staring at the wall, trying to force his eyes into becoming accustomed to the light. Now, so slowly as to be unnoticeable, trying to resemble nothing more than shadows shifting because of changing window light, he was moving his head. He was turning his head and then he was looking at the thing perched on thin covers that separated the tender flesh of his belly from the hard darkness of that thing that now opened its mouth and revealed all those teeth. It was one of those things Jacob had removed from within the foundation stones. It doubled up its neck and hissed at him, its teeth extending even farther into the dim streak of light from the window.

Then a baseball bat came out of the darkness and swatted it off the bed. Jacob materialized out of the dark and stood over the bed, grinning. "Been chasin' that damn critter all over this goddamn hotel. Think it's the last one. I think."

Then the thing was scrabbling at the door, its teeth prying at its edge. Then the door was open, the mad ball of teeth and fur racing away.

"Ho ho!" Jacob shouted, jumping onto Richard's bed. " 'Scuse me," he said, then bounded after the thing.

Somewhat incoherently Richard began thinking of Serena, asleep in her room with this thing roaming the halls, and how Jacob seemed to be making a game of the whole thing, and it made Richard furious, more so because he didn't exactly know what to do about it all. And it seemed strange even at the time, to be worrying over this small creature, however ferocious it might be, when there were other things, his guests, who might be far worse, whatever system of etiquette they all subscribed to. And he felt a rage toward himself for bringing his young daughter into this terrible place, where there were things with teeth and things with claws, and worse. Where there were werewolves.

He jerked himself out of bed and ran after the thing, ran after Jacob, in his underwear.

He could hear, somewhere in the darkness ahead of him, the rhythmic pound of Jacob's feet on the carpeted hallway. And beyond that the fading but still nerve tickling scrape of claw and tooth against walls and baseboards. And below all that he could just barely detect a chaotic murmuring, like animal thoughts amplified.

Richard followed the sound to the staircase, over the landing, and to the rear hallways of the second floor. Here the electricity was rationed. Two of the rooms back here were more or less permanently occupied, but Richard hadn't yet met those occupants. Jacob had told him he might never meet them, that he himself had only caught a brief glimpse of one of the pair, and that years ago. "I hear them, now and then, one of them crying occasionally, the other tapping the bed with something metal, I guess," was all he would say. So there were only nightlights protruding here and there from the baseboards, and some of those dead, to light the way. "Those two wouldn't take to the light anyway," Jacob had said.

Richard's bare feet seemed to float from shadow to pooled light to shadow again—each time they reappeared was almost a surprise. As if they were someone else's feet, and he was just an anxious head floating through the dark.

You just don't think, Richard, she whispered inside his head, and, though he could not see her, he knew she was there.

He concentrated on the trail of pounds and scrapes.

What did you think you were trying to do, Richard, bringing her here? Look at the danger you've put her in.

He tried not to speak it, but softly he was saying. "No, Addie. Not now." He tried not to plead, but even more softly he found himself saying, "Please."

The air around him shimmered lightly in amusement. *You've no sense anymore,* she said, and the voice was sad now. *You'll get both of you killed.*

"I'm her parent," he said, straining to hear what might be ahead of him. "The only one she has now."

The air was suddenly ice that adhered to his skin. His underwear grew stiff and slightly abrasive. . . . *no* . . . The word caressed his numb face.

He was in the red corridor on the third floor now, the walls a dark burgundy, the long crimson rug glowing. He didn't understand how he could have gotten here—he hadn't climbed any more stairs. But he had to listen for the trail. Serena depended on him, maybe more than he could manage. But he was all she had.

No! The burgundy walls lightened and ran. The ice evaporated from his skin.

Bathed in sweat, he ran around a bend he could not remember. He could hear a dry scrambling in the walls.

Dust spread like lace over his cheeks and forehead. Debris covered the corridor. He stumbled. Something warm and wet smeared across the bottoms of his feet, collecting grit as he ran. He realized he'd never been in this part of the hotel before.

He passed under a low arch into a night cool and wet with earth. The flavor of it filled his lungs, then turned candy-sweet, burning up his sinuses.

He paced through rooms and corridors burned to a pale, geometric skeleton, clamping his lips against the flying ash.

He ran into indistinct sleepwalkers, clothed and bare, trembling if the feel was wet or hairy, racing harder if it was hard and dry.

It was only when he found himself in a great emptiness, when he had lost the very walls of the Deadfall, and the sound of the trail, that he stopped to consider. Where was Serena?

He had left her back there alone in their suite of rooms while he chased shadows through the multitudinous intersections of the Deadfall's skewed geometry. He had run off half crazed in his underwear, he had ignored his dead wife's proddings and proved her right. Where was Lovelace?

Richard had begun to turn, crouching, seeking the clearest way back. "Got you, you devil!" It was Jacob's shout, close by him. Richard turned to the left and strained forward. An inestimable distance away he could see a vague rectangular outline in the darkness. He walked toward it. The floor felt seamless and without texture under his feet. He encountered no furniture, no obstacles of any kind.

Richard ran his fingers along the vertical edges of the outline. His hand found an irregularly shaped lump of metal—he clutched it in both hands and yanked. The door scraped and whined. He yanked it again.

The door jerked open with the sound of breaking rust. Jacob sat on the floor with his back against the blue-papered wall, stoking his pipe. At his feet lay an old grass sack decorated with spreading bright red spots. Some of the red had dripped out and stained the indigo rug. The baseball bat lay a couple of feet away, several inches missing from the thick end.

Jacob slipped the pipe from his mouth and sighed. "Hope this last one didn't have babies." Richard was back on the second floor, the wing above his quarters. Jacob stared at the ancient door behind Richard and nodded. "Myself, haven't used that way in years." He looked down at Richard's bleeding feet. "Where's Serena?"

"I—I was following *you.*" His own voice sounded ragged to him, with an edge of hysteria.

He'd barely gotten it out before Jacob was on his way. "Come on!" The sudden quickness frightened him.

This section of the hotel was quite familiar to Richard, but after only a couple of jags he felt confused again. He wondered if he would ever feel at ease again, even in the most-used sections of the Deadfall. In minutes they were standing in front of one of the closets. Jacob dragged him inside. "Wake up, Richard!" he hissed. The closet appeared to be empty. Jacob felt the wallpaper on one side. "I don't like doing this, mind you. But it's necessary." A horizontal split of graying opened in the dark wall. Jacob put his eyes to it. "Come here," he whispered. Richard awkwardly pushed his head alongside Jacob's. On the other side was one of the better rooms. Richard thought he recognized it. A dark form had spread itself over the bed.

"Seems okay," Jacob said.

The head of the dark form fell slowly to the side. Richard felt his breath swell in his throat. "Lovelace."

In sleep, he didn't look the same. He looked like an old man. His long red hair was pulled back from his face, and trapped under his head and shoulders. What little of it Richard could see looked pale, a silver color. The lines of the face were thin and long, and fell together into a sharp bundle when he snored. It was an old man's snore, congested and throaty, and it made the man's narrow chest tremble.

"Not so threatening now, is he? Not the broad-chested, flame-haired terror?" Jacob whispered.

"He hardly looks like the same person."

Jacob snorted softly. "They seldom do. They're like children, asleep. Until they dream. They may hunt safely in their dreams. They may howl at the darkness because the dream howl is silent. And most of them carry the sleep through most of their days, I think, when they seem no different from you or me. And perhaps they *aren't* that different from you or me."

Richard didn't buy that, but he didn't have the words to argue with the old man. Something was happening to Lovelace now that made it impossible to see any such resemblance.

Arthur Lovelace was apparently dreaming—at least he resembled a man troubled by a bad dream. His head moved slowly side to side as if in denial. His hands clutched and unclutched. His brow gleamed. A low moan stirred in his throat. His bare feet made small kicking motions, as if in some other world he were running. And his hair, his hair had begun to redden again, evolving back to its familiar daylight color of flame. Richard looked away. It was like blood oozing out of the scalp, out of the brain, to fill the elderly man's translucent hair.

"The old tales got it all wrong," Jacob said. "The werewolf coming out of his clothes. And no wonder."

Richard pressed his eyes against the slit. Lovelace's motions of denial had grown more vigorous; the fine red hair filled the air above his head like a cloud. The lines of his face had blurred, and doubled.

"Richard—behind the bed."

Richard looked beyond Lovelace's thrashing form to the far wall. A face stared at him. A pale face with sections of skin missing from cheeks and forehead. A wide red mouth. Dark, obscured eyes. And the tatters of uniform. "The chauffeur." Richard felt a flash of anger. "Isn't that enough, Jacob?"

"No, my friend. Not necessarily. As distasteful as it might be, there is always the possibility she knew exactly what she was getting into. I've known Arthur to make such arrangements before."

Lovelace's mouth had fallen back, and now it filled with an odd combination of sounds, guttural background highlighted by occasional high-pitched notes. His skin broke out into a heavy, syrupy sweat and then appeared to melt. His long, crooked fingers pulled at collar, at sleeves. His ears fell back. His face fell back. And something like a ghost of skin, like skin turned to damp vapor, began to separate out of him, began to spread like wings from shoulders and head and hips, wrapping him in mist, all his secret fluids suddenly taken flight, fleeing the old man's body.

Richard felt his own back straighten, his shoulders curl forward, as if he had suddenly lost control of his body. His tongue was dry; he craved something wet for his throat. His nerves began a violent dance.

Distantly, he could feel Jason's fingers wrapping his arm, steadying him.

The white vapor floating over Lovelace began to congeal. Unseen forces appeared to grab each smoky curve and pull it, shape it. The lines of the form grew more distinct. Jagged edges rose out of the mist. The lines appeared vaguely shiny, electrified.

Richard felt himself backing away from the closet wall.

The white form turned its head. Wolf eyes burned like dark coals in hollows of ice. The pale wolf raked its claws derisively across the old man's puny, laboring chest. Shallow rivulets of blood welled up. Then the pale, translucent wolf was leaping in slow motion out of Lovelace's body, this movement seeming to pull a film of blood out of the flesh, splattering walls and sheets, the lines of the room distorting with its passage.

Richard tried to follow with eyes forced to an unblinking stare, but Jacob was already pulling him from the closet and across to another door. "We have to beat the thing to Serena's room!"

He took Richard down a narrow spiral staircase, through a room empty of furniture except for hundreds of glass bottles filled with a murky green liquid, and, suddenly, into Serena's room. She was sound asleep, two rag dolls tucked against her chin. She always tried to hide the fact that she still slept with them.

There was a vague scratching at the door.

Jacob moved quickly and grabbed the knob. "Jacob?" Richard moved in front of Serena's bed. Jacob began to open the door. "Jacob! Are you crazy?"

But he had already flung it open. The wolf crouched there, back rising like a white, foamy wave. Sharp-angled smoke made its long, mouth-filling teeth. Jacob clapped his hands together sharply in front of its face.

The clouded face of the wolf seemed to separate a little. The wolf howled from its head, a cry something between a baby's scream and an electronic whine. It twisted up into the air like a mad wind and then it was gone.

Serena was crying softly in her sleep. Richard stroked her hair. "It's gone, then?"

"These are dream things, see? They're all cowards when surprised by anything awake. Not that that means they're harmless. They'll get you good enough, if you happen to be asleep. Can't stay awake all the time."

Richard gathered his daughter closer to him. "So what do we do?"

Jacob looked at him as if the answer should be obvious. "Tomorrow's Serena's birthday. So we have a party."

The party was to be held at twilight. It had been Serena's request; she said that the sky behind the gazebo was prettiest then, the light just the way she wanted it. She had her mother's eye for the small details.

The timing made Richard anxious. The Deadfall was at its most ethereal then, its most ambiguous. At that time of day it could look most like a normal hotel, but that was only because there was enough gray shadow to obscure its odd angles and other eccentric aspects of its architecture. That also meant it was easier to lose your way. Walls suddenly became new passages. Passages suddenly became solid walls.

All that day Richard tried to find out more of what Jacob knew, if indeed he knew anything concrete at all, about Lovelace.

"We'll just need to watch him, Richard. I'm still thinking this thing out. Act, if it seems absolutely necessary, but only at the appropriate time."

"Then you have some sort of plan?"

"I'm always making plans. You'll learn to do that, too, running the Deadfall.

Richard *was* watching for the thing, but Lovelace had proved difficult to find most of that day. He had used the passkey and been relieved to find the chauffeur's body gone, but there had been no signs of Lovelace, except for small threads of bloodstain on the quilt. Then at lunch Lovelace suddenly appeared in the dining room, as if nothing unusual were going on. The old man ate a hearty meal.

"You know, he may not remember much, if anything, of last night," Jacob said, as they watched him devour his food. Richard wasn't comforted by the idea—it made Lovelace seem even more out of control. And he himself felt more and more impotent.

He sometimes wondered if Jacob had seen a certain passivity, a certain pliancy in his character that had led the old manager to choose him as his successor over all the others. Certainly he treated him like a child much of the time, withholding information as if it were gold and he a miser, as if he couldn't trust Richard with the responsibility of knowing. Someone with backbone might have left a long time ago. Someone with backbone probably wouldn't have taken the job in the first place. Not with the restrictions.

"There are certain rooms, certain locks, where you'll find your passkey useless," Jacob had said. "In due time you'll receive the keys to some of those locks, but perhaps never for others."

Richard had been surprised. He had come into the hotel assuming that he was to be some sort of owner, with privileged access. But they hadn't signed anything, and no money actually changed hands. "Your services shall purchase your way," the old man had said. It was a ridiculous way to do business, but then Richard had never been much of a businessman. He just needed a quiet place to stay, something to do, and in a quiet, secluded environment. He was unlikely to find another place as secluded as the Deadfall.

For all his anxiety, Serena's party was actually a pleasant affair. Serena and Ms. Rutledge had baked several platters full of cookies, far more than the small party could eat. Serena kept pushing them on Richard, and he kept politely refusing, but she didn't seem to mind. She wore a rather grown-up dress Ms. Rutledge had made for her as an early birthday present. She looked gorgeous. Richard had felt somewhat self-conscious about the meager gifts he had selected—a small flute and a stuffed giraffe—but she was enthusiastic about both of them. Her delight seemed genuine; she was a joy to give things to. He was very proud of her.

For his present Jacob had given her an intricately carved wooden necklace, primitive-looking, with symbolic fruits and animals. He also provided the musical entertainment: an ancient accordion he hauled out of a trunk that had been hidden in one of the small storage closets under the stairs. It had a strange, tinny sound. When Jacob squeezed the instrument, great dark clouds of dust blew out. Serena laughed until she cried, and after a moment of false consternation Jacob laughed with her.

The clouds were dark that evening. The final rays of sunlight left a liquid crimson rim around them that gradually blackened, blending with the night.

An hour after dark they all gathered the things from the party and went inside. Serena seemed mildly disappointed, but when Ms. Rutledge promised tea in the formal parlor, her mood quickly picked up again.

"I'm going to go change for the parlor, Father."

Richard looked at her, amused. *"Father*, eh?"

Serena laughed. "I'll just be a minute. Sandy—Ms. Rutledge—made me *two* dresses!" She could barely contain herself.

"Well, Lord knows a woman needs to look her best on important occasions like this. But don't be too long."

"I won't. Promise." She forgot herself momentarily and went around the front desk at a dead run.

Richard settled into a chair in the front lobby to wait. *No . . .* He hadn't thought of Addie all day. *Richard . . .* But as Serena grew older, it was as if the memories of his dead wife became more real.

Serena . . .

The dim light over the lobby reddened. Richard was already out of his chair when he heard Serena's scream.

When he got to her room, Serena was standing behind her bed. Jacob was standing beside her, whispering to her, apparently trying to calm her by stroking the side of her head.

Richard strode toward the bed. "I thought you were going to be watching her," he said.

"I was," Jacob said softly. "I was right here." He nodded toward her closet.

Richard turned slowly. He could feel the thing before he actually saw it. Standing inside the closet door, its back drifting upward like an arch of smoke, was the wolf. The wolf's jaws drifted apart. The mist inside them was burning. Richard raised his hands stiffly and clapped them together with as much force as he could muster.

The wolf's eyes burned a brighter red. Its head twisted on the neck like a snake, whining and snarling. The edges of its form grew firmer as it began to slice the rug apart with its claws.

"Won't work, Richard. It's got too good a hold. Arthur must be pretty bad off for this to be happening like this."

The wolf began to creep forward, leaving a trail of mist that settled into the floor like acid.

"Pull back with us, Richard. Behind the bed."

Richard did as he was told.

The wolf raked its ghost teeth against the steel bedpost. Sparks flew. Richard was beginning to worry about a fire when Jacob pulled all three of them down to the floor and rolled. Suddenly they were under Serena's bed, staring up at the springs.

"Jacob?" He could hear Serena whimpering, but he couldn't see her. A white muzzle suddenly gaped open a few inches from his face, at the side of the bed. "Jacob!"

White fire roasted his face. He began to scream.

And then was falling through black. He could feel Serena next to him. He grabbed her and waited for the fall to end. It seemed to go on for a very long time.

At the bottom there was light. And a hallway. Before he could think about the implications, Jacob had them running again, down a snakework of tangled passages and stairs.

And into the rented room of Arthur Lovelace.

"Daddy! That poor man . . ."

Lovelace was spread-eagle on the bed, head back, mouth peeled open. His skin appeared shrunken, tight enough to break the underlying bone.

"Grab his feet!"

Richard hesitated. He imagined touching the man's paper-thin flesh, the skin breaking open, and things . . . coming out.

"Richard! Do it now!"

Together they pulled the old man off the bed. He was stiff, and he spasmed as they moved him, almost bringing them down. Serena helped where she could. Jacob led the way down the corridor. Richard was amazed by Jacob's strength: he practically dragged the rest of them with him.

They turned at two bends of the corridor, then at the third bend Jacob didn't turn. He backed through solid wall. Richard and Serena slowed, confused, but Jacob pulled them through as well.

They were suddenly within a passageway lined with ornate doors, and elaborate carvings over each doorway. It was too dark to make out many of the details, but Richard had the sensation of being stared upon by hundreds of tiny faces. Jacob opened one of the doors and they entered.

The room was empty except for a rough plank laid across two ancient sawhorses. Jacob guided them as they laid Lovelace's body on its length. Richard and Serena stood holding each other, exhausted, unable to move. Jacob pushed them back toward the door, and they stumbled awkwardly in that direction.

The wolf drifted through the door. Its face howled and vibrated, the misty contours of its head breaking apart, then drifting back together again. Jacob tried to shove them back, but they couldn't keep their eyes off the thing.

The wolf's teeth grew like fast-freezing icicles. Its head spun madly around. It reached back with teeth grown too long for its mouth and began ripping pieces out of its own torso. Luminescent blood filmed the room. The wolf's head turned and stared at them. It stopped, statuelike, and stared at them.

Then the wolf began its leap.

Arthur Lovelace's emaciated arm reached out and grabbed the thing, pul-

ling it to him. The wolf thrashed and bit. Blood flooded Lovelace's face.
"Go . . ."

Jacob was the last one out. He slammed the ornate door and locked it. In
the shadows the elaborate carvings writhed. Sculpted eyes blinked. He
pushed them through several more doors before they could no longer hear
the wolf's frenzy, the snap and splash of Lovelace's embrace.

"That man," Serena said later. "Mr. Lovelace. He still isn't dead, is he?"

Richard stared at Jacob.

"No," Jacob said. "But as terrible as that might seem, he's where he
wanted to be. In that room, where he can't leave. I suspect he even had that
half in mind when he came this season."

Richard held his daughter in his arms. He looked down at her: she was
older, noticeably older.

"You didn't lose her, son," Jacob said softly.

But Richard wasn't listening to him. There were other sounds to hear.
There was the soft inner breath that drifted through the Deadfall, higher
pitched through the halls, dropping lower in the stairs and secret passages.
There was the light tapping of guests who never left their rooms, their
frenetic thoughts in tune with that breath. There was the soft crying of a
white wolf with dying eyes. And there was the soft laughter of his wife, his
beautiful wife Addie, growing madder with every day of her death.